Books by Carrie Merrill

Angel Blade
Book I in the Angel Blade Series
Daemon
Book II in the Angel Blade Series
Archangel
Book III in the Angel Blade Series

The Key, The Outlaw, and the Treasure

# THE KEY, THE OUTLAW, AND THE TREASURE

CARRIE MERRILL

SOUL FIRE
PRESS

an imprint of
Christopher Matthews Publishing

Boston, Massachusetts

The Key, The Outlaw, and the Treasure

Copyright © 2018 by Carrie Merrill

All rights reserved. Except as permitted under the U.S. Copyright Act of 1976, no part of this publication may be reproduced, distributed or transmitted in any form or by any means, or stored in a database or retrieval system without the prior written permission of the author. All characters appearing in this work are fictitious. Any resemblance to persons, living or dead, is purely coincidental. This book is a revised edition of the original book titled *The Secret of the Hooked X*.

Editor: Jeremy Soldevilla
Cover design: Neil Noah

ISBN 978-1-948146-43-5
ebook ISBN 978-1-945146-44-2

Published by
Soul Fire Press

an imprint of

CHRISTOPHER MATTHEWS PUBLISHING

http://christophermatthewspub.com

Boston

Printed in the United States of America

This work is dedicated to my own six furry rescued outlaws:

Jesse James
Billy the Kid
Wyatt Earp
Doc Holliday
Sundance Kid
And Butch Cassidy (my only little girl)

Keep running around the house and
playing with your toys, you little bandits.
(Yes, like Anna, I, too, am obsessed with outlaws)

# ACKNOWLEDGEMENTS

This project was an act of love and many years in the making. First of all, thanks go out to my parents. They fostered my interest in reading at an early age, and that included a book that they had on the shelf that I would pick up and read often. It was a historical account of various outlaws throughout the Old West. This is what started my passion for the stories about Jesse James and Billy the Kid.

My first audience for this work was my niece and nephew, who insisted that this was their favorite of all my tales and that I should get it published. Their input was invaluable, especially since they were the ages of the kids in my story.

And thanks, of course, to my brothers and sister, who keep encouraging me.

None of this would be possible without the aid and superior knowledge of my editor, Chuck Sambuchino. His insight into the characters and the story made this a much better manuscript.

Last, but not least, thanks to Jeremy Soldevilla and to my cover designer, Neil Noah. Thanks for bringing this into the spotlight.

# TABLE OF CONTENTS

Gaily bedight,
A gallant knight,
In sunshine and in shadow,
Had journeyed long,
Singing a song,
In search of Eldorado.

But he grew old—
This knight so bold—
And o'er his heart a shadow
Fell as he found
No spot of ground
That looked like Eldorado.

And, as his strength
Failed him at length,
He met a pilgrim shadow—
"Shadow," said he,
"Where can it be—
This land of Eldorado?"

"Over the Mountains
Of the Moon,
Down the Valley of the Shadow,
Ride, boldly ride,"
The shade replied,
"If you seek for Eldorado!"

**"*Eldorado*" by Edgar Allan Poe**

# CHAPTER 1

Anna stood at the entrance of the mineshaft, the two great doors open beside her, and the rusty hinges creaking in the breeze. The heavy, dank air breathed from the depths of the tunnel before her. She held her breath and tried to steady the lantern in her hands, but the glass rattled inside the metal casing and echoed like chattering teeth against the rock walls of the cavern. Her eyes followed the two iron rails that started at the mouth of the tunnel and disappeared into the dark, well beyond her small circle of light.

She had wanted to enter this place from the moment she first saw it, but now she wasn't so sure. The lantern light glinted off the iron rails and beckoned her forward. This place had been abandoned for so long; there couldn't possibly be anything or anyone in here. There was nothing to worry about. Right?

With a trembling breath, she steadied her lantern-holding hand and stepped across the threshold of the mine. The damp air tickled her shins just under the long skirt. The heel of her boot tapping against the rock echoed back to her with each step. Gold light fell from the lamp and circled at her feet, lighting the way as she stepped further into the tunnel. The thick rails guided her path forward into the blackness ahead. She glanced back as a little voice in her head urged her to leave this place now. Daylight burned bright just outside the opening of the tunnel, around the heavy gates that she had pulled open to reveal the mouth of the mine. She could still go back there, to the warm sunshine and back to the farm where her mother, brother and uncle stayed, safe and unaware that she had kept this little secret. There was still time to turn around, shut the doors, and never think of this place again.

Just as she thought it, she knew it would never happen. The intrigue of the abandoned Appleton Silver Mine would plague her forever unless she continued onward. And what if her little brother William found it? He would most definitely enter the mine without any supervision and probably get himself hurt along the way. She could only imagine what her mother would say to her then. Why didn't you stop him? How could you just let him go in there like that? You are old enough to know better. At sixteen, Anna was practically his second mother.

That settled it: she had to go on further. She turned away from the door and started along the mine tracks.

It didn't take long before the comforting light of the entrance was too far distant to be of any help. She swallowed against a dry throat and continued to follow the tracks further into the cavern. Each step echoed louder down the curving tunnel. Her eyes squinted against the light, trying hard to peer into the inky darkness ahead, but her small circle of lantern light was all that she could see. The mine forbade her from seeing any further.

The walls closed in tighter as she moved further down the tunnel, the small bubble of light keeping the darkness from completely swallowing her. The glow about her now trembled with the shaking in her hand.

She stopped and glanced back. The curves of the tunnel had now obscured the entryway, and she was surrounded by black. It occurred to her that if she were to get confused somehow that she would never know which way to go to escape to the outside world. But only a coward would turn back now. Whatever lay in the dark of this place would be hers to find, her secret alone.

A secret that she could have shared only with her father . . . if he were still alive.

She never would have thought that she would be here, like this right now. Only six days ago, she was just leaving Boston. Six days was all it took for her to find herself on this kind of adventure.

# CHAPTER 2

Boston, Massachusetts, 1891
Six months earlier

The night the constable came knocking was no different than any other. The rain fell and flooded some of the lower streets of Boston, and the thunder rumbled against the window panes, but other than that, there would have been no reason for Anna to worry.

The knock came as three sharp raps. Anna laid in bed but still felt wide awake despite the late hour. The grandfather clock chimed at 11 p.m., just minutes before the knock. *What callers could be coming at such a time at night and in this weather?*

Anna slipped from under the down blankets and walked to the door. From here, she peered down into the parlor on the lower floor.

A flash of lightning illuminated the room from the great windows that looked into the atrium of their three-story home. She could see Lupe, the Mexican-immigrant servant who tended to the main rooms of the house, walk to the door with her oil lamp in hand. When the woman opened the door, the spattering downpour of rain roared into the house. The clean, sharp fragrance of it drifted into Anna's room from where she watched.

"Is Mrs. Holloway about?"

"She is taking tea in the study. May I ask who is calling?" Lupe said, her voice nearly as small as her tiny waist and slight shoulders.

"Constable Kramer, ma'am," he said with a nod of his head.

Lupe stepped aside and motioned the constable into the atrium. Rain dripped from his dark blue coat and puddled on the oak floor. Mother would be upset when she saw how the water soaked her Persian rug splayed out over the floor in the atrium. The constable remained silent, his hands clasped before him, as he waited for her mother.

It was only a minute or two before Mother appeared in the atrium. She had already let her hair down and now wore her white shawl over her shoulders. The constable nodded at her with a tip of his hat.

He spoke so low now that Anna could barely hear him except for a few murmurings and a stray syllable here and there. But reaction from her mother chilled her. In front of company, Mother was always quiet and composed, a picture of still calm. Now, her shoulders trembled as though she were crying. The constable stopped talking to her and merely gazed as she continued to slump forward, her face in her hands.

Anna couldn't watch this anymore. It felt wrong so see her mother this way, but whatever the constable had told her, it was terrible. She closed the bedroom door and remained at the threshold, listening through the thin crack between the door and the jamb. The voices in the atrium were so quiet.

She was sure that her little brother, William, had heard nothing. He was likely still asleep; that boy could sleep through anything.

The constable's voice echoed louder now, his tone taking a very official sound. "You will be able to see the body in the morning."

Anna's blood ran cold under her skin. *Body?*

The door of the atrium clicked. The man must have departed, leaving her mother alone in the atrium.

*Alone in the atrium? Where was Father? Why had the constable not asked for him?* Anna knew that he had planned on staying late at the university tonight. He was working on something very important and had stated that he had made a wonderful breakthrough in his research. But he must have come home by now.

He wasn't down there with Mother.

And somewhere in Boston was a body.

# CHAPTER 3

Anna stood behind her father's desk as the house staff finished covering the furniture in his study with large white sheets. She tried to disregard them, but it was difficult because they were leaving the entire house like this: a realm of ghosts in white sheets. The place was covered as though she was supposed to forget everything and leave it behind. It was now her former life, and it was meant to remain here. She gazed up to the painting of her father and watched his eyes, as though he looked down into his study with disapproval.

It had been months since they had received the news of her father's murder, but the ache still remained. That night, when returning home from work after being there particularly late, he was robbed in the street and shot in the back during a rainstorm. The doctor said he had died instantly and the murderer was still at large.

Everything changed after that. Her father had saved enough finances for the family but willed many of his work-related items to the university or had them shipped away to some unknown destination. And what was worse, her mother fretted over where these items had gone. They certainly were not given to his wife and children. They had disappeared on that fateful night. Not that her mother would have the slightest idea what to do with these trinkets. Things like maps and codices and dusty old books written in Swedish had never held her mother's interest.

Anna turned to face the things in her father's study, but she hoped it wouldn't be the last time she would ever see them. The servants had packed most of their things and loaded them into the trunks bound for the train station.

"Anna, it is time," her mother's voice echoed up the stairs.

Perhaps for the last moment, she studied her father's face; the paint looked like it was still wet. He had had the painting commissioned just months before his death, so it appeared that he had not aged a day.

She turned away from the study and closed the door. The servants would shut up the rest of the house after they left.

Anna met her mother on the ground floor.

"Why must they cover everything?" Anna said, looking at the furniture draped in white linens.

"To protect from the dust, dear," her mother said. "And to dissuade thieves."

Just three weeks ago someone had broken into the house and had ransacked Father's study. The burglars had left everything a mess, and although the constable called the intruders "thieves," she was sure that nothing had gone missing that night. That was when her mother made arrangements to leave Boston. The incident had rattled her mother's nerves enough to decide to take her family elsewhere. There was nothing left for them here. The house was only an empty carcass, the bones of a once happy memory.

And then there was the strange telegram that came about that time.

The messenger arrived at the door on a stormy August evening and delivered the note, which was a request from one John Holloway.

That evening would be burned into her memory forever, and not only because it was another rap on the door that brought her chills. The late summer winds had swelled a stormfront over the East coast, and heavy rains threatened to flood the streets. Lightning and thunder assailed Boston that day, and Anna thought it was unusual that a postman would bother delivering a note on such a stormy evening.

Mother had opened the door and accepted the telegram. She unfurled it with her thin fingers and read it to herself.

"What's it say?" William asked first.

Anna tried to hang back, but now that William had intervened, she stepped into the parlor as well.

Mother cleared her throat. "Well, apparently, your father had a Last Will and Testament drawn up a month prior to his death."

"Didn't you know about that?" Anna asked.

Her mother feigned a smile. "I did not. It has expressed his desire for Mr. John Holloway to care for us in the event of his death."

Although Anna never said it, the timing of the will and his death just seemed a little too coincidental. But the messenger wasn't bothered by this, and neither was her mother.

With a creased forehead, Anna accepted the telegram from her mother and reread it. "Who is John Holloway?"

Mary had turned away and was almost out of the room when she said, "He's your uncle."

Anna and William looked at each other in awe. "We have an uncle?"

That was the first time either she or William had ever heard of John Holloway, and now they were leaving their home in Boston to seek a man they only knew by way of a single telegram. To New Mexico: a place in the West that she only knew by reputation from the books she snuck into her room and read by candlelight.

# CHAPTER 4

aves of heat rippled from the train platform, and the air was thick with the humidity of late summer in Boston. The stewards had already taken away and loaded their baggage, including the two large trunks, thankfully leaving them without much to carry in the stifling heat.

"Now loading tha' three o'clock train ta' Chicago," the platform steward shouted in a heavy Massachusetts accent, followed by a harsh trill from the silver whistle that hung from his neck.

Anna grasped at the fabric of her skirt and lifted it just above her ankles as a breeze teased across the platform.

As quick as a snake, her mother slapped her hands, and she dropped her skirt.

"That is not what a lady would do in public," she whispered to Anna, her eyes darting to the others on the train platform.

"Sorry, Mother," Anna said, but rolled her eyes and tugged at her lace collar as the sweat continued to trickle down her neck.

"Stand up straight, chin up," her mother's voice came again. "You must never slouch."

Anna sighed. "Yes, ma'am." She forced her spine into the straightest position she could manage but still breathe in the tight corset.

The steam engine puffed once more like a great dragon exhaling from a long journey across the mountains. Another cloud of steam drifted over the platform, enveloping them in a haze that smelled of cedar and coal.

They were about to leave Boston, maybe for good. Anna couldn't think of any of her friends that she would miss much. After all, most of the girls she had associated with at the boarding school never really shared her interest in the history of ancient Europe or studying the writings from the great libraries of Egypt. Any of her male acquaintances were better left far away from her on the other side of the country.

Anna's thoughts drifted to Mister William J. Gibbons, a 19-year-old gentleman who would often come calling at their home, usually in response to an invitation from her mother. He was unusually tall but handsome, with a tuft of thick, dark hair atop his head just like his father.

"You look particularly lovely in that dress, Miss. Holloway. An absolute picture of virtue," he always said, no matter how much she hated the gown her mother picked out for her.

Although her mother would never admit it, the woman arranged the meeting with Gibbons in hopes that Anna would marry him in a year or two. Undoubtedly, the choice of the young man had very little to do with his nice smile, but more with his father's wallet. While he currently attended the university and headed the cricket team, his family's fortune had swelled with the growth of the iron industry. They owned most of the iron warehouses in Boston as well as New York and Connecticut. Anna would surely be well-off for many years to come if she were to marry into the Gibbons family.

As appealing as that might have been, she could feel William's attentions drawn elsewhere when they would walk through the park, and another pretty young woman happened to be standing along the path. He had very little interest in Anna, and she felt it every time he held her hand.

Her father's death had interrupted any further contact she would ever have with Mr. Gibbons. The event had sent shock waves through the community, and either William had respected her family's privacy, or he now used it as an excuse to look elsewhere for a wife. And for that, she had to admit, she was relieved. And now, travelling to the New Mexico territory, she would never have to worry about him again.

In that moment of solitude, Anna took the time to readjust the back seams of the tight dress and tug at the ribbon under her chin that held her hat in place. Then she stole a glance at her mother to see if she had noticed. Not at all. In fact, she had barely noticed anything in months.

A man with a woman on his arm stepped past them. He tipped his bowler hat to them, and her mother nodded, although William seemed to be fidgeting enough to bump into the man as he passed by them.

Without a flinch, she whispered again to Anna. "A curtsy, dear. You must always curtsy to a gentleman."

"And you, King William," she said as she nudged her brother at her other side. "Take your hat off in the presence of strangers."

A faint grin appeared at the side of his mouth at the mention of her nickname for him. He grasped the brim of his hat and slipped it from his head. His mess of blonde hair stood up in different directions, but he looked up at his mother as if she was the source of all knowledge.

Anna once thought that too. Mary Elizabeth Holloway. Her mother was always so perfect, like a china doll, hair like silk and the color of straw set in ringlets without a single strand out of place. A lace collar was placed ever so carefully around her neck and her grandmother's ivory pendant at her throat. Even in the hot sun beating down upon the train platform, she did not break a sweat across her perfect skin. A lace and silk broad brim hat shaded her blue eyes that gazed upward to an approaching train.

Anna always had envied her mother's silent beauty and her golden locks, whereas, she had been born with dark brown hair and brown eyes. She looked more like her father in many ways. Her brother, William, had many more of her mother's qualities. Blonde hair, blue eyes. All except her mother's stillness and poise, which Anna sometimes wished he would soon acquire when he was being his most obnoxious. Yet, he had the unnerving ability to control himself when he wanted.

The steward called their ticket number, and they were finally able to board. He showed them the quarters they would be sharing for the long ride to Chicago, where they would change trains for another to New Mexico.

William bounded into the room. "Why is it so small?"

"The cabins are just the right size for what we need," Mary said.

The room had three beds and clean linens and drapes. The accommodations could have been far worse, considering that they could have been taking this entire journey by stagecoach. With the summer heat and the musky smell of horses that made Anna get a small gag in the back of her throat, the train was a far better option.

Their mother motioned them into the cabin and then followed the steward as he offered to show her the location of the dining and leisure cars. William rushed into the cabin, brushing past her in his haste and nearly knocking her against the wall.

"You need to calm down," Anna said to him, fuming as she untied the ribbon under her chin and tossed her hat on the narrow bunk. She loosened the collar at her throat, anything for some relief when her mother wasn't looking.

"Why?" he said with a laugh and jumped up the small ladder to the upper bunk. He pulled off his boots and let his feet dangle over the edge of the bed, right in Anna's way.

"You know, New Mexico is nothing like Boston," she said and shoved his feet away as she rested on her own bunk.

"How do you know?" he said. "You've never been there."

Anna rolled her eyes. It seemed like the only logical thing to do when dealing with a 10-year old child. "I read, you know. You should try it some time."

"*I read,*" he mimicked and leaned down to face her, his blonde hair hanging down in wild strands.

"Well, then, you would know that we are heading right into the Wild West," she said and dropped her voice with a hint of mystery. Anything to make him listen to her, and it wouldn't hurt to scare some sense into him.

"What does that mean?"

"It's an untamed place where cowboys and Indians battle it out on the desert plains," she said and made a dramatic gesture with her hand. "Where outlaws ride into the sunset, escaping the sheriff close on their heels."

"That's not true," he said.

"Yes, it is," she said. "Billy the Kid and Jesse James lived out there, and you've heard of them."

"Well, yeah . . ."

"Then you know I'm not making it up. We will probably even see an outlaw or two. They're all over out there," Anna said with a final nod.

"What did I say about those stories, Anna?" Her mother's stern, tight voice startled her. Anna glanced to the cabin door to see their mother standing there with her hands resting on her hips. "You are filling your brother's head with nonsense."

"See," William said, "I told you." Then he disappeared onto his bunk above her.

Anna shook her head. What did they know, anyway? Her mother was prim and proper, and William was just plain dumb, as most boys were. They never read the books that she enjoyed and knew nothing about the many tales of gunfighters and train robbers that populated the West. When they arrived in New Mexico, she was sure that they would need her help in adapting to the new environment. She was the only one of them that knew anything about it.

A knock sounded at the door, and William jumped from his bunk, landing with a thud. Before Anna or her mother could react, he rushed to the door and opened it to see the steward. William was barely half the man's height, but he puffed up his shoulders, straightened his back and gave a little bow.

The steward held a bronze key with a number stamped in it. "Your luggage case key," the man said and glanced over the boy and then to their mother.

"Thank you, sir," William said and took the medallion from the man's hand. He reached into his own waistcoat pocket and pulled out a coin, but leaned away from his mother so she couldn't see him. He placed it in the man's palm and gave a little nod. "For your trouble."

The steward's eyebrow cocked to one side, and he waited for a moment. Then his fingers curled over the coin as he bowed. William shut the door, his posture just as straight as when he had opened it, and turned back to the bunk and climbed up the stepladder.

Anna watched him with narrowed eyes. Their mother said nothing but just went back to arranging the things on the bed. When he finally settled onto the upper bunk, Anna nudged him with the heel of her hand.

"What was that?" she said with a whisper.

"What?"

"Where did you get the money?" she said and glanced back at their mother.

A smile formed on his thin lips. "You're not the only smart one."

That was when she realized that he had pilfered the coin from the man on the train platform—the man that had tipped his hat to them. And this wasn't the first time he had done something like that. He was charming and sweet and had an uncanny knack for kleptomania. Anna used to bring it to her mother's attention, but he so rarely got reprimanded for doing such things that she stopped wasting her time.

William had a way with adults, something she would never understand. He got along so well with Mother, yet he was always moving or making noise. She could never get away with that without a stern look from her. He rarely got reprimanded for being such a brat. And today was no different. Anna stepped away from his bed while he still smiled at her.

She settled back into her bunk and ignored her mother placing her things on the bed in such a way as to not disturb the linens. It would be some time before the train would depart, and it was best to rest a little if she could.

Sleep was difficult, though. Random but troubling thoughts continued to plague her as they often did when she was alone in her head. This adventure, traveling across the country by train to the fringe of the Wild West, should be exciting, but she was nervous. Her mother had found a single photograph of Uncle John among her father's things in his study, and this was all they had to go on when they would eventually arrive in New Mexico. How could they have lived this long and never known that their father had a brother? But their mother had known about him all along. There was very little explanation from their mother, despite how hard Anna had pushed to learn more.

The night before they had left Boston, she had sat with her mother in the lounge as she examined her uncle's portrait.

"Who is Uncle John, anyway?"

Her mother worked on her lace under the light of an oil lamp. "He is a cattle rancher and farmer in the territory of New Mexico, and he is your father's younger brother."

"Why have I never heard of him?" Anna asked.

Mary tatted her lace, never looking up. "That is just the way it is. Your father has not been in contact with him for years, nor has the family."

"Why not?"

"His family doesn't speak of it," she said, her voice smooth as a lake on a calm day. "And neither shall we."

"Did they have a fight or something?"

Mary sighed. "Anna, we will be done with this business of family feuding because it is none of ours."

Anna could only deduce that there must have been some kind of fight and nobody had seen him in years.

And now they were going all the way across the country to live with him. Not only across the country but to the very edge of the Wild West. What if John was deranged and belonged in a hospital for the mentally ill? Then where were they to go?

"He has offered us his home," her mother said in her soft and hushed tones. And that was all she would ever say about it.

Anna didn't push it. She could see her mother was scared too, despite her prim and proper manner. It was still there, though, hidden within the fine contours of her carefully pinned hair and perfectly placed lace. Boston had become for them a terrifying place, and they had to find something different.

The train ride was long and very boring. Thankfully, the luggage attendant had brought their things to their cabin not long after they had boarded. William had burrowed into his trunk and found his toy soldiers, some of which appeared mismatched, and, undoubtedly, they were "borrowed" from his friends.

Anna discovered the bag with her books, particularly the penny novels her mother disapproved of. She tucked these into the pages of the more appropriate books, and while the train rattled down the tracks and her mother tatted her lace, she secretly read the harrowing tales of the gunfighters of Arizona and Texas. Yes, she was nervous about leaving Boston, but she was going to see the West for the first time in her life; a place that she had only read about in her penny novels. This would be a land of cowboys and Indians and beautiful women in fine silk dresses that swooned when their gallant man walked by in his boots with a lasso and revolver at his hip.

At least she hoped it would be like the books.

Then there was that other nagging problem: Uncle John.

It was strange, though, and Anna continued to think back on the telegram. Why would their father wish for them to stay with his brother if they hadn't spoken in years?

# CHAPTER 5

The trip to Chicago took two days, and then the change-over to the next train went smoother than expected. They were set up in similar quarters, and the voyage continued southwest, bound for New Mexico territory, to a strange frontier Anna had only read about.

She took her book and left the cramped room that seemed to grow smaller every hour. Her mother's silence grew louder than if she screamed. Perhaps if she would talk to her children about how nervous she was or about what they might expect in this new place, it might be easier to handle, but her silence made this trip almost unbearable.

Anna clutched her book to her chest as she walked down the narrow aisle between the cabins. The car rocked back and forth, and she caught herself against the wall once but continued forward to the seating car. Perhaps if she could get out of the cabin and to a car full of windows, it wouldn't feel that the world was collapsing.

She pushed through into the seating car and felt the open, sunny feel of the atmosphere. Plush, red and gold velvet seats greeted her as she moved into the car and found an empty spot. She sat near the window and opened the silk embroidered blinds to look out into the morning.

No buildings. No carriages. No people. Only rolling hills and grasslands. There was nothing out there but wilderness and this train. What if their train was robbed by highwaymen with guns and bandanas covering their faces as they waved their shiny pistols? But that was a silly idea.

Her fingers moved to the pendant at her neck; it was something her father had given to her, a "good luck charm," as he had called it. He had found it during one of their many trips to Sweden. Ever since then, she never took it off and often found herself reaching for it in times such as these when she wished he was with her.

She felt the curious pendent, a symbol he once said that was given to him by a priest in honor of his visit. It was molded in solid iron and was a simple cross of two equal length bars meeting in the exact middle. Small symbols decorated its smooth exterior surface, but they were nothing that she could read or had even seen anywhere else before. Every time she rubbed it, he said it would bring her luck, and her father said it would bring even more luck if she always remembered that he was "two steps to her right." She only wished that were true now.

The train car rocked again, and she tucked the pendant under her bodice. She opened the book she had brought with her and peered over the edge of the tome, ever so careful that nobody could see what she was really reading. Of course, it was not *Hester*, as the cover said, but it was the latest novel she had picked up at the train shop and was the gossip stories of the Western crime sprees. She had tried to read *Hester* once, but it never held her interest. She now only kept it to hide her penny novels.

The most fascinating gunslinger since Jesse James had been terrorizing the West for the last ten years, robbing banks and trains with his notorious gang. He was Diamond Dave Thibodaux, so named because of the diamond-studded pistols that he had special-made and carried in his holsters. Born in New Orleans, an orphan of the Civil War, he pick-pocketed his way across the frontier until he came to the Western towns of Missouri where he met up with his right-hand man, Johnny Holiday. Together they robbed more banks, trains and stagecoaches than any other outlaw pair that had ever lived.

Then, about ten years ago they robbed the Bulwark Express, a large armored train filled with a government payload going from California to Washington. Their entire gang was captured except Dave and

Johnny, and nobody had seen or heard from them since, and the whereabouts of the payload remained unknown.

Anna could not help it. Anytime she saw a new penny novel on the shelf about Diamond Dave she had to get it, even though she knew they were probably just fictional stories about a real man. Her mother had scolded her about them ("because ladies do not read such horrible things"), but she kept them hidden under her bed or among her other books. She only hoped that she could still find the newest editions out in New Mexico. And why wouldn't she? She was going to be living in the heart of outlaw territory, where the gunslingers roamed, robbing from the rich to give to the poor, just like Robin Hood.

Days and nights blended together as they travelled, but the train eventually rolled to a stop, and Anna felt butterflies in her stomach.

Her mother worked at pinning her own hair into a perfect mound of curls atop her head. Anna tried to mimic it, but it just didn't work as well. As soon as Mary had finished with herself, she stepped to Anna and began to curl and pin her hair until she had a masterpiece.

"I would like you to wear your blue dress with the cream lace," Mary said.

"But that one's so difficult to wear," Anna said, looking at her mother's reflection in the small hand mirror. "I can't breathe in it."

"Shallow breaths, then. Make sure your corset is laced properly."

Hair in place. Hats straight. Dresses pressed and not a single wrinkle. William's shirt was white and perfectly in line.

Her mother looked like an angel and not the nervous wreck that Anna knew she was. Anna hoped that her own nerves didn't show. Her mother helped her place her blue silk and lace hat in order.

The attendant aided the ladies from the train's car and out onto the platform. The day must have been going on toward evening because the sun appeared almost red, and the light cast across the platform at odd angles.

Boston was hot, but this was different. Dry. Parched. Despite the steam erupting from the engine, the air remained still and scorching as an oven.

Through the thick steam, they couldn't see much farther than the train station platform where they stood. Anna glanced up to her mother as she cleared her throat with a small but ladylike cough, something her mother only did when she became nervous. She started to move forward but then stopped.

The steam began to clear, and the New Mexico landscape revealed itself. The red-brown mountainside curled like a chunk of Dutch chocolate behind the station. The steam rose like fog around the pillars of the main building and licked about a pair of dusty boots. Silhouetted against the station, a figure stood in a long, dark brown, leather duster. His shoulders were broad and stooped to one side as he leaned against the hitching post. His head tilted against the evening sun, and his face remained half-shadowed under a cowboy hat.

As the steam cleared, he lifted his head, and a single finger tilted up his hat just a little, revealing soft brown eyes, ruddy brown hair, a square jaw and a face close to needing a shave. This man was the perfect picture of the Wild West; it was far better than Anna could have imagined. Boots. Hat. Duster. It was all true.

"Is that Uncle John?" William asked from beside his mother.

Anna had seen the old photograph her mother had shown her. There was a definite resemblance to the picture of their father's brother and the man standing before them.

"I believe it is," Mary responded, and she sounded just as surprised as they all felt.

# CHAPTER 6

John strode toward them with all the confidence of a western cowboy through the steam of the train. Even his swagger was exactly as described in her penny novels of the gunfighter that had ridden for days and stopped at a saloon for a drink.

He removed his hat and placed it against his chest. The setting sun made the red in his hair even ruddier. "Ladies, welcome to New Mexico."

Mary nodded, tilted her head to the side and smiled. "Thank you so much for the invitation."

What had gotten into her mother? The woman had just relaxed a little bit. Anna rolled her eyes, and William laughed at her. She nudged him to keep quiet.

They followed Uncle John to the hitching post where he had tied his wagon. Two sable-brown quarter horses waited where they were hitched to the wagon. John loaded the trunks with William's help as Anna looked around the corner of the wagon. That was all it was. Just a simple wagon with one uncomfortable bench in the front and space for their trunks in the back. Somewhere in the back of her thoughts, she had expected a coach, covered from the setting sun, with velvet cushions and silk curtains, just like in her novels. Not this simple wooden carriage. She and William would have to sit on the trunks if they were to ride to the ranch house.

She watched Uncle John lift the gate in the back and chain it as his coat drifted back a bit from his hip. For that moment, Anna didn't believe what she saw. The glint of metal blinked fast in her eyes. But as she moved back up to the front of the wagon, she was sure.

It was a gun.

This made her shudder, but why should she be surprised? This was the Wild West. Pretty much everyone carried a gun here; at least that is what her novels had suggested. She approached the front where the iron step had been folded out for them. Somehow, John had already made his way there and held his hand out to help her up into the wagon.

She met his eyes as the dry desert air blew his hair under his hat. A subtle gold flick in his irises sparkled in this fading sunlight. The memory of the gun in the holster at his hip flooded to the surface again, and she hesitated. Then she accepted his help and stepped up into the wagon.

William climbed in after her, and they did their best to get comfortable on the luggage in the back. William took off his hat, and his blonde, tousled hair already looked so messy. Anna rested back against the trunks and gazed out across the desert.

"Hope you ladies and gentleman had a good trip from Boston," John said from where he sat, the reins comfortable in his hands as the horses plodded forward down the road.

"Very good, thank you," her mother said with a nod and almost-pursed lips.

"Is this your wagon?" William said.

Anna shot him a glance: *why did you ask such a stupid question?* But Uncle John simply nodded. "Why, yes sir, it is. My horses, too."

She felt nervous to ask him anything but now felt that she had to since her entire family already had done so. "Is it true that you have a cattle ranch?"

"Yes, ma'am. But it's more of a farm," he said, his eyes still trained on the trail.

"With cows and chickens?" William asked.

"Cows, chickens, horses and lots of corn."

"I've never seen a chicken," William said with a smile and a glint in his eye.

"Well, you're about to see a bunch of 'em," John said.

"Do you milk your own cows?" Anna asked.

"Indeed, we do."

William pushed his way up toward the front of the wagon. "We? Who else is there?"

"Oh, I have lots of help," John replied. "One man can't do the whole thing himself."

A real farm! Again, it was something that Anna had read much about but had never seen growing up in the city and moving around in Europe so much. Jesse James and Diamond Dave had been raised on farms. She wondered if they milked cows and tended the chickens, out in the thick of farm life with open fields of corn or wheat waving under the summer sky.

Golden sunlight turned to hues of orange and pink that settled across the salt brush and sand. The light gave way to twilight when they approached the outskirts of the farm, allowing the desert air to cool a little. The horses led the wagon between fields of corn that stretched as far as Anna could see. The corn stalks rose almost as high as their seats in the wagon. The road wound around the fields and then dropped into a clearing.

A barn rose out of the cornfields, and not far beyond it stood the house. It was not at all what Anna had expected. The Western deserts had seemed so barren and unsettled, but this home appeared like an oasis in the sand with fields of green cornstalks and a beautiful house in the center of it all. So often in her books, the farm houses were simple one-room log cabins with dirt floors.

The home stood with two levels and a broad porch that sprawled around the entire structure. The closer they approached, the more they could smell the aroma of a fresh meal, signaled by the smoke puffing from the top of the chimney.

Uncle John walked the horses to the front of the home and pulled the wagon to a stop. As the wheels ground to a halt in the dirt, a woman stepped from the front doors. Her once-black hair, now peppered gray, was pulled back into a braid, exposing her brown, weathered face. Her eyes lit up into a smile as she saw them pull into the driveway. Her wrinkled, knobbed hands clasped against her apron and she walked to a solitary and heavy bell mounted in the center of the circular drive-through. She rang the bell which signaled others to emerge from the barn and surrounding structures about the farm.

John climbed from the wagon and helped Mary down first. Then he turned to the children. Anna eyed him as he lifted William down and turned a hand to her. She took it and stepped onto the gravel and dirt of the driveway.

The woman approached the wagon, her face in a wrinkled smile.

"Ah, *muy bonita,*" she spoke with a thick Mexican accent. "You must be Anna."

Anna smiled and took her smooth hand. "Yes, ma'am."

She then turned to her brother, crouching down to meet his height. "And young *señor* William."

William smiled and nodded.

"I am Maria," the old woman spoke and led them to the open porch. "Welcome to New Mexico. We are so excited to have you here."

Every wrinkle in her sun-licked skin told them she meant it. She then turned and signaled the group to follow her into the house.

The house loomed like a warm smile upon the twilight desert. The two stories were framed in thick dark wood and the stucco walls painted brick-red. A heavy wood door with a single stained-glass window in the center opened to the front room.

Hand-woven rugs adorned the floor before the empty hearth. Anna gazed at the comfortable furniture set about the room and the wall of shelves filled with books: *Robison Crusoe, Treasure Island,* the works of William Shakespeare. So many titles she had read or wanted to read. This place was nothing as she had first expected.

"You are welcome to any of the books that you would like," Uncle John's voice came from behind as he carried in a load of their luggage. "I love to read, myself—sit by the fire every night and read something; that is if I can find my glasses."

For some reason that made her cringe a little inside. He was a dusty cowboy; he should not need glasses to read. Old people need reading glasses.

Maria moved to the back of the room to a stairway that ascended to the second floor. "Upstairs are your sleeping quarters. Anna and William's rooms are on the left. *Señora* Holloway, let me show you to your room."

Her mother, pretty and demure as always, nodded with grace that came so easily to her and followed the Mexican woman. William followed, and Anna took the back of the line.

They finally found their rooms as they parted ways from their mother. William ran inside his room and leaped onto the down-stuffed mattress as Anna stood at the doorway.

"Wow, this bed is better than at home," he spoke, excited.

For some reason, that had hurt her. "Don't say that."

"Don't say what?" he said, not paying her any attention.

"This place is beautiful, but it isn't our home."

"Yes, it is. Mother says we're going to live here now."

Of course, mother said that, but it had to be only temporary just until they could get their affairs in order at the home in Boston. They would move back some day. Anna just knew it. That's why they left father's study just as it was. This place was amazing, and New Mexico was bound to have some great adventures, but William now acted like Boston never existed. That they hadn't just left their entire life back on the East coast.

"William, stop it."

His brow furrowed and then his eyes saddened. "*You* stop it," he responded. "I like it here, and Uncle John is nice. And I like Maria too."

"We can't stay here forever," she spoke, perhaps harsher than she intended because his eyes began to fill with tears. "Uncle John is not our father, and this isn't our home."

"I don't intend to replace your father," John's soft voice came from behind them.

Anna turned and felt her cheeks flush with embarrassment.

"I only want you to have a safe place to live. Your father was my older brother, and I made him a promise to care for his family if anything should happen to him," he said and placed the trunk down at the doorway.

His brown eyes seemed sad below his ruddy brown hair.

Anna's cheeks burned. She stammered for words. "I—I'm—sorry. I didn't mean to offend you."

"No harm done," he said with a forced smile. He turned to go down the stairs. "I will bring the rest of your things after I have seen to your mother's accommodations." Then he was gone.

With slumped shoulders, she turned to face William.

"Way to go, Anna," he said and went back to his bed.

She hung her head and leaned against the door jam. Everything had gone so wrong since they had left Boston. No, since her father had died. Why did he have to leave them like this? None of this would have happened if he were still alive. Why did he have to go to the university that night? Why did he have to get shot? Everything would have been perfect if he had just stayed home that evening instead of going out in the rain.

Anna turned and stepped into the adjoining room, which was arranged in a similar fashion to her brother's room. A single bed below a window and a small table and chair with a candle and flint.

She stepped to the pane glass window that overlooked the farm and to the last embers of the fading twilight. William was right, but she would never admit that to him. They were never going back to Boston. This was going to be their home now. As much as she loved the romance of the Wild West, those were just stories. She wanted everything to go back to normal. But that was never going to happen.

After a meal of fresh tortillas and chicken roasted with a sauce of peppers and tomatoes, the family and ranch staff turned in for the evening. As she walked up the stairs behind her mother, Anna's stomach rumbled with all the new flavors and spices that she had tasted tonight.

Her mother slipped into William's room, and she could hear them through the wall as she spoke in soft tones to him. This happened every night: William would act like he needed mother before he could sleep, and she would stay with him while he settled into bed.

Anna slipped into her nightgown and crawled into bed, under the hand-sewn blankets as she found the pendant at her neck. She rubbed its familiar contours and bit her lip. She knew that her mother would step into her room tonight too, as soon as William pretended he was going to sleep.

When the sound stopped in the next room, she heard the opening click of the door latch, and candlelight flowed into Anna's room. She lifted her head from her pillow.

Her mother approached her bed and sat down on the edge of the soft, down mattress. She curled her fingers through Anna's dark brown hair.

"I need you to be strong right now, my sweet," she said in a whisper. "William needs your help. He looks up to you more than you realize."

Anna barely nodded. *Oh, heavens.* "I know. I'm trying. It's just—I miss Father so much. I just wish everything could go back to the way it was."

"I know you do." Mary noticed the pendant in her daughter's fingers. She smiled. "I remember when he gave that to you. He got it while we were in Sweden, and it was only for you. He had so many stories, and you listened to them all. You learned the languages. I can't believe you even learned to read some of the old tablets he brought home."

Her mother's eyes grew distant as if she could still see that memory. "You are just like him. I know you will be strong." She leaned down and kissed her forehead.

This was the type of conversation she craved with her mother. It was something true, devoid of any need to be proper. She was more like this when Anna was younger, and they were all together in Europe. Maybe that was why she missed Sweden so much. Those were the days when they were the happiest.

Then Mary blew out the candle and slipped out of the bedroom. Anna remained in darkness, seeing only the moonlight filtered through the lace curtains on the window. Her eyes grew heavy, and she left behind the anxiety of this new place. But, her dreams carried small glimpses of a pistol and the sound of gun shots firing in the distance.

# CHAPTER 7

"Good morning, *mi hija*," Maria's voice boomed in the dark bedroom.

The early morning hours barely allowed a wisp of light on the horizon as Maria called out to her. Anna propped herself up onto her elbows and cringed at Maria's bright lantern.

"What time is it?" Anna said with a croak in her voice.

"It is time for breakfast and then work," she spoke with far too much cheer for the early hour.

"What are you talking about?" Anna muttered and covered her head with the pillow.

Maria snatched the pillow away and lightly patted Anna's leg until she sat upright. "Work, my dears. A farm does not run itself."

Anna rolled her eyes. It must be too early in the morning to be that cheerful and alert.

She climbed out of bed and changed into her clothes. William appeared at her door. Maria must have awakened him as well. He had covered his messy hair with a broad-brim hat, and Anna braided her hair to keep it out of her eyes. After a quick bite of biscuits, eggs and bacon, they followed Maria out to the barn.

As the sun rose over the edge of the mountains, William and Anna were put to cleaning out the horse stalls with a few more of the farm hands that seemed to populate this place. The other two men worked on moving a few of the harnessed mares from the stalls and out to the pasture.

Anna watched them walk the animals through the main door while she stood next to Maria. The first mare, her coat a dark sable to match her eyes, glanced about the space outdoors. Without warning, she skittered to the side and pulled against the harness, threatening to rear back. The man holding onto her turned, sensing the danger, tugged at the rope and spoke forcefully in Spanish to her.

Maria shook her head and leaned in to Anna. "You see, you must be very careful around these creatures. A spooked horse can be a deadly horse." She turned to face Anna. "Have you ever ridden?"

Anna wrinkled her nose at the familiar smell of the horse. "I learned at the preparatory school in Boston, but I never much cared for it."

Maria smiled and laughed a little. "Well, it is a good skill to have out here." Then she turned and led Anna beyond the horse barn and to the structures at the south end of the farm.

If the smell in the barn wasn't bad enough, Maria took her to the chicken coops, where she showed Anna how to clean the pens and feed the birds.

She had never hated chickens so much in her life.

When her boots, dress and apron smelled like the chicken coop, and the sun rose high and hot, Maria showed her to the cattle barn, where the cows stood waiting to be milked.

The chickens weren't enough?

Maria laughed as she watched Anna's shoulders slump and she dropped her head.

"Well, the cows will not milk themselves," Maria said and demonstrated the procedure. She pulled a stool up to the cow's udders and placed a silver bucket next to the stool. After positioning herself upon the stool with her elbows on her knees, Maria cleaned the teats with a damp cloth and placed the bucket underneath the udder. With a firm grasp, she proceeded to extract the milk from two teats simultaneously. The milk flowed easily into the bucket with each squeeze.

The woman stood with the bucket in hand. "Then you dump the milk in the can." She carried it to a hip-high silver can across from the stalls. The milk sloshed about in the bucket she placed on the ground beside the can. Maria opened the can, exposing a layer of cheesecloth held by a ring over the opening of the can.

"What is that?" Anna leaned over the can, gazing at the loosely woven cloth.

"It filters anything that might be in the milk," she said and poured the milk through the cloth. Bits of hay and other debris got caught in the cross fibers of the cloth as the milk poured from the bucket. Anna felt a little bubble of nausea grow in her stomach. It was not so much the small pieces of hay that bothered her as much as the other stuff. Heaven only knows what else could be in that milk.

As soon as Maria had closed the lid back on the milk can, she turned her smiling face back up to Anna. "Carlos will help you carry the can to the spring house when you are done. Come, I will show you."

Leaving the barn was the best moment of the morning because Anna could finally breathe fresh air. She followed Maria to the spring house, which stood behind the barn and under a small grove of trees. The brick and stone structure was but a single room with two windows and a shingled roof. The door creaked open on rusty hinges as they entered.

Unlike the rest of the farm, this room smelled clean with cool, damp air. The tinkling of spring water popped in the small space. The house had been erected over the spring, with the edges of the water source lined in smooth brick to prevent the ground from eroding away with the water. Two individual milk cans sat upright in the spring water, cooling the milk inside the cans to the water's temperature.

"The cans get placed here where the milk and cream separate as the cans cool in the water. They stay here for a day until they are cold. Then we can skim the cream off the top, leaving the milk for us," Maria said.

Anna listened to her as she gazed out the window, her eyes following the course of the stream as it wound its way around the edge of the cornfields and into the distance.

"What do you do with the cream?" Anna asked.

"Well, when you are done with the milking, I'll show you how we churn the cream into butter and buttermilk. It's the secret to my wonderful biscuits."

Maria stood upright and stepped back out of the spring house and closed the door as soon as Anna followed her. "In the meantime," she said as she walked back to the cattle barn, "you will have four cows to milk, every twelve hours, and the stalls need to be mucked every day."

"Mucked?" Anna said, her nose wrinkled in a grimace.

"Cleaned. There is a rake and shovel in the back room of the barn. You will find a pitchfork there as well to add the straw into the stalls. The best time to muck is after milking, then let the girls out to the pasture to eat while you clean."

*Ugh.* This was turning into so much more than just chickens and milk cows.

"Well," Maria said, the bright colors on her skirt catching the morning rays of sunlight as she turned. "I will leave you to it." The woman left her in the barn as the cow in the first stall glanced back to Anna with its big brown eye.

She turned and looked at the cow, which stood patiently against the harness.

"I hate this place," she mumbled and sat down on the short stool at the cow's midsection. This was not her idea of the Wild West.

She hated milk now, too.

Anna leaned down, holding her breath against the odor of cowmusk, urine and cow poop that littered the place. The pink teats felt rough and warm to the touch. She cringed as her hand wrapped about the flesh, and she squeezed, just as she saw Maria do, but nothing happened. Again, she tried, but the cow only glanced back at her in curiosity.

"What? I don't want to be a part of this any more than you do," she spoke to the animal.

She wriggled the cramps out of her fingers and tried again. Again and again. She repositioned her hand and squeezed again as her hand dropped.

A squirt of milk hit the bottom of the silver bucket with a sharp tink sound.

Anna laughed and hopped on the stool a little bit. The animal glanced back at her again.

"Ha ha! Did you see that?" she exclaimed and did it again with her other hand.

But the joy of the singular experience soon disappeared as her hands ached and her joints began to swell, and that was only after the first cow. Thankfully, the stink of the cattle soon faded or she was just getting used to it. One thing was for sure, though: she was never going to get the smell out of her hair and clothes.

She moved on to the next cow and started with her just as Maria had. The damp cloth the woman had used was draped over the stall, and she wiped down the teats of the next cow. The animal turned its head to watch her as she cleaned the udders and then repositioned the bucket. She started the milking process all over again.

Tink. Tink. Tink. The milk hit the bucket with each squeeze of her hands. The sound and the feel of the milking began to be rhythmic. And boring.

So boring.

A meow of a cat caught her attention, and she glanced behind her to the stall barrier. An orange tabby stepped daintily along the edge of the wood, its yellow eyes looking down on her with curiosity. The cat's tail curled and swished as he rubbed his cheek along the supporting beam of the stall.

"What are you doing here?" Anna said, smiling up at him from where she sat.

A rattling purr grew from his throat, and he jumped down with finesse beside her. He arched his back and leaned against her leg, his eyes looking up to her again.

"You want some milk?" She stroked his back and the tabby lifted is head to meet the palm of her hand. "Okay, sweetie." The barn was littered with all sorts of cups and containers. There had to be something that she could use. Then she found it, a stoneware bowl on the upper shelf above the stalls where the stall cleaning implements were located. She pulled it down and poured a little of the milk from the bucket into the bowl.

The tabby seemed to forget about her for a moment and lapped at the bowl.

"What? No 'thank you'?" she said with a smile and got back to working on the udder again.

Well, at least she had a little buddy with her now. Having this kitty with her would be some small amount of company in this disgusting work. She concentrated on his purring while she continued with the rhythm of milking again.

After the last cow was milked and she had filtered and filled two cans, Carlos arrived and helped her carry the silver cans into the spring house. Walking into the spring house was a welcome relief from the heat and smell of the barn. But just as she was enjoying it, Carlos suggested that she begin the chore of mucking the stalls. The thought of more work for her sore hands was too much right now.

"I need a break," she said and wiped the sweat from her face with the back of her hand.

"But the cows need to go out to pasture for the day."

"Fine," she said. "I will take them out, but then I need a break. I will clean the stalls when I'm done." She turned and stormed out of the spring house, leaving Carlos standing at the door and laughing at her.

The hot sun pounded down on her as she ran away from the spring house and to the barn, unlatching each of the four pens as the cows wandered into the corral. She didn't wait for them to get far before she escaped into the cornfield along the edge of the spring that burbled into the spring house, the last echoes of Carlos's laughter still piercing into her ears. She wanted as much distance as she could get between herself and that building right now. Unfortunately, the smell of the barn followed her. It was stuck to her hands and her clothes, and it was probably permanently seared into her nostrils too.

Her mind fumed in anger as she slowed to a fast pace through the field and emerged into the pasture at the far reaches of the farm. She ducked between the lines of the barbed-wire fence and walked. She didn't know where she was going, but it was good enough to just get away from everyone else.

All the important conversations she had had with her mother since her father had died now raced through her head as she stormed through that field. She was angry at everyone right now. Mad at her father for leaving them all alone. This was not how New Mexico was supposed to be. Why did Uncle John bring them here: to be farm hands? For a brief while, she had been optimistic about coming here, but this was nothing like her novels. Running a farm was too hard, and that was not what she had hoped for when she stepped off the train. And she was angry especially at Maria right now—because she had actually liked her at first, and now she was the Devil in a Mexican dress. And she was angry at all the cows and chickens around the world, too.

When she finally looked up from the ground, she had crossed the pasture to a thicket of trees. Beyond the edge of the woods, she heard a burbling stream.

She entered the grove and saw the sparkling silver water. Kneeling down at the water's edge, she dipped her aching hands into the water. The cold stream soothed her painful joints, and she hoped it would wash the smell away as well. She splashed some against her sweaty face, and the refreshing chill cooled her mood somewhat.

Sitting back against her heels, she rubbed out her shoulders and leaned into a tree. She gazed up into the canopy of leaves and then realized she didn't remember seeing this thicket of trees upon first inspection of the farm yesterday. She must have walked further than she originally thought. She may not even be on the farm any longer.

*Oh well,* she thought. *Maybe Maria won't be able to find me then.*

The thought made her smile, and she leaned back deeper against the tree.

A soft breeze rustled the leaves, and it reminded her of the park in Boston just outside their home. Sometimes the odor of fresh baked bread drifted on the wind from the market up the street. The air here had no such fragrance, but it was fresh and filled with the perfume of flowers and trees. Perhaps that wasn't so bad.

A faint squeak caught her attention, a sound like a rusty hinge. She opened her eyes and glanced around her. Had someone followed her out here? The stream continued to gurgle and the leaves rustled, but she heard nobody else around the thicket. Another breeze stirred the trees again.

And the squeak happened once more.

Anna rose to her feet and glanced through the trees along the stream bank. If that was William, then he was going to get it. He had no business following her out here. She stepped through the brush, the branches scratching her arms and catching on the edges of her dress until she emerged into a clearing. It had been well-hidden from the bank where she had stopped to wash her hands.

The source of the sound soon became evident, and she was positive that nobody had followed her out here.

Within the clearing, beyond the thick wall of green shrubs and trees, stood the chained doors to an abandoned mine shaft. The doors held closed by a heavy rusted chain, shuddered against the breeze and squeaked with the slight pivot in their rusty hinges.

# CHAPTER 8

The great gates to the entrance must have hung on those hinges for a hundred years. The wood had long since grayed and splintered with years of sun bleaching, heat and other elements.

Iron bars, brown with layers of rust, closed two smaller windows cut in the doors. The chain clinked at the gust of wind that shook the gates like a big exhale from a sleeping giant.

As Anna moved in closer to the gates, her boot caught something in the ground, and she nearly stumbled. A set of iron rails, now covered in a layer of dirt, vines and rock, snaked across the rock and plunged under the gate. She kicked at it, sending a reverberating gong deep inside the shaft.

She moved up to the great gate and stood on her tip-toes, peering into the barred windows. Beyond the gate lay a gaping, dark tunnel, silent and still.

Nothing. No vast underworld stacked with gold and sparkling gems. Disappointing.

The gates shifted with another breeze, and the chain clinked against the wood. The chain was heavy in her hands, caked in rust and grime. But the lock bore only a minimal amount of wear. Perhaps it was a stronger metal. It couldn't be a new lock, not with all this vine growth and rust on everything else. Nobody could even care that this old place was out here.

She followed the twisting and curling growth of vines above the door when a glint of metal sheeting caught her eye. The vines tore away in a blanket of green with minimal resistance and collapsed to the side of the track. With a step back, she saw the metal sheet, a large iron-plated sign bolted above the gates and stamped with thick lettering: Appleton Silver Co.

A silver mine, long forgotten and chained shut so that somebody like her could never re-enter. But that only made it more interesting. Beyond these gates and the heavy iron chain lay a vast network of tunnels and tracks that would provide much in the way of adventure, so long as she was brave enough to explore them. If only she could get past the chain.

She wasn't about to give up that easily. All it would take is some ingenuity and patience. She stepped away from the entryway and scanned about the track. There had to be something here. It was the wilds of New Mexico, and a rock should be found anywhere. She shuffled the tip of her boot around the rails, under the vines and around the planks.

*Thunk.*

There it was. She stooped to pick up the stone, thick enough to carry the gravity needed but not too heavy to lift. It was worth the try.

She raised the rock above her head and dropped it against the chain. Nothing else happened except for a shower of brown-orange flakes of rust falling from the chain and the threat that smashing her finger doing this might cause some trouble. Hey, maybe that would get her out of milking cows, though. Again, she dropped the rock, the impact reverberating into her palm.

The rock dropped again, but this time a link of the chain bent, showing a fissure in the weather-softened metal. Once more should do it. She dropped the rock with all the force her tired arms could gather, and the chain link cracked. The rusted chain fell to the ground in a heap.

Blood pounded in her head. *Keep calm.* She slid the chain out of the way and grasped the iron latch of the gate. With all her body weight, she heaved the door open, and the hinges creaked in protest. The sound rebounded through the miles of tunnels dug into the hills and then into the dark. Anna cringed at the sound. Anybody within a mile of the tunnel could have heard that.

A waft of cool, underground air gusted out from the black tunnel, blowing back a strand of her hair that had teased at her cheek.

"Hello?" she called out, and the echo bounced back to her. *Silly girl. Nobody was in there.* And if someone answered back, she would probably just drop everything and run back to the farm.

Inside the tunnel, dust and vines covered the tracks that curved into the darkness along the rocky earth. She stepped inside and paced along the track planks. It was so black in there. The darkness could swallow her whole if she went in too deep.

She bit her lip. The stalls at the farm still waited for her, and she had been gone longer than she had planned. Someone would eventually come looking for her. Her fingers still grasped around the edge of the gate, though. She wanted to see more, to walk deeper into that darkness. But if anyone else came, she would lose it all. Her secret place, gone.

And she needed a light anyway. *Can't get too far inside the tunnel without a lantern.*

That was it. She pulled the gate closed and rested the chain back through the latches. *Close enough. Wait, the vines were still piled up along the track.* She pulled some through the gate windows and across the latch. *There. Now it looked untouched again.*

As she backed away from the gate, she smiled. So many possibilities for the cave. A place to read her books. A place to draw. A place to just get away from William and her mother and Uncle John. And especially Maria.

Her lungs filled with the fresh air and she started back to the farm, ready to take on the cows and chickens again.

Thoughts of the mine filled her head for the rest of the day. At least the work was bearable now, as long as she kept her thoughts distracted. It didn't keep her back from hurting after mucking the stalls, and every creak of the barn door reminded her of the mine gates shifting on rusty hinges.

The sun came close to the mountain tops by the time Maria rang the dinner bell. The crew gathered toward the house, and Anna met William as he started up the porch.

He scuffled his feet up the stairs and took off his hat. His hair had matted with sweat against his head.

"You do okay today?" she asked him.

"I guess," he said and looked up at her. "I'm kind of tired."

"I'm hungry," she said.

"Me too."

"I fed the horses today," he said and looked up at her with a smile. "That was fun. What did you do?"

A grin played at the edges of her mouth. *Oh, if he only knew.* "Nothing much. Just cows and chickens. They smell awful." She scrunched up her nose, and he giggled.

They washed up at the water basin and sat with the rest of the crew for dinner. The hardest thing to do was to eat slowly and keep her manners. Her stomach growled so much while Uncle John said grace that she thought everyone would look up at her. Offending the Lord wasn't a good idea tonight.

Maria might be a difficult task master, but she made a delightful dinner. Anna broke into a soft, warm roll when Maria spoke. "I wanted to say how proud I am of you two today," she said with a smile. "You both worked so hard."

William and Anna glanced at each other. *Why would she be proud?*

Maria continued. "Both *Señor* John and I thought it was a good idea for you to understand a little about how the farm worked. One person alone cannot do it all by himself. That kind of work won't be required of you every day, but now you see."

So, some of that was Uncle John's doing. All that work, for what? To teach them a lesson?

Anna's jaw tightened and her fingers clenched around the fork in her hand. It didn't matter now. *Just think of other things.* The kitty in the barn was cute, and she planned on making it hers. She touched the fork to the ceramic plate and the little squeaky sound it made caused her heart to speed up. It was like the creak of the hinges. The thought of the gaping, black entrance to the cavern filled her thoughts, and her grip on the fork relaxed. At least she had found a secret hiding place.

Tomorrow she could return to the mine.

The morning didn't begin as early as it had the day before, and as she rose, her sore muscles responded. The hard work from yesterday had finally caught up to her. There were the same chores to do today and apparently every day. But the sooner she finished it, the sooner she could disappear into the field and toward her secret destination. Despite her aches and pains, she dressed and raced down to the kitchen, grabbed a quick breakfast of eggs, biscuits and bacon, and then went back out to the barn.

There would be no more chicken coop cleaning for her anymore. Thank goodness. That was the worst. No, Maria informed her that if she could just milk the cows every morning and again in the evening, then that would be just fine. She would have to learn to work a little faster though, but that would come in time. If she had to trade the chickens for cows, she would take it any day. Those stupid birds were bound to be the death of her anyway.

Her sore hands didn't want to move well at first but soon warmed up to milking the cows. Now that she knew how to do this, it moved a little faster. Her cat friend swung by for another bowl of milk. Once the cans were filled, Maria helped her haul them into the spring house and then skimmed the cream and buttermilk from yesterday's batch. With such an early start, she had the cows and the milk finished well before lunch.

*Plenty of time to go visit the mine today.*

Now, to find a lantern for her trek. She glanced about the barn for any sign of Maria or Carlos, but they remained along with the milk cows. Good. They didn't need to know if one of their lanterns went missing anyway. She slipped into the tack room, found the medium lantern with a piece of flint that she tucked into her apron pocket and then made her way out the barn door.

It wasn't long before she spied William and some of the other teenage boys that worked around the farm all huddled together near the horse barn and probably getting into no good. Whatever they were doing, she didn't really want any part of it.

William saw her, and a quick smile spread across his face as he motioned her toward them. She rolled her eyes but approached the little band of mischievous boys. *He better not be stealing something.*

"Come here," he said with a grin. "You've got to see this."

The boys opened up their circle and greeted her but then got back to work with their no-good doings. She gazed into their space and watched as the oldest of the boys worked with two wide-mouth, glass screw-top jars.

"You take the smaller jar and fill it about half full of this," he narrated as he held up a pungent clear liquid in a bottle. He proceeded to fill the jar just as he described. "Then you take the large jar and put in equal parts of these," he said and motioned to three cans of a white, green and black powder each. Once he was done filling the large jar, he then picked up the smaller one and placed it carefully inside the larger jar.

"You have to be careful not to spill any when you put it inside, or it will ruin."

Anna crinkled her nose as she smelled the liquid from where she stood. "What's going on?" she whispered to William who stood beside her.

"Shhh," he said with a mischievous smile. "Just watch."

"Now," the older boy spoke and picked up the jar-in-jar concoction with steady hands, "make sure you don't shake it up until its time." He walked up to the open barn doors, and the crowd followed him. Anna peered inside the barn, now cleaned and empty of all the horses.

The boy bit his lip, and she could see the spark of evil that she recognized in William's eyes just before he was about to do something awful for which mother would barely scold him. The other boys in the crowd hushed as they waited for something amazing.

*This had better be good.* She needed to get going and standing here just burned daylight.

The older boy threw his jar collection into the center of the barn and the concoction shattered. And then something unexpected happened. The chemicals, whatever they were, mixed in that instant and exploded into a burst of the thickest white smoke, filling every crevasse in the barn with the noxious fog. The entire group backed away from the barn door as the smoke rolled toward them. The boys laughed and jumped with a parade of clapping hands.

"What is that?" Anna plugged her nose as she smelled the chemical fog spilling from the barn.

"Bug bomb," the older boy said, his Mexican accent similar to Maria's. "Mister John taught us how to make 'em. We use 'em in the barns about every three months or so. It keeps the scorpions and spiders away from the animals."

"It smells terrible," she said.

"That's the sulfur, but it won't hurt you. Just the bugs," he said and went back to putting his ingredients together for another bomb.

"Do you want to make one?" He glanced back up at her and held an empty jar, squinting against the sun.

"Oh, I really shouldn't," she said.

"Come on," he said and stood up next to her. "It's simple."

The boy placed the ingredients along the upper board of the fence. He talked her through the mixture, and she tried to follow exactly.

"Okay," he said. "Now carefully place it in the larger jar." She tried to control the shaking in her fingers as she slipped one jar into the other.

"Do you want to throw it?" he asked.

Her lips curled into a smile, something that seemed too foreign as of late. "Of course I do." She grasped the jar.

The boy stepped behind her and looked over her shoulder as he searched for the right target. He pointed over her shoulder. "Right over there. Throw it real hard."

Her fingers grasped around the jar, and she hurled it. The bomb hit her mark and exploded into a puff of white.

That was when she realized she couldn't stop smiling. The farm might not be as bad as she had once thought. The other boys cheered and then clambered for their turn at putting the ingredients together for their own bombs.

She turned away from the crowd of boys as they all shoved toward the ingredients, took her lantern in her hand and faced the daunting cornfield that separated her from the mine.


A breeze rustled across the sun-drenched cornfield in a subtle murmur as she moved toward the foothills. When she got into the thick of the cornfield, she concentrated harder on the terrain. It was too easy to fall or get lost among the corn. It was taller than her, and she couldn't see the horizon at all. With the lantern in her left hand, she imagined all the things its light could see in the darkness of that tunnel. *But what if there were bugs in there? Or something else much bigger?* Maybe she should have collected one of those bombs to use in the mine. Just in case.

A sudden chatter of squeals and screeches startled her as she stepped into a patch of nesting crows. The black birds flapped in terrified confusion as the flock scattered out of the cornstalks and took flight. Anna stopped abruptly, her heart pounding against her ribs at the sudden scare of the sound. She took in a controlled breath to stop the shaking in her fingers.

"Stupid birds," she said and watched them fly away above the field. But the birds weren't the only thing that made her shake. The anticipation of the mine now flowed with the adrenaline in her veins.

She started back on her path. The barbed-wire fence appeared at the far edge of the field, the same fence she had crawled through the first time she came this way. At least she was on the right path. The shaking nerves jangled by the crows eased with each step toward the thick of trees at the base of the foothills. The familiar tinkling of water in the creek whispered across the pasture.

A thrill of dizziness spun around her ears. She shouldn't still be shaken by the crows, but it wasn't the birds anymore. In the copse of trees ahead of her lay the mouth of the cavern, an unknown place barred to keep people like her out. And she was about to break the rules.

She pushed through the brush, grateful to now be shaded from the hot sun. The gurgling of the creek guided her to the overgrown rails. Then, the opening of the mine appeared through the thicket. Her foot stopped just short of the edge of the hidden rails that fed into the mouth of the mine. The lantern rattled in her trembling hands.

The two barred windows in the old gate gazed at her with aged but knowing eyes. She gripped the handle of the lantern with a clammy hand and then closed her eyes, feeling the cool of the breeze against her cheek.

Just do it, she told herself. It's like a pirate cave. Just like in *Treasure Island.*

Opening her eyes, she steeled herself, marched to the great doors and yanked the chain free from the handles and the vines away from the latch. She pulled the door open on the rusty hinges and stepped across the threshold.

The air inside was still and stagnant, the cool and damp of a place closed up for so long. Her eyes adjusted to the dark, and she fished the piece of flint from the pocket in her apron. With shaking fingers, she lit the lantern and held out the light before her.

Thick rails guided her path forward into the blackness ahead. She glanced behind her as a little voice in her head urged her to leave this place now. But the lantern burned bright around her feet, leaving an orb of light along the curved walls of the cavern. She turned away from the door and started along the old mine tracks. *It's silly to be scared. It's just the dark, and there was nobody else here.*

The comforting light of the entrance grew too far distant to be of any help. She swallowed against a dry throat and continued to follow the tracks further into the cavern. Each step echoed louder and louder down the curving tunnel. Her eyes squinted against the flickering flame within the lantern, trying hard to peer into the inky darkness ahead, but she could only see within her small circle of light. The mine wouldn't allow her to see any further. The walls closed in tighter as she moved further down the tunnel. Only her small bubble of light kept the darkness from completely swallowing her. The light about her now trembled with the shaking in her hand.

She stopped and glanced back. The curves of the tunnel had obscured the entryway, and only blackness surrounded her. If she got confused or turned around, she would never know how to escape to the outside world. Lost forever in the depths of the mine, and then, someday, a teenage girl would come wandering by and find her dried up bones just lying on the tracks.

The image made her stop.

"What am I doing?" she asked aloud, her voice echoing down the tunnel. "There's nothing down here."

She licked her dry lips and glanced into the tunnel ahead. If her father was with her now, he wouldn't turn back. The intrigue of the dark ahead would keep him going, just to see what treasures lay ahead. Hesitating, she kicked the tip of her boot against the track. Dust trembled from the rail, and the glint of shiny metal flashed at the edge of her light.

Curious. She approached the small glint of metal and stooped down beside the track. A flat, round object lay against the track under a layer of dust. Her fingers grasped at it, brushing away the dust with her thumb to reveal a silver coin. The face stamp shined in the light like a brand new coin.

Dated 1882, only ten years prior. But this mine had been closed up for far longer than that. And why would a fully minted coin just be lying here?

She slipped the coin into the pocket of her apron and stepped deeper into the tunnel, her eyes focusing along the track. The echoes of her steps changed, and she sensed an alteration in the tunnel ahead of her. Holding up the lantern, the bubble of light illuminated a fork in the cavern.

The tracks curved off to the right. The left tunnel, however, remained dark and solitary, supported by a frame of heavy wood beams in case of tunnel collapse. She glanced back and forth to both tunnels.

Her shaking fingers rose to touch the wooden beam that framed the left tunnel. The structure felt firm and stable, at least she hoped so. She rapped her knuckles on the wood for good measure. No motion in the beam. No creaks or grumbles from the rock above her. Hopefully, that was a good sign that the tunnel wouldn't collapse.

*Okay, the left tunnel,* she decided.

She lifted the lantern to the cavern and proceeded through the left tunnel. Without the track to guide her, she kept a hand along the wall to feel her way. The stone was cold and slippery in some spots where condensation trickled down the wall. She moved her hand along the wall until another object lying upon the cavern floor caught her eye.

A wrinkled, brown paper. Her fingers brushed over the brittle surface and grasped at the edge. Dust fell from it as she lifted it into the light, a shred of paper discarded as trash. Green ink curved across the top and arced around a printed word. There was a "B" printed at the edge, but the paper had been torn away from the rest of the word.

She tossed it aside—just a piece of refuse. She continued onward, but the echo of her footsteps changed, indicating that this tunnel was likely much shorter than the main cavern. This was probably just a side tunnel created while following a vein of silver in the rock. She had read about some aspects of mining in the preparatory school in Boston last year before everything had changed. Within those books, she at least learned that the silver mines could run deep and go for miles, and a tunnel collapse was not unheard of.

The tunnel turned sharply, and her lantern lit up a rusted iron door along the cavern wall.

No locks. Just a single handle. No window in the door to peek inside.

She grasped the door latch, but the door was much heavier than she could move with just one arm. After setting the lantern on the ground, she used both hands on the latch and a foot against the tunnel wall. The door heaved open with a deafening creak of the hinge, the sound roaring and rebounding down the tunnel. If someone hadn't heard the main gate opening, they definitely would have heard that.

The shadow cast from the opening door fell back from the contents of that small room like a great black curtain, opening to reveal the grand scene. The lantern light flooded into the room, a stark contrast to the black shadow of the door.

Her mouth felt like cotton now. *Oh, this wasn't good. Not good at all.*

# CHAPTER 9

A few scattered pieces of the same brown paper with green print littered the floor at the threshold of the door like a bread crumb trail leading to what lay in the vault.

Anna grabbed up the lantern and stepped into the room. The littered paper crinkled under her boot as she moved across the cold stone floor. Her shoe brushed the edge of a burlap bag with a heavy thud and clink.

Stacks of these bags lined from the floor to the wall. This room was so full of them that she couldn't tell how big this vault actually was.

The few scattered bits of paper led to a single bag with a tear in the corner seam. She kneeled down and ran her fingers along the tear and found another, more complete piece of the brown paper. As she pulled it out, a few scattered silver coins fell from the tear. The same as the coin she had collected along the track. She drew the paper to the light and unrolled its curved shape, following the green printing, the words complete in bold ink.

**Bulwark Armored Rail**

Her brow furrowed. Bulwark. A name she recognized. She rose and flashed the lantern about the room, noting how the same phrase was printed upon each bag. She set the lantern upon the heap of bags and gazed out across the room.

The adventure of this place had just turned much darker. She now wished she taken the right-sided tunnel. Somebody had intended this to stay hidden. Locked away in an abandoned mine forgotten by time.

Her shaking hands moved to the pile before her and untied the cord that cinched the bag closed. The burlap then gaped open. Her shoulders fell. Yes. This was exactly what she had suspected.

The bag was filled with a collection of silver coins rolled into a hundred short stacks and sealed in the brown and green printed paper. If these were all the same coins as she had in her pocket, the one bag alone would have over a thousand dollars. And there were hundreds of bags in the room. She picked up a single roll of coins and felt the weight of it in the palm of her hand. A crime had brought all of this stuff here. At least she could bring a single roll with the Bulwark printing to the sheriff, and then maybe he could take care of it.

From the corner of her eye, she spied another glint of metal that she had not seen before. It had come from against the wall and behind a stack of bags. She pulled a bag from the top of its stack, the burlap sagging as soon as the full weight of it dropped into her hands, nearly dragging her down with it. The bag fell out of her hands, but she hardly noticed as she gazed to the thing beyond the space where the bag had once rested.

A gleam of bright gold met her gaze, reflected as an orange glint in the lantern light. Her fingers grasped at it, lifting it from its space. The gold bar rested in her hands, the metal smooth and colder than she would have thought. The bar filled her hand like one of her mother's bread loafs.

A single imprinted stamp across the top of the bar erased any further doubt she had about this place: Washington Mint.

With trembling hands, she replaced the bar, hoping that this would save her from being detected.

This was bad. Very bad.

The penny novels she had read so many times had detailed it all: Diamond Dave Thibodaux and his right hand man, Johnny Holiday, robbed the Bulwark Express of its treasure en-route from Washington to California ten years ago. Nobody had seen the treasure or the outlaws since that time.

The cargo had come from the Washington Mint, dated 1882. It was loaded onto the Bulwark Armored train.

This had to be Diamond Dave's stash.

She grasped the lantern and rushed from the vault. The door squealed closed with her heave of desperation. Maybe if she could close this room up fast enough, it would be like it never existed and she never saw it.

How could this be? Why did she have to find this? Did Uncle John even know about this place, so close to his own home?

The breath rushed in and out from her lungs as if she had been running, but she didn't move, frozen as she leaned back against the cavern wall.

Then her back stiffened and her ribs seized. A second door further down the tunnel, in the shadows where she hadn't seen it before.

*Oh, no. No more, please.*

Another iron door latched on rusty hinges just like the first one. Another room of horrible things that she wasn't supposed to see. She glanced back to the first door, and she closed her eyes, but she could still see the stacks of burlap bags inside that room, the black stamp of Bulwark Armored Rail still fresh in her mind. Yes, it would be best to speak to the sheriff. He would know what to do, but he would also need to know what was in that other room. Her eyes opened again, and she turned toward the second door, all the reluctance of what she had to do now urging her back to the fork in the tunnel. But she couldn't move, not until she opened that iron door.

She pulled away from the damp rock wall and moved toward the door. Anna took in a careful breath and pulled open the heavy latch, just as she had the first. The lantern weighed heavy in her hand now, unwilling to look into the darkness of a second vault. The stash from the robbery was so much bigger than she had ever suspected; two rooms of it would be too much.

The air wafting out from the room smelled of leather, dust and old wood. A fragrance she had become all too familiar with when frequenting old libraries in Sweden with her father.

The light shone into the room and illuminated the edge of a desk. No burlap bags. No stacked bars of gold. The lantern cast across the surface of the desk and into the room, against dark wood furniture placed about the room. Stacks of books, parchments, paintings and etchings, frames and other artifacts had been placed along the walls. Everything stuffed into this space as though it were a storage locker. Only a fine layer of dust covered these things, unlike the thicker layers that had fallen over the burlap bags in the first room.

This room was much different but much worse.

Her heart sank. Yes, Uncle John knew about this place. He knew everything about it.

A writing desk rested along the side wall with dusty books stacked upon its surface, the spines of the books creased with use. Ancient Languages of Europe. History and Culture of Sweden. Other books in foreign languages she couldn't understand. But she recognized them, nevertheless. She had seen them all before.

These things, every book, framed painting, and piece of furniture had belonged to her father. These were the things he had supposedly willed away. They had all disappeared from his office at the university the night he was killed. But all of this had allegedly been in the possession of other universities in New England, not hidden away in some dark abandoned mine. At least, that's what her family had been told.

No. It had been given to Uncle John . . . or he had taken it and brought it here himself.

How could that be? They didn't even know about Uncle John until last week. And her father had not spoken to him in years. What business did he have with her father's things?

Anna's fingers ran along the edges of the desk and found the corners of the drawer. She pulled it open and immediately felt sick. She had hoped it would not be there, but it was anyway.

Protected in the drawer, her father's personal journal rested with various other papers. It had been the very thing he had kept with him all his life, all his notations from his travels across Europe. Her eyes filled with tears as she grasped it and held it to her chest. Uncle John couldn't keep this. She wouldn't be able take all these things with her, but she would keep this. This was not Uncle John's business.

# CHAPTER 10

nna stormed from the grove, the mine shaft entrance closed up again and the vines arranged around the gate. The single roll of coins she took along with her father's journal weighed heavy in her apron pocket. Tears threatened the edges of her eyes, but the tightness in her jaw wouldn't allow them to come. Each stomp closer to the farm house made her fists clench, and her nails dig into her hands.

Time must have moved faster inside the mine. The early evening sky had begun to cast tired and lazy shadows across the cornstalks. She moved with singular purpose: to the farmhouse, to her mother. This information was too important to keep to herself. Her mother needed to know that her husband's most sacred belongings were somewhere very close. The mystery of their disappearance had been solved. Instead of being cared for in a quiet museum or university, they were hidden in dusty shadows among other things of nefarious origin. Uncle John had lied to them about everything. He didn't want them here because he cared. He must have had other intentions, or he needed them for something.

The only thing on her mind was getting to her mother and warning her about what she had just found. Then, they could get to the sheriff, show him the coins and set everything right. She needed to take care of her father's things first, however. Then Uncle John would have to answer to the authorities about the other vault.

Smoke puffed out of the chimney already. From the fragrance of grilling meat and onions, dinner would be ready soon. Hopefully,

Uncle John was still in the barn or out in the field and Maria in the kitchen, and her mother would be alone.

Anna's pace quickened as the house loomed closer. She rushed into the kitchen but slowed when she spied her mother arranging the table for dinner.

"Mother," she said, "I really need to speak with you."

Her mother smiled and continued to arrange the plates. Maria entered from the kitchen door with the silverware in hand and smiled at Anna as well.

"Sure, honey. What is it?" Mary said.

Maria moved about the table and set tin cups with each plate.

That woman never left the house. "In private," Anna said with a drop of her voice.

A wrinkle of concern formed at her mother's brow. She stepped away from the table and walked out to the front room with her daughter. "What's wrong?"

"It's about Uncle John," Anna started in a whisper. "I think he might be . . . bad."

Her mother's eyes narrowed, and she turned away in a sigh. "Anna, stop this right now."

"But—"

"No," she spoke. "No more of this. I know you miss Boston, but this is our home now."

"But, Mother—"

"Do not interrupt me. If you cannot deal with this and be nice to your uncle, then maybe you need to spend some time in your room."

"But I know something very important about him." Her hands clenched together and her stomach dropped. Mother wasn't listening.

"Go now," her mother spoke, the crease between her eyebrows now a deep furrow, and pointed her thin fingers up the stairway.

"Mother, please—," she pleaded.

"Anna, now."

She held back the tears as she turned away from her mother. This wasn't what she had expected at all. If her mother had known exactly what she knew, there would be no question about leaving tonight. But her mother shut her out; end of discussion. All those hundreds of pounds of coins and gold settled in her gut like a stone. She trudged up the steps and to her room where she sank into her bed.

Tears flowed despite her best effort to stop them. If only her mother would listen, just for tonight. The images of what she had seen in the mine boiled to the forefront of her vision, and anger flooded her thoughts. Uncle John had wanted to take all her father's things: that was the only explanation as to why they were even here to begin with. *Fulfill my brother's last wish,* she remembered back to the telegram. Ugh. John's charade made her sick.

Anna stepped to her window and pulled back the white lace curtains. Silver moonlight spilled over the cornfield and faded into darkness at the edges of the property. Far beyond that edge of black lay the mouth of the mine, closed up but never silent. It still spoke to her in whispers of horrors and secrets, leaving that empty hole in her stomach. Her fingers played at the edges of her apron and felt the leather cover of the journal.

She pulled the book from her apron pocket, its edges worn in the silver light that poured through the window. Her eyes had never before peeked beyond the dark green cover. Even now, the book still held the scent of her father's cologne within its yellowed and frayed pages. It had traveled across the globe with his drawings, the notations of his findings in his various library and ancient church stops, all of his passions poured out at the tip of a fountain pen.

Perhaps nobody but her father had ever looked inside this book, but the memory of him hunched over its pages couldn't stop her from doing so tonight. She pulled up the simple wooden chair to the table, lit the oil lamp and set the journal in front of her. Gold light danced over the cover as she stared at it.

Maybe it was the fear of hearing her father's voice in her head like a ghost that made her hesitate. Her fingers touched the leather cover and, with a shaking hand, opened to the first page. Only three words printed in her father's hand: *Thomas George Holloway.* Nothing scary or life-changing. She let out the breath that she'd been holding and allowed her shoulders relax. The next few pages held drawings of symbols and hieroglyphs accompanied by his small writing on the edges, describing the location where they were found and the possible interpretation of the symbols. Then, more pages on the history of the monastery in Sweden where he had studied while they had lived there. Anna lifted the book toward the light to read the small print when a piece of folded yellow paper fell from deep within the book. It drifted across her lap and landed against her boot.

She placed the book on the table and stooped to pick up the paper, the edges fragile and thin as if it had been opened and re-folded many times. The paper was thicker than the journal pages. Like vellum. She unfolded it across the table under the light of the lamp. A drawing unfurled before her, the black edges curling in jagged lines indicating roads and trails, land borders and stars blooming where cities would lie. A map, likely the eastern half of the United States and its bordering territories. Words and small sketches filled in the edges of the map, all in her father's handwriting. Blossoms of red stars dotted a few places on the map, stretching across the middle section of the country to the northeast coast.

Her fingers followed a line up to the top of the map, where a single red star carried the number "1" next to it. She tilted her head to read the script beside it: *Kensington, Minnesota.* Her brow furrowed. The town didn't sound familiar, and as far as she knew, her family had never traveled there. Above the marked location on the map, her father's writing curled in black ink: *Journal Entry #1.*

The tension in her shoulders eased when she pulled the journal out from under the map, the memory of her angry mother now a distant thought. She opened the book and paged through the first several drawings until her eyes fell on the title, "Entry #1," at the top of the fifth page. His writing was just like his university discourses—serious and precise.

*This is the journal and notations of Thomas Holloway. These writings and clues are the collection of my life's work, an investigation of the world's most secret society, the Knights Templar.*

Footfalls echoed up the stairway and to the landing. She glanced back, and her heart almost fell to the floor when she saw the glint of lamplight shine through the space under the door. With quick fingers, she collected the book and the map, moved to her bed and stuffed everything under the covers just as the door creaked open.

William's small frame filled the doorway.

"Mother says you can come down for dinner if you want to," he said.

Her heart still pounded in her chest, and she faked a smile toward him, the objects under the covers still palpable against her arm. She had done a lot of work around the farm today, not to mention the anxiety of her visit to the mine. All of that had left a rumble in her stomach.

And Uncle John would be down there. As much as she didn't want to face him, she needed to keep an eye on his activities, at least until she could tell mother everything and then turn it all over to the sheriff. She no longer trusted John around her family. The journal and the map would have to wait for now. She straightened her dress and followed William down the stairs.

Supper tasted as good as usual, with the typical tortillas, sauces and roasted pork. But after only a few bites, Anna no longer wanted it. Eating was too difficult when she had to watch John for any signs that he may know what she had been up to. He sat across the table, laughing and telling stories about things that had happened around the farm. All of this made her mother giggle as well, something she never did at a dinner table. It wasn't polite, or so she had once told Anna. Even William leaned over his plate to smile as John regaled them with a tale about a young colt that couldn't be tamed.

But Anna knew better. This was a farce, a carefully constructed play by Uncle John to lure them and keep them here; but for what purpose she wasn't sure. He would never be able to lie to her, though. She could see through his mask of frivolity now, each smile on his face brought more memories of her father's things collecting dust in the abandoned mine.

Mary laughed again, throaty and loud as Uncle John's face reddened with laughter. Something he had said was so funny he could no longer speak. Watching her mother behave this way made Anna's fingers tighten around the fork that pushed the food around her plate. It was like she didn't even remember that her husband had died. Not just died—murdered in the street, shot in the back and his possessions stolen away by his own kin.

She looked back down at the plate again, unable to watch this fake display any longer. A long steady breath moved into her lungs, and she loosened her grip on the fork. If she was the only one that would remember him, then so be it. The journal still waited for her upstairs, the last thing that held her father's words and his voice.

The sound of it rattled around her brain, the last words she had read in the journal before William opened her door: *The Knights Templar*. The laughter at the table faded into the background as her mind swam around what she had learned about the knights in school. These were the very men who had inspired the Knights of the Roundtable, and she had devoured the King Arthur stories as soon as she had learned of them. But the Templars were real, a group of courageous men who traveled from Europe with the king to fight a war —the Crusades—in the Middle East. They were very wise and saved all their earnings, collecting a vast wealth as a group, and started the first banks and savings accounts in the world.

But she never recalled her father ever saying anything about studying such fanciful things. He studied linguistics and writings of the ancient people of Sweden, not adventures of pre-Arthurian crusaders. Now, only the journal could possibly explain any of this to her.

Supper ended, and Anna helped to clear the table with Maria as her mother retired to the sitting room to work on her lace and Uncle John departed to the front porch. Without John there, her mother was now alone with the exception of Maria in the kitchen. Anna washed the plates and cutlery with Maria at her side, the sight of the front room in the corner of her eye.

Anna winced as the tip of a knife poked at her finger in the soapy water.

"Oh, be careful, Miss Anna," Maria said and stepped up to her side to gaze at the trickle of blood that beaded at the tip of her finger. "Dangerous things in the water."

The pain had already subsided, but Maria still insisted upon wrapping her hand in a clean towel.

Maria sidled in her way before the tub of water. "Never you mind the rest of this. I will take care of it. You just take care of yourself."

"Thank you," she said and stepped back from the basin, the towel still wrapped around her hand.

She slipped into the shadowy recesses of the back porch and turned to glance out the windows. Nighttime had descended on the farm, leaving the broad porch dark and empty since the remainder of the help had retired to their cabins about the farm. The lamps had been turned out in the back rooms, leaving only the moon and stars to light space around the house. Uncle John had left the sitting room and just vanished. He sometimes did that after dinner and then often came back smelling like pipe tobacco.

Where had he gone? She didn't dare speak to her mother about dangerous things until she knew that John wasn't listening in on them.

She let the towel slip from her hand and tucked it into a window sill as she opened the back door and stepped out onto the porch. The darkness that crept through the cornfields oozed toward the house in hot bands of ink as she searched the property for any sign of him. She imagined him standing like a scarecrow among the stalks, watching and just waiting to jump to life to grab her. She pressed back to the wall and slid along the length of the porch as she scanned the dark field that reached out toward the abandoned mine.

What if he disappeared to the mine at night, running off to inspect the spoils of his evil trade? If so, he might discover that someone else had been there, and it would only be a matter of deduction to learn that it was her.

Everything remained still and quiet, though. Silent except for crickets and the occasional yelp of a coyote.

She rounded another corner and stopped before a tall, dark form framed against the porch rail. Anna gasped, but it was too late. Uncle John leaned against a supporting post, a puff of blue-silver smoke drifting from the end of a pipe in his hand. He gazed out into the dark and didn't move or flinch when she had come around the corner.

"You don't have to sneak around, you know," he said and didn't turn to face her. "You are free to explore wherever you wish."

If only he knew.

*Maybe he did know. Oh no!*

"I'm sorry," she said, her fingers clenched together before her.

"No need. I understand the young desire to spy on me," he said, and she could hear the smile in his voice. "I am a stranger to you. You don't trust me. But I'm not what you think I am."

Her throat tightened. Did he know that she suspected him of unspeakable evil?

"I am not trying to replace your father. You are family. I am trying to do right by my family. I care about you and William and your mother." He finally turned and peered at her with those soft, brown eyes that just looked more tired than anything else.

"I would be more than happy if you would like to run around out here after dark, but I am sure your mother wouldn't agree, so you probably ought to return to the house. It wouldn't do to have a woman like that angry with me for letting you loose," he said with another smile.

Anna forced a fake smile in return. Oh, he was sly, smooth and careful. Keeping her under his watch and within the confines of the house. He may think that he had her family under his control, but she could outsmart him. She had to. "Okay," was all that she could say.

She turned and went back into the house and hurried to her room. As soon as she shut the door, she turned the lock and leaned back against it with her eyes closed. Her stomach swirled into knots that almost made her sick. That was a close call. He might be watching her tonight, and any attempts to speak to her mother again could have unfortunate consequences, for both her and her family. Those thoughts brought the memory of the gun he always carried at his hip. From this point forward, she had to tread carefully.

With worried thoughts floating about her head, she readied for bed and then rechecked the lock on her door one more time. Secure, and hopefully safe. She slipped onto the bed and slid under the covers beside the hidden pile of the map and the journal. Trembling settled into her bones as she lay there in the dark, listening for the sounds of the house. Doors closing and opening. The stairway creaking when her mother finally went to bed. The last embers of light shining from under her door until it extinguished when Uncle John closed his bedroom door for the night.

But she waited even longer, hearing the sound of her own breathing over and over again until nothing else slunk along the floor boards outside her room. Hours must have drifted by until she finally sat up, lit her own lamp and brought the journal out from under the covers. The book splayed open to the last page she had read:

*These writings and clues are the collection of my life's work, an investigation of the world's most secret society, the Knights Templar. Which means that if you are reading this, I must be dead.*

Anna's spine bolted up straight. How could he have known he was going to die, and if that was the case, why didn't he go to anyone for help? Nausea welled in the back of her throat, and she swallowed.

Her father knew something was going to happen to him, and yet there was so much more written in the journal beyond this point. She couldn't stop now, not even at this late hour. Her eyes drifted back to the cursive writing, which now took on a frantic characteristic.

# CHAPTER 11

## Journal of Thomas Holloway
## Entry #1

*Unfortunately, the things I have discovered in my investigations were so great that it has brought the attentions of some who would choose to steal rather than to study. It is for this purpose that I keep this journal. But with this book, I have attached my map and notations. Without the journal, the map is useless, and the converse is true as well.*

*I wish this world were different, but circumstances have forced me to hide these discoveries until the parties searching behind me have been taken by the authorities. My family is most important right now, and this is the best protection I can offer them.*

*Set within the pages of this journal are the items I have discovered that led me to a series of clues. These clues, when translated properly, have indicated the site of possibly the world's most deeply held secret: the location of a treasure so great it would boggle the mind and tremble the spirit.*

*But I must start at the beginning.*

*The Knights Templar were also known as the Poor Knights of Solomon. They were a large group of soldiers who travelled across the Mediterranean Isles and to Jerusalem. It is said they made a pact: one of unity and one of silence and learning. Their travels over 200 years of Crusades brought them to many lands. In all that time, the legend states the brotherhood collected many artifacts and treasures, returning everything to a sacred place somewhere in Europe. It is even said their treasure may contain the Holy Grail and the very Arc of the Covenant spoken of within the pages of our Christian Bible.*

*In 1307, King Philip of France knew of the Templars' vast but hidden treasure. He owed money to the Templars as well. He came up with one solution to his problem of debt: he would disband the Templars, then find and take their treasure. That way he would owe them nothing and become rich in the process.*

*On a very dismal October 13th, King Philip's men arrested the Templars all over the countryside. Many knights died that day and in the days to follow. But after the arrests and murders, the king's men could never find the treasure.*

*What King Philip did not know was that a band of knights got word the day before the arrests that the king was coming for them. There was known to have been a Templar ship in the harbor on October 12th. It is rumored that the treasure may have been loaded upon this ship that very night. At dawn the next day, the ship had vanished, and the treasure would not be found by the king.*

*The Templars often wrote their messages in code so that, if intercepted, they could not be deciphered by the enemy. The code has many identifying characteristics.*

*I first came upon this code in Sweden, in a church on the island of Gotland. This place was a well-known location for Templars to hide, especially after the arrests. One particular mark stood out to me, found in many Templar texts and nowhere else: an X with a notch hook on the upper right arm.*

*This was merely an interesting historical finding until I received a message from a colleague in Minnesota who related a fascinating story to me.*

*About two years ago, upon this American soil, a farmer in Kensington, Minnesota, was clearing his field of trees. There was a particularly large aspen tree that he and his team of horses pulled out to the roots. Upon clearing the roots, he found a most curious discovery: a stone tablet. This slab weighed over 200 pounds and had been densely tangled in the roots of the tree. With the aid of his two sons, the men brought the stone to the house.*

*At first, they supposed it to be an Indian tablet, but after my colleague inspected it, he contacted me straight away due to the crucial nature of the find. He recognized the writings to be runic inscriptions, much older than the Indian tribes in that area and in a language he had seen in Europe whilst travelling with me.*

*I now proclaim that I have seen this tablet with my own eyes and have translated the writings. The tablet is a curious thing, with a paragraph of old Swedish inscribed across the face. But it is also framed in a numbering system. The writings and numbering system were consistent with the medieval system found in Gotland in Sweden, to the very same codes used by the Templars. Upon interpreting this stone, I absolutely believe it to be a marker placed by the Templars themselves, and this case was made stronger when I found the same unusual X inscribed in the stone.*

*I am also able to date the stone, using the numbers inscribed on the sides, to the early 1300s.*

*The inscription on the stone began a series of clues leading to another stone, and for the safety of my family, I will not include this here, as it is the first step along the path to the Templar treasure, which I will state that I have discovered its location but have not yet seen it, given its very difficult location.*

*With best regards,*
*Thomas Holloway*

# CHAPTER 12

*o wonder this book was hidden in the mine. A buried treasure at the end of this map! Uncle John wanted to keep it all for himself. He had the map and the journal and hadn't told anyone.*

Shudders moved down her spine as the memory of Uncle John's gun catching the sunlight when they had first met him flooded her thoughts. That could be the very weapon that may have killed her father. He carried that gun everywhere, and it was always within his reach should he ever wish to use it on her or her family. After all, he had probably killed his own brother. He wouldn't hesitate to murder the rest of his family. She would have to make her mother listen, for the sake of them all. Perhaps if she read this journal entry to her, then she would understand that they had to get away as soon as possible.

She examined the drawing below her father's signature, a symbol she saw every time she looked in the mirror. Her fingers found the chain that always dangled around her neck and pulled the pendant from under her nightgown. The symbols matched, and he had obtained this curious charm while in Sweden. Gotland, as a matter of fact. She scanned through the previous pages again and found the reference to the notched X symbols found on the tablets during his time while in Sweden. Now she understood why they had lived there for months while she was a child. He researched these things the whole time but never spoke a word of it to his family. Not even to her, and they shared every secret.

Tears flooded her vision again, making it impossible to read any more of the print. Nor did she want to. Not tonight. This was too much to take in all at once in such a short time. With shaking hands, she folded up the map and tucked it under her mattress. She closed the book but held it close to her chest. Even though she could no longer look at the words, she didn't want to let it go quite yet.

She rested back against the pillow with the journal clutched to her chest, her ears still sensitive to any sounds outside her door. With everything she had just learned, she would have to be vigilant from now on.

Anna swallowed the last bite of her breakfast just as Maria entered the dining room. The men and women that still sat around the table barely glanced up as she slipped between them to fill their coffee cups from her steaming pitcher.

"We will be leaving at noon," she announced to them all.

"Where are you going?" William asked between bites.

"To town," Maria said. "Every Wednesday we take a wagon full of the farm's goods: grain, corn, milk. Some of my specialty cheese. The mercantile sells them. It is our job to keep them supplied. You and Anna are welcome to come, of course. We could use all the hands we can get."

Her mother walked into the room just as Maria had finished her sentence. "That sounds like a very good thing for my children to witness."

"Well, there is plenty of room in the wagon, *Señora* Holloway," Maria said.

Although it sounded like more work in the hot New Mexico desert, the thought of getting away for a few hours appealed to Anna more than she had expected. She hadn't been in town since the day they had arrived on the train, and this could be her chance to find a sheriff and tell him what she knew. He needed to know about the stash in the mine, but also that she suspected her uncle of murder. Maybe it was best to talk to him before talking to mother anyway, just to be safe. The dry air and change of scenery would do her well too and hopefully clear her thoughts of these darker happenings that had recently emerged from the book.

Many of the farm hands had already settled into the wagon by the time Anna arrived. Even William had found a seat and chatted with another boy that she recognized as one of the group that had made the bug bombs just outside the barn. Anna climbed into the back, and Maria gave her a nod and a smile as soon as she had secured herself into the back of the wagon.

With a flick of the reigns, the driver started the horses, and the crew headed off down the rutted road. Another wagon just ahead of them led the train, carrying the supplies destined for the store in town. Two wagons with most of the farms workers, including Maria. That left mother at the house alone with Uncle John.

Anna glanced back to the house, nearly obscured by a cloud of ruddy dust left behind from the wagon wheels. The gnawing ache of dread settled into her gut as the wagons drew further from the homestead. Her fingers clutched the back edge of the wagon wall, tight and cold despite the growing heat of the morning.

"Everything all right, Miss Anna?" Maria's voice chimed toward her.

Anna turned and faced her, painting a smile on her face as she squinted to the eastern horizon that silhouetted Maria's frame. "Fine," she lied, her fingers still clutched to the wood. Hopefully, it would be all right in a short time. Find the sheriff, and then escape with her family back to Boston.

After about forty minutes of a bumpy ride over the dusty road, the edge of the town came into view. The road opened into the main street edged by shops, barns and corrals bustling with people along the boardwalks. A saloon. A blacksmith's shop, with the proprietor deep inside the building banging away at another horseshoe. The mercantile. All with painted exteriors and swinging signs above the boardwalk. But no evidence of the sheriff's station or the jail. Anna craned her neck around the men in the back of the wagon to scan the other side streets as they rolled deeper into town and toward the mercantile. It had to be here, maybe further into town where she hadn't been able to see.

A booming whistle sounded, catching her attention. A plume of steam rose above the edge of the rooftops at the other end of town, evidence of the soon-departing train. She recalled leaving the train station in the wagon the night her family arrived, and nothing stood out from that ride that indicated the location of the sheriff's office.

The wagon rolled to a stop before the mercantile, and everybody climbed out. One of the farm hands held his arm out to her and helped her down from the back gate and onto the dusty main road.

Everyone got to work unloading the first wagon as if they had done this a hundred times by now.

William sidled up beside her as they walked together to help. "You're quiet today."

"I'm always quiet when I'm thinking," she said and dusted her hands on her apron.

"So, nothing's wrong?" he asked.

"If there's something wrong, I'll tell you," she said but felt the pangs of the lie. She couldn't tell him. William was too much of a tattle-tale to share anything this important with him. She glanced down at him, but then saw his fingers and thumbs rubbing together. "Oh, no you don't, William."

"What?"

"I know what you're thinking," she said and stopped him. She leaned down to look him in the eye and lowered her voice to a near-whisper. "Whenever you do that thing with your fingers, I know you're thinking of stealing something."

"I was not."

"You can't lie to me, stupid. Don't you dare nick anything. Remember: we're in the Wild West. Thieves get hanged here."

The color drained from his face.

She pointed her finger in his direction. "Just remember that. And Mom will skin you alive if she knows that you did something bad. Promise."

"Okay. I promise."

Anna stood straighter and gave him one last look from the corner of her eye. She turned back to the wagon where Maria gave assignments to take items into the store, but she needed to keep a peripheral eye on William.

She carried a wooden crate of Maria's wrapped cheeses into the mercantile. The heat from the desert sun vanished on her skin as soon as she entered the store. The heady fragrance of fresh-baked bread danced across the threshold. A young girl at the far end of the mercantile fingered through a bowl filled with rock candy, the pieces clinking against the glass. Anna's mouth watered with the memory of the peppermint candies she used to get at the store around the corner from her house in Boston—the same store where she used to buy her penny novels.

Maria continued to the cashier at the front counter. Anna turned away from the girl and the candy and followed the others to the rear of the store, where they stacked their supplies in the storage room.

"We'll take care of the wagon," one of the farm hands said as he brushed past her. "You two browse if you want until it's time to go."

William turned and dashed back to the front of the store. Great. He had the freedom to wander all over the mercantile with his sticky fingers. Mother would never let her hear the end of it if he got caught stealing something here. Anna marched back to the cashier's counter and craned her head around the first aisle of groceries. William stood at the far end, looking at the glass case of hunting knives. He stuffed his hands in his pockets as he leaned down to examine each one.

Good. Nothing that he could easily swipe. Maybe he had listened to her after all.

She allowed her shoulders to relax and wiped her sweaty palms over the front of her apron. The spicy tang of cinnamon tickled her nose as she wandered down the aisle. The smell intensified as she approached a glass bowl of cinnamon candies. Her stomach rumbled at the sight of them, but she turned away. No. Mother wouldn't allow either of them to have any of the candy even if she had given them money.

She rounded the aisle and stopped at a table. The breath caught in her throat. Thin-leaf penny novels and newspapers lay across the surface, the decorated covers of the books staring back at her. So many books, with adventures of the western territories. Gold strikes. Train robbers. The same novels that graced the insides of her more proper books. Her fingers danced over the covers, the rough brown paper tickling against her skin. Tales of Billy the Kid, Wyatt Earp and Jesse James. All of these she had read before. She brushed aside the top books, counting through each one that she had already read.

The sixth book down caught her attention, the red ink lettered in a title she didn't recognize. She picked it up and thumbed through the pages.

"Sorry, honey. No reading unless you buy it," the shopkeeper called out to her from behind the counter.

The sound of his voice made her heart skip and her hands shake. She placed the book back down on the table and tucked her hands into her apron, but her fingers brushed against a heavy weight in the front pocket.

The roll of coins. She stuffed her hand into the pocket and palmed the roll, its weight firm against her skin. Silver coins, taken from a stash of thousands of rolls. One coin would be plenty to purchase a single novel. Nobody would care if she used just the one, a single piece that nobody even knew she possessed.

Her fingers worked at the end of the coin roll and loosened one, the silver cold in her grasp. The knot of worry tightened in her chest, but the novel she wanted stared back at her from the table. The coin rolled between her fingers again. It was just another book; she had hundreds of them. But not this one. Heaven knows when she would come across it again. Mother didn't need to know, and neither did William.

Before worry twisted her thoughts again, she grasped the novel and marched to the counter, her glance fleeting back once to William, who still hunched over the glass case of knives. She placed the novel in front of the cashier with the single silver coin next to it.

She didn't care that he gave her a smug look as he handed her the change. The book was hers now despite the cashier's derisive glance her way. She tucked the novel into the pocket of her apron and turned away from him with a smile.

The remainder of the farm crew gathered outside the mercantile according to Maria's directions. She called once again to William, who dashed from the store.

As they climbed back into the wagons, Anna's hand snuck into the apron pocket and rested on the surface of the novel, safe from Maria's eyes. Her secret. Was this was how William felt every time he stole something? It left a thrill in her body that made her hands tremble a little. Maybe that's why he did it so often.

No. She would never do it again. Just this once. The rest of the coins would stay put in the roll in order to show the sheriff. Ugh. The sheriff. Her eyes wandered back down the street as the horses started back toward the farm, back toward Uncle John. Speaking to the sheriff couldn't happen today. There was no way to wander around the town looking for him with Maria and the crew so close. Maybe another day.

The cashier opened the cash drawer. The delivery crew had finally left, and the mercantile stood quiet, at least for now. He picked up the single silver piece the girl had used to pay for the novel. At the time, he wasn't sure, and he needed another look. The silver was bright, not tarnished like the other coins in his drawer. Like it had never been used before. He held the piece up to the sunlight and read the words stamped onto the face: Washington Mint 1882.

After all this time, he had found it. It had been months at this post, and he finally could say that it was productive. This was the one thing his real boss had placed him here to find. Evidence of a single coin, the proof of a hidden stash missing for ten years now.

The girl that had given it to him climbed into the wagons with the others from the farm down the road. And that was all she was. Just a girl. Not the one he expected to be in possession of the coin. Nevertheless, the silver looked back at him from the palm of his hand. The wagons rolled away from the mercantile and into the morning sun, but it didn't matter. He had a good inkling of the location of the farm.

He watched the wagons vanish down the road and turned around the "Open" sign. He wouldn't be gone long. Just a quick trip to the telegraph to send a message to his real employer. Finish his duty to inform him of the coin and where it probably came from, then get out of this God-forsaken town and back on the trail with the boys.

# CHAPTER 13

Anna leaned back against the head post of her bed, the penny novel across her lap. Every sound outside her door caught her attention. But nobody knocked on it. Nobody even cared that she had shut herself up in her room after dinner. William's voice sounded from downstairs. Everyone stayed in the parlor after the farm hands retired back to their cabins. Good. All alone now with her secret book under the light of her oil lamp.

She turned the lock of her door and moved toward the bedside table and lamp when the edge of her apron knocked on the leg of the table with a thud. The coin roll, still heavy inside the pocket of the apron. Her fingers wrapped around the roll with the edge frayed from the single coin she had removed.

No more temptation. She pulled open the drawer of the table, dropped the roll inside, and shoved the drawer closed. This is where they had to stay until she gave them to the sheriff. It wouldn't be wise to keep them in her pocket and risk the draw to spend another coin, even if the book she bought today was the best one she had ever read.

The days had been so busy she could never find the right moment to tell her mother. But it may be that she didn't know the best way to tell her. She would have to go about this carefully because her mother was already defensive regarding Uncle John. Furthermore, she hadn't decided to tell William about the mine yet. If she did, she knew he would want to see it, and then he would want to see Father's journal. That was a whole Pandora's box of problems she didn't need right now.

She kept the penny novel in her apron. William didn't need to see it and go blabbing off to their mother. It would bring up too many questions, like where did she get the money to pay for it. And of course, she would get in trouble for it, unlike William and his mysterious ability to obtain things that didn't belong to him in the first place.

All in good time. Just needed to wait a little longer.

XXX

Maria made the announcement of another trip to the mercantile while they were all assembled for breakfast.

It had been a week since they last went. One long week. Maybe this would be the day Anna could finally speak to the sheriff if she could find him.

Maria poured a pitcher of coffee for Uncle John and then glanced to Anna and William. "You children do not have to join us today for the delivery."

Butterflies swarmed in Anna's gut. "But I would like to go."

Maria's eyebrows rose. "It is not necessary."

"I want to go too," William said.

Anna could have kissed him right now. Not a big affectionate one, just a little peck on the forehead. If William wanted to go, then at least it would take off some of the attention from her if she tagged along as well.

"You do?" Maria asked.

"Yeah," he said. "I like riding in the wagon."

Anna sat up straighter. "Me too." The lie came out faster and smoother than she had expected.

Maria smiled. "Very well. The two of you are welcome to come along." She patted Uncle John on the shoulder. "*Señora* Holloway has some eager children."

John smiled and nodded and then sipped at the steaming cup of coffee. Anna forced a smiled back to him, even though it made her gut do somersaults.

Just a matter of time. Then this façade can end, and she and her family could leave this place for good.

The farm hands loaded the wagons before the morning sun grew too hot. The trip back into town was just as dusty as last time, with the smell of the horses in front of the wagons leading them all the way there. The routine was the same, even though Maria insisted that she and William did not need to help unload the wagons. This was a good thing; it gave Anna a moment to walk down the street and look for the sheriff's office.

Women with their pretty skirts and hats walked past her with a smile, trailing the wonderful scent of lilac perfumes behind them. Anna smiled at them and continued down the boardwalk, glancing into windows and reading the door signs. A barber shop. A bakery. The telegraph operator. The sinking crept into her bones. This town was too big to just wander and not have Maria curious as to what she was doing. And she didn't know if she could wait another week. All this time knowing what she did about Uncle John gnawed at her.

She pulled the edge of her necklace from under her bodice and rubbed with her fingers. She needed all the luck she could get today, and hopefully, the charm would work.

XXX

The girl stepped away from the wagon, a lamb wandering away from its flock. Unlike the others, she didn't walk into the mercantile. Instead, she took off down the boardwalk, in search of something else. Her sable brown hair fell down the middle of her back in a single braid, likely something that her mother had created for her.

Nothing about her screamed devious or cunning. Nothing about her revealed itself as an accomplice to one of the grandest outlaws he had ever had the pleasure to know. She was just a child. Fifteen, maybe sixteen at the most.

"That's her," the mercantile cashier's voice spoke to him as he leaned against the post along the boardwalk. "The one I told you about. She's the one that traded in the coin."

The cashier's voice grated against his nerves. A slack-jawed idiot. But he did have to give him some credit. He'd recognized the coin when it came into his possession and then notified him, just like he had paid him to do.

He lifted the brim of his hat with a finger as he watched the girl stop along the boardwalk and peer into the windows of the telegraph.

"All right," he said to the cashier. "Get back into the store. Don't draw any more attention than you already have." His Louisiana drawl came out thick despite his best effort to calm it down. It was no use trying to stop it, nor did he really want to anyway.

The cashier stepped away and crossed the street like an obedient dog. The man continued to watch the girl from under his hat—at her confusion and frustration. Whatever she sought, it wasn't to be found on the streets of this dusty little town today. One glance at the wagon and the people with whom she had traveled told him this was his moment. Everyone had gone into the mercantile. Every last one of them. Leaving the lamb out in the wild. Alone.

He squared his shoulders and tucked his long duster around his hips to conceal the guns on his belt. No matter how hot the desert sun grew, the coat never failed him. He stepped away from the boardwalk and crossed the street, his eye trained on the girl.

XXX

Anna lifted her hand to her brow and shaded her eyes as she gazed through the glass of the telegraph office. Maybe there was someone in there that could direct her to the sheriff, and hopefully before Maria came looking for her. But the place appeared empty for now. By the placement of the sun in the sky, it must have been near noon, and perhaps the clerk had left to eat lunch.

She stood straighter and stepped back from the window, right into a man who walked down the boardwalk. Her heart nearly stopped as she tripped against him. His strong arm caught her before she fell on her bottom against the hard wooden boards.

"My apologies, young lady," he said, his Southern accent thick, as he stopped to help her get her balance.

"I'm so sorry," she said and took a step back from him as his grip loosened from her forearm. "I'm just clumsy sometimes."

A faded brown leather hat rested atop his head and shaded his blue eyes from the New Mexico sun. Dirty blonde hair fell in wavy strands to the back of his neck. Under that hat, in partial shade, the glint of sun from her necklace shimmered against his blonde mustache and goatee.

"Are you injured?" he said, tilting his head down toward her.

She shook her head. "No. I'm all right. Thank you."

This was the moment she noticed his long rawhide leather coat that framed his tall form, down to his dark boots and silver spurs.

"You seem lost. Anything I can help you find?" His voice was smooth as New Orleans silk.

The flutter of butterflies turned into a swarm of bees. A tingle of anxiety pinched at her chest. As nice as this man had been, something about him made her palms damp, and her fingers shake.

"No thank you," she said, wringing her hands together. "I really need to be on my way."

Before she could turn, his hand moved to the charm hanging from the chain at her neck. She froze, the breath catching in her throat.

"My, my, that is a very nice pendant."

The warmth drained from the sun with the faintest pressure of his fingers against her chest as he touched the charm.

"Thank you." She grasped the pendant with a trembling hand and tucked it back into her bodice.

The man smiled, a thing that would probably make the ladies melt, but it only chilled her further. "Where would a man like me get a necklace like that? Perhaps I should want to buy one for a pretty gal such as yourself."

Cotton filled her mouth and dried her tongue. "I don't think you can buy one. My father gave it to me."

He took a single step back and tipped his hat to her. "Well, it looks very nice on you. Have a lovely day."

She nodded her head and painted a smile on her face as she turned away from him. The penetrating stare from under his hat still burned at her back, and she quickened her pace to the mercantile. There was no reason he should make her nervous. He had been nice enough. After all, she was the one that had tripped into him. Sure, he was kind and handsome for a man as old as Uncle John. Maybe he wasn't as bad as she had thought. As cuddly as a rattlesnake.

The tight muscles in her shoulders eased as she approached the wagons and Maria and the crew came out of the mercantile. Even William came running to her side. She let out a tight breath and glanced back down the boardwalk. The stranger had gone, disappeared into the New Mexico desert. Despite the heat of the noonday sun, goosebumps rose on her arms.

Even this town no longer felt comfortable, just like the farm. New Mexico was no longer a place where she wanted to stay. Not for one more day.

They arrived at the farm, and as Anna stepped up to the porch, the cornfield stood at the periphery of her vision. She stopped and then lingered, gazing out across the field. The breeze drifted over the cornstalks and rustled through the trees. Beyond that field, through the grove, lay the opening to the mine, like a sleeping monster within the mountain. The wind like a breath from the depths of the creature, a place she knew she would never visit again.

She slipped into the house and into her room. Daylight fell from the window onto her bed, and she lifted the mattress where the journal rested upon the bed ties. The map had come loose from the pages again. Mother would only need to see the journal and then she would understand. The map might be a little too much right now. She gathered the book and tucked it back in her apron pocket, placing the mattress over the map.

Just as she stepped away from the bed, a single thought made her stop. Mother probably didn't need to know about the roll of coins, either. And Maria could easily find it in the table drawer if she came in to clean. That wouldn't be the best scenario—to have to explain stolen money to her mother.

Anna turned on her heel and pulled the drawer open. She grasped the roll of coins and tucked it into her apron pocket again. If anybody was going to tell mother about the stash of stolen silver in the mine, it would be her. But it had to be at the right time.

With the journal and coins in her apron, she marched down the stairs. Her fingers clenched into fists. What would she say to her mother? Was she ready to hear about the horrible things Uncle John had done? It didn't matter if she was ready; she needed to hear them and soon.

Anna lighted onto the landing and turned the corner into the sitting room. Mother sat here every afternoon, working on her lace creations. But as Anna entered the room, her gut dropped, and she held her breath. Uncle John sat across the room with her today, talking and smiling with her mother.

Why did he always have to be around? Especially now. There was no way to speak to her now, not without drawing more suspicion from him.

# CHAPTER 14

"You haven't touched your meal," Maria said.

Her voice drew Anna's attention away from mother and John as they conversed at the dinner table.

Anna glanced down at the pile of rice and beans that her fork had managed to scatter all across her plate.

"I guess I don't have much of an appetite."

"Probably too much sun today," Maria said. "Let me get you some more water."

She wanted to tell her "no thanks," but the woman would have done it anyway. She returned to the table with a glass of clear water drawn from the kitchen pump. With Maria's eyes on her, she took an obligatory sip but continued to watch her mother.

"Are you feeling sick?" William's voice came from beside her.

"No."

"Well you're not acting right," he whispered under the chatter of everyone at the table. "Not since coming back from town."

"I'm fine, okay?" She gave him a pointed glare. "Just drop it."

"I knew it. You're sick." He stuffed his mouth with a spoonful of rice and then spoke again, his voice muffled with the rice that danced behind his teeth. "Sick in the head."

She rolled her eyes at him and took another sip of water. Anything to please Maria and keep her eyes away from her.

Dinner felt like hours, with the things she wanted to tell her mother burning in her chest. Finally, the table had cleared, and the farm hands returned to their cabins. Mother took to the sitting room again, her lace tablecloth draped over her lap as she started working on it. The oil lamps glowed on each side table next to the chairs. John busied himself on the back porch, putting away coats and aprons from the day's work.

Anna entered the sitting room and stood before the bookshelves, feigning an interest in any of the dozens of books that decorated the shelves.

William entered the room with one of his many toys and stretched out on his belly over the center rug, his tousled blonde hair almost covering his eyes.

*Great. Everybody was down here tonight.* There was no being alone with Mother. She let out a sigh and pulled a book from the shelf, not even reading the spine. It didn't matter what the book was about. It's not like she was going to actually read it anyway.

She settled back in the settee with the book on her lap, casting an occasional glance toward her mother.

"I am so glad you are joining us tonight," Mother said, her fingers still working the tatting hooks. "I feel as though we haven't seen much of you lately."

Anna bit her lip and looked up from her book. "I'm sorry about that."

"That is quite all right, dear. As long as you're feeling well."

That was all a matter of perspective. Right now, she didn't feel well at all. Every minute of every day that ticked on made her sick.

Uncle John sat in a chair beside a table lamp, a newspaper that Maria had purchased in town spread across his knee and his reading glasses on his face. Minimal conversation. Everyone in their own space, quiet and content.

The knot in Anna's stomach tightened. She folded the book closed and stood to place it on the shelf. The weight of the journal tugged down her apron pocket. Again. Another night of keeping her secret.

"I think I'll turn in for the night," she said.

Her mother never looked up from her work, but Uncle John peered over the edge of his paper. "G' night, Anna."

She swallowed the dry lump in her throat and turned toward the stairs. With each step up, it became easier to breathe.

Until the knock sounded on the front door.

Everyone looked up and to Uncle John, expecting that he might know who it could possibly be at this unusual time of night. In the time they had lived there, nobody had come calling after dark. But John appeared as confused as the rest of them.

Anna paused on the stairway, her eyes trained on the door. John rose after removing his reading glasses and approached the door. He hesitated, his glance drifting toward the coats and his gun holster that hung on the rack across the room. Even from the staircase, Anna saw the handle of his pistol against the fabric of his coat.

The knock came again.

John opened the door, and a chill ran up Anna's spine when she saw the familiar hat, long blonde locks and dark coat of the mysterious stranger from town standing at the threshold. In the shadow of the darkness outside, she could see his steel-blue eyes. And he wasn't alone. Three other men stood behind him, out of the light cast from the doorway. She froze, her fingers tightening around the iron stair railing.

"Well, boys," the stranger said to the men who were with him. "Look who it is."

"What are you doing here?" John said, his voice with an edge of anger.

"Now, where is your hospitality?" the stranger said, his Southern accent thickening. He pushed his way past John and into the house.

Mother stood, and William moved to his feet. Anna's hand trembled, and she forced her foot up another step. Anything to get away from him. His gaze fell upon her from where she stood on the stairway, and he tipped his hat at her, just as he had done on the boardwalk.

"Well, hello again, purty lady," he said with a slight smile.

John looked at her, and she saw the surprise and confusion in his eyes. He intercepted the stranger midway through the room. "Can we talk about this outside?"

"Why would we do that, Johnny Boy?" he spoke, his voice laced with a hiss. "Why don't you introduce me to these charming ladies?"

He approached Anna's mother and extended his hand. She took it reluctantly. "I'm Mary," she said. Anna had never heard her voice sound so tight and scared. "Mary Holloway."

"Holloway?" he said. He turned back to John, and they shared a knowing look. "What a unique name."

Anna caught his glance again, those eyes as determined as a pit viper. "Well, then, that makes you a Holloway, too. What's your name, honey?"

"Anna," Her throat had gone dry, and she almost choked on the word.

He stopped and faced the room again. "Well, why don't you join us down here, Anna?"

She shook her head and said, "I don't want to."

As fast as a spider strike, he reached into his coat and to a gun holster. The pistol aimed at her before she even knew what was happening. A gasp escaped her throat, and a knot tightened in her stomach. She had never looked down the barrel of a gun before, especially not one pointed right at her. Somewhere in the room, her mother cried out, but Anna couldn't look away from the gun.

"No, I need you to come on down and join us," the stranger spoke. The smile faded from his lips, and his eyes stared at her with ice and fury.

Anna stepped down into the sitting room, her knees weak. Each step threatened to drop her to the ground in a bundle of crying nerves. But she didn't want to do that in front of this man who had just invaded their home.

At some point, Mother had grabbed William and pulled him into the corner of the room. Uncle John now stood in front of them, between these men with the gun and her family.

She eyed him with each step she took. John signaled to her to stand behind him, her mother and brother. Each second that ticked on droned like hours as she moved to the corner of the room. In that slowed time, her gaze fell on the stranger, and something caught her eye. His coat fell back from his hip in the breeze that came from the open door. The golden lamplight glistened upon the objects at his hip and in his hand: twins, two parts of a whole. Like a thousand stars shimmering in one collected space.

*Diamonds!*

Diamonds encrusting the handles of two pistols.

She looked up from the blinding shimmer and to his rough but handsome face.

Could it possibly be true? But he was a legend. Somewhere in the depths of her consciousness, she had always suspected him to be a work of fiction. He couldn't be real and standing in the parlor right now.

The crooked smile and shine in his blue eyes as he stared down the iron barrel of the pistol told her that the outlaw west had just crashed into her life.

This was most definitely Diamond Dave Thibodaux in the flesh. A very real and terrifying flesh.

The gun then shifted to train on Uncle John. "Why you been hidin', Johnny?"

"Whatever this is, let's take it outside," John said. "I have all the money stashed if you want it. Take it all."

Dave laughed, and the pistol shook. "Come on. You know this is not about the stash. You earned your share. You always did, and I was grateful. I wouldn't have been able to do half those jobs without you. You were my right hand, Johnny."

*Wait a minute,* Anna thought as she sidled in beside her mother, who was now shaking so hard that Ann thought she might fall apart. *This was Diamond Dave, without a doubt. All the tales and newspapers, however, told of Dave and a partner, the infamous Johnny Holiday. What were the chances that Uncle John was Johnny Holiday?*

*Johnny Holiday—John Holloway!*

It couldn't be true.

"No, Johnny." Dave stepped forward. "You know why I'm here. You ran away and hid because of this. Now, where is it?"

"I don't have it," John said and stood his ground before Mary and William.

Dave lost his smile and cocked his head to one side. "Go search upstairs, boys. You know what you're lookin' for."

Like hungry hounds, the three men smiled and bounded up the stairs. Within seconds, the crashing and rumbling from upstairs sounded like bulls tearing through the rooms.

"I call your bluff," Dave spoke, and his narrowed eyes fell upon Anna.

Uncle John tried to step in his way, but he pointed the gun at him again.

"Leave her alone," John spoke.

"Don't worry. I won't hurt her, but she has something I want."

With the gun still fixed on Uncle John, he reached for the chain at her neck. The pendant emerged from under her bodice. He pulled the necklace free, breaking the chain, and examined it in the light.

"I'm pretty sure this will be useful to me," he said with a smile and pocketed the necklace.

The men came storming down the stairs.

"What did you find?" he asked.

One man, dirty with sweat and smelling like horse and leather, held up the object in his hand.

Anna felt her heart nearly drop to the floor. It was the map. They knew about it. What else did they know? She couldn't breathe and caught Uncle John at the corner of her eye.

The disbelief in his face was evident. Then he looked at her and at that moment they both knew each other's secrets.

"And the book?" Dave asked, an exasperated sigh leaving his lips.

"No sign of it."

Dave glared back at John, who looked away from Anna. "Where is it?"

Fear gripped her. With the gun pointed at John and the rest of her family in danger of the same treatment, she couldn't speak even if she wanted to. Those men had the map in their hands. A map, it seemed, that they already knew about. And now they wanted something else, and she could bet good money that they wanted the journal.

Her heart sank when something else drifted into her thoughts. John was trying hard to protect her and her family right now. He wasn't one of them, even though he knew about the stash in the mine. Something else was going on.

"I don't have it," John spoke.

Dave's finger remained steady on the trigger, never a flinch or a tremble in his hand. This man was going to shoot Uncle John, and for the first time since she met him, she cared about him. She didn't want him to die. Her hand slipped into the pocket of her apron and grasped the spine of the journal from where she stood behind John.

The outlaw smiled and moved faster than she could. The butt of his diamond-encrusted pistol struck out and hit John against the side of his head. John fell to the ground, and her mother cried out, crouching down to help him. But this left William and Anna exposed.

Dave lashed out and grasped the collar of William's shirt. Her brother yelped for a moment as the man dragged him across the room. He drew the boy in close and backed away from everyone.

Anna nearly choked and stood alone in the corner. Her brother watched her with wide eyes, a glisten of tears at the edges. John lay on the floor with mother crying over him. She could only stand there and watch Dave back away with her brother toward the door.

"You have 'til sun-up to bring me that book, Johnny Boy. I'll be at the saloon in town. I'll have that book, or at dawn, the kid gets a bullet."

Shadows fell across her brother's face as a tear finally ran down his cheek, and Dave pulled him out the door. The other men exited with him, and they disappeared into the night on the sound of hoofbeats.

Anna's legs shook beneath her where she still stood, gazing into the empty doorway with her hand on the journal in her pocket. She hadn't acted fast enough. Maybe if she had given them the book, they wouldn't have taken William. Dave wouldn't have hurt Uncle John. Maybe they would have just gone and left them in peace.

But she knew that wasn't true. She had read enough of the tales of Diamond Dave to know that it wasn't his style. He believed that they all knew about the journal and the map and everything to which it would eventually lead. After all, they found the map upstairs. He would have killed them all if she had given them the journal.

This was all her fault. If she had never gone into that mine, if she hadn't taken the journal and map, they would never have found it.

She couldn't breathe and her knees buckled below her. The tears fell as she stared through the empty threshold where her brother had just disappeared.

# CHAPTER 15

ary's crying echoed in the room, hollow in Anna's ears. From the corner of her eye, she saw a streak of blood trickling down the side of John's head from where her mother cradled his head in her lap, her hand on his cheek.

Her mother's trembling hand waved absently in the air. "I need towels. Water."

Of course. What was she thinking? She needed to help John, and not sit here like a whimpering fool. She dried her damp palms on the front of her apron and stood. Her head spun when she got to her feet, but she caught herself on the edge of the chair before she ran into the kitchen. Although the room was dark, she had enough light from the parlor to draw water from the pump into a metal bowl and grabbed a handful of flour-sack towels from the cabinet. Her hands were still shaking when she rushed back to her mother and knelt at her side.

Anna dipped a towel into the water, rung it out and then handed it to her mother. Blood smeared across Uncle John's forehead as Mary placed the damp towel to his skin. His eyes remained closed, and his lips open as her mother tapped his cheek.

*Oh, God, please don't let him die.* Anna clasped her fingers together and held them up to her lips as she muttered a silent prayer.

"Why did this happen?" her mother cried. "What do they want from us?"

*I know what they want,* Anna thought. The ache twisted in her stomach again.

John's eyes fluttered open, and his unfocused sight gazed at the women looking down upon him. Anna nearly gasped and dropped her hands when she saw him awaken. His hand fumbled up toward Mary's arm, confused and agitated.

Anna's hope crumbled into desperation. John might be awake now, but there was no way he could ride into town, stop Diamond Dave and save William. He barely knew where he was. That blow to his head was even harder than Anna had initially suspected. And Mother was just a bag of nerves, nor would she be a force to confront the band of outlaws to get her son back.

She sat back on her heels and took in a deep breath. Maybe it could calm her racing heart. There was no other way. Nobody else could help William now. Only she had the key to getting him back, but she was no gunslinger. The furthest from. But it didn't matter now. She had to go and hope that she could save him.

With the back of her hand, she wiped away the tears that had stained her cheeks. She let out her uneven breath through shaking lips and looked up from John's pale face.

"I have to leave, Mother," she spoke.

"What?" Mary looked at her, eyes wide and glistening with tears. Her thin fingers clenched into white knuckles. "No, Anna. You are not allowed to go anywhere right now. One of Maria's people can ride into town and get the sheriff."

Anna shook her head and glanced to the floor. It was too hard to look at her mother, especially now that she was ready to defy her orders.

"I'm sorry. I have to go. I know what they want, and I can get William back."

"What are you talking about?" Mary grasped her forearm with her thin, shaking fingers. "How do you know them? What do they want?"

Anna pulled her arm free and stood on trembling knees. She wished she could tell her mother everything, but not until she straightened this out. Then, when she returned with William, she and Uncle John would have to have a long talk about things. She turned away and marched to the porch as her mother called after her with ever increasing cries to "get back here now."

Someday, she would understand why Anna had to go. As she grabbed her coat and stepped out of the golden glow of light from the parlor and onto the deck, she knew that things would forever change between her and her mother. She only hoped she could come back and find that John was okay after all and that William would survive this.

Her mother's voice faded into the distance as she hurried to the barn, the weight of the journal in her apron tapping against her leg. There was enough moonlight pouring through the door of the barn to prepare a horse with a bridle and saddle. But there was one last thing, one hope for making this all right, and it was in the far closet at the end of the barn. She ran through the recipe from her memory of when the boys showed her how to make the bug bombs. With a burlap bag, she found hanging on a nail, she collected the ingredients and then tied the bag to the back of the saddle. As the mare tapped her foot, ready to start her journey, Anna mounted the saddle and nudged the horse from the barn and into the road outside the house.

Just before she kicked the horse to start into the night, a dark silhouette stumbled and fell to his knees in the doorway to the house.

"Anna, stop," John's voice boomed into the dark.

The sound made her nerves twitch as the horse shifted its weight under her. "I'm going to save my brother. I'll take care of this."

Her heels flashed against the horse's flanks, and it bounded off into the darkness. Thankfully, the horse had taken this route many times because the stars and moon offered very little light. With every pound of the animal's hooves, her heart raced faster. The scenario of how things could go rushed through her brain, but all of them ended very badly. If she was going to get William out of this alive, she would have to be smart. The bug bomb could come in handy if things got out of hand, but hopefully, it wouldn't come to that.

The horse slowed as it neared the edge of town, and she hesitated to nudge it deeper into the streets. If her plan was going to work, she needed to stay hidden from the men that had William. She dismounted and led the horse to a hitching post in the shadows of the silent and closed mercantile. Just as she tied the reins to the post, the boarding whistle of the train across town jangled her nerves and made her jump. The animal jostled against the reins as well, startled by the sound. After she removed the burlap bag of ingredients, she tucked them into her coat and slunk into the shadows behind the mercantile.

It didn't take much imagination to figure out where the saloon was. Piano music and raucous laughter led her through the back alley and between another two stores where she could see across the street to the saloon. Gas lamps lit the street, giving her a view of the horses tied to the hitching posts outside the building.

Music from the piano in the bar seeped out of the doors and windows every time patrons moved in and out of the glass-paned door. Cowboys with gaudily-dressed women on their arms exited the doors, stumbling off the boardwalk and staggering into the night. Anna pressed deeper into the shadows when they crossed the street. *Just need to stay in the dark.*

A man walked past the window inside the saloon, and she recognized him from the gang that had come inside her house and ransacked her room. They were definitely in there, just like Dave had promised, poised to stay until sun-up when he would do the unspeakable act of murdering her brother if he didn't have the journal.

Nobody else walked through the front doors for several minutes as she watched from the shadows. She had to move, and it had to be now. A quick breath in as she clutched the burlap bag inside her coat. She crouched and moved across the street, finally sliding between two horses hitched in front of the saloon. The horses shifted and glanced at her with curiosity as she let out a nervous breath and peered over the hitching post and into the window.

A quick survey of the room revealed the piano and bar on the back wall with only a few patrons and ladies dressed like peacocks. Most of the tables were empty except one in the center of the room, and that one made her heart wiggle in her chest. William sat at the end of the table, facing the window. His face was pale and scared blue eyes watched from under tousled hair. One of the men sat at the table, several chairs down from William. Others that she recognized were scattered throughout the saloon: one leaning against the piano and another with his arm around a woman as they sang off-key with the music.

And then there was Dave, his blonde hair evident under his hat as he leaned back on a chair next to the fireplace, his feet propped up on a table as he polished the diamond-studded handle of the pistol in his hand.

All the players of this little game present in the saloon. Now she had to move them just right.

She crept to the window, her gaze fixed on William. One look at her. That's all he needed to do. Her eyes bored into him, willing him to look to the window. None of the other men even noticed anything beyond their little circles of drunkenness and debauchery. She raised her hand beside her face and waved it. He had to see her, or none of this would work.

And then it happened. His small eyes looked up for one moment, and her heart leaped into her throat. The veil of fear slipped from his face, and he almost smiled when he saw her. Anna placed a finger to her lips to signal him to stay quiet, and he bit his lip to hide his smile.

He would understand everything when he saw what she brought. She felt around the burlap bag and withdrew the two glass jars, holding them up to the window so he could see. His cheeks turned red, and his face nearly glowed. Then she motioned to the fireplace, and he gave the tiniest nod of understanding.

Thank heavens William was smart for his age. He played the part of a stupid kid most of the time, and now Anna was sure that it was just to get Mother's attention. He understood far more than he let on, and this was his chance to put it into action.

Anna stuffed the bottles back into the bag and slipped away from the window. The smile fell from his lips when she disappeared into the shadows again. She crept back to where the horses stood at the hitching post, and a sudden bloom of an idea occurred to her. It wasn't part of her original plan, but the grin formed on her lips when she thought of it. The laughter and music continued in the saloon. Good. Nobody would hear the horses wander away after she untied their reigns.

With a little slap on their hind ends, the horses all trotted down the streets to freedom. After the last horse vanished, Anna crept into the shadows of the back alleyway behind the saloon, letting her eyes adjust to the dark once she was away from the lamp light of the street.

She kept close to the wall. That was the best way to not trip on something in the dark until her hand found the firm attachment of the roof access ladder. Every one of these buildings had them. She hooked the burlap bag over her shoulder and hurried up the ladder. A cool breeze danced across her face along with the shrill whistle from the train station. The platform attendant called out into the night for final boarding. She stepped over the edge of the rooftop, the breeze carrying the scent of the train steam through the town and over the top of the saloon. The plume of steam rose on the north side of town, the sound of the engines a welcome deterrent to any of her footsteps that creaked as she walked toward the chimney jutting out at the far end of the roof.

Although it was dark, she thankfully remembered the order of the contents in the bug bomb: large jar with the powdered contents and the liquid in the smaller jar, slipped carefully into the large bottle. Don't let them mix until its thrown. Hold the bottle straight. She screwed the lid onto the bottle and then turned back toward the chimney. She peered down into the soot-covered hole to see the last embers of the burning logs in the fireplace down in the saloon.

This was it. Once the jar left her hands, that would be the end of the relative peace downstairs. Anna closed her eyes, running through her plan in her mind one more time. The inner jar clinked against the outer glass as her hands trembled. She let out a shaking breath and positioned the bomb just above the chimney hole.

Ready for the chaos. Then get William and run like hell.

Her trembling fingers opened, and the jar dropped straight down onto the embers.

She didn't wait to watch the glass shatter. There was no time to scale the ladder back down. Not this time. She leaped over the edge of the rooftop facing the front of the saloon and fell onto the awning that shaded the front doors from the daytime sun. No time to wait here either. She rolled over the edge and jumped to the boardwalk with an unsteady landing.

The music had stopped and the once-clear windows looking into the saloon were now clouded. Shouts rang out from the bar, and the clatter of tipping chairs echoed into the night.

*Come on, William.*

Another man shouted to get outside, get the horses. That had to be Dave.

*Come on.*

The door burst open, and she jumped. The white cloud of smoke swirled like a parting curtain as William stumbled out onto the boardwalk. The family hug that she wanted to give him would have to wait. She grasped his hand, and together they ran, his shorter legs keeping up well with her as he led them into an alley. The sound of the door crashing open behind them fueled her to run faster. Boot falls pounded on the boardwalk, heading in their direction as Dave's voice shouted orders at his men to find them. Then more curse words followed. They must have noticed that their horses were gone.

She rounded the corner to another street. The one that would take them straight on to the train station. Dave and his men wouldn't dare to grab them, not with so many people at the station. The platform attendant had to still be there too. William kept up with her, his hand so tight in hers.

The ricochet of gunfire sounded behind her. That kind of surprised her. For a little while, she thought they wouldn't dare to shoot at them. They were just kids. Another shot rang out, this time with the whistling of it a little too close to her head. So many voices shouted behind them now, too many to be just Dave and his gang. People screamed and ran from the violence that now followed Anna and William down the street.

Another whistle of the train and the screeching of wheels spinning on the track. *Oh no!* The train was leaving the station. Leaving with anybody that could help them. The train started off in a slow roll.

An idea came to her. A desperate one, but it might be their only chance to lose the men behind them.

"I need you to trust me, William," she called out above the screeching of the train wheels.

His hand squeezed hers tighter. "Okay."

She veered away from the platform, and he kept up with her. The ground sloped down under them as she ran toward the moving train and the track. The train accelerated, and Anna pushed harder. His hand tugged against hers as he stumbled on the gravel slope. He would never make it, not without her help. She reached back, placed an arm around his chest and lunged toward the last cargo car, the only one with an open door. His small hands grasped the rails along the door, and he pulled himself inside.

The effort to lift him into the car had taken so much energy, and the train accelerated. She had to push so much harder to keep up with it, and William now poked his head out and held out his hand to her. That was a nice gesture, but there was no way his small body could help her into the car.

A man's voice shouted from behind her, coupled with the sprinting of boots in the gravel along the track. The race of her heart quickened as she glanced back. Even in the dark, she knew it was Dave, his silhouette like a terrible ghost bearing down on her. His long dark coat flowed behind him. The grim reaper on her heels.

"Hurry, Anna! He's coming!" William pleaded and reached his small hands out to her again.

The train began to slip further ahead of her. She had no choice but to lunge for the open door. She dug her boot into the gravel, one last surge of strength. She leaped for the door, and her hand caught the railing. The momentum of the train pulled her forward, and her feet slipped from under her. She cried out but kept a hold on the railing and heaved her torso onto the floor of the car. The breeze swirling around her became a wind as the train moved faster. Her fingers found a notch in the floor boards, and she used it to pull herself along her torso deeper into the car.

A hand grasped the heel of her boot, dragging her back out the door. She screamed, and her fingernails scraped across the floor, desperate to find a gap in the planks. Her hand caught the edge of the open door.

*Can't hold on.* His weight pulling at her was too much.

The journal fell free of the apron and slid across the floor and toward the door, hanging half-out above the chugging wheels of the train. In that instant, she glanced back at him, the flash of recognition blazing across his face. His grip loosened as he tried to lunge for the journal. That was all the leverage she needed. She kicked her foot out, striking him in the face. Her boot slipped out of his grip, and he lost his balance in the gravel. With a heave, she pulled herself back into the car and grasped the journal before she turned to glance back out the door.

The gusty wind blew her hair around her face as she leaned out to see the last of Dave and his men trying to run after the train, but it left them behind in the town. The car lurched from side to side with the increasing speed. The lights of the town quickly dimmed the further they moved down the track, away from Dave and his gang.

William scrambled to where she stood and wrapped his arms about her waist. This almost made her lose her balance, but the white-knuckle grip she still had on the railing kept her upright. She looked down at him, his head buried against her abdomen, and his small frame shaking against her. Or maybe that was *her* trembling in *his* grip. The vessels in her legs still pumped with fury and fear, twitching with each beat of her heart.

She placed a hand on his back, something that her mother would have done. But she wasn't sure it was the right thing to do. This wasn't exactly the escape she had in mind. Sure, they were out of Dave's clutches, but now they were captives of this speeding train bound for some unknown station in the dark of night. Mother and John would have no idea where they were. All they knew was that her children were out there somewhere, hunted by a murderous outlaw who now knew that she had the journal.

Dave pushed himself up from the gravel along the track and brushed the dust from his coat. He watched the train accelerate away from him, the very train that carried away the book he had been looking for. That girl had had it the entire time. It had been right under his nose when he was in John's house, and he missed it.

With the back of his hand, he wiped away the streak of blood flowing from his nose. The cooling night air burned in his lungs and threatened to make him cough after the irritation of the smoke from the saloon. The throbbing in his nose where the girl's boot made contact fueled his anger even more as he watched the train vanish into the night.

Two of his men ran up behind him, their boots crunching in the gravel.

Dave didn't turn. He didn't have to. "Anybody know where that train is headed?"

"Kansas City, I think," one man said and gasped for breath.

"We got men in Kansas City?"

His man stood straighter. "I believe Bob Pickett and his boys are still there."

The train had nearly become a black shadow in the distance. "Good. Send a telegraph first thing in the morning. Tell them to meet our special cargo at the station. They're to hold 'em until we show up."

A fading sound of metal against metal was the last that Dave could tell that the train had even been there. That, and the blood that still flowed from his nose. At least he knew where to find the book. No more searching with John. The man had been his friend once, and he really didn't feel like putting a bullet in him tonight.

Whatever had happened here, John had missed it.

His head ached with a powerful, throbbing pain. His hand moved to the linen dressing around his temples. At least the bleeding from his scalp had stopped.

The gaslight lamps of the town appeared fuzzy and out of focus as he approached thanks to the pounding blow Dave had given him. Wisps of smoke billowed from the saloon at the west end of town, and the shadier patrons of the bar stood along the boardwalk across the street.

John dismounted and tied his horse within the shadows of the alley. Surely, with all this commotion, the sheriff would have been bothered to get out of bed and see what was going on. John stepped past the shops, hearing the chatter of the people along the street. The sulfurous odor of the smoke brought a small smile to his lips when he recognized that awful smell. It was his own concoction that he had taught the boys at the ranch to rid the horse stalls of poisonous insects. He hadn't even known that Anna was aware of the bug bombs. *Brilliant. Wish I'd been there to see it.*

From what he could make out, there had been a tussle at the saloon with a rough-looking band of men, undoubtedly Dave and his gang. But what about the children? Nobody said anything about two kids escaping these men.

He scanned the many faces that had gathered outside the saloon, but none of them were William or Anna. If Dave and his men had indeed been here, William at least would have been here too. He kept to the shadows and behind the crowd, all the time listening to the gossip.

And then he heard what he had waited for.

"Well, I saw them heading out of town," one woman spoke. "They were in quite a hurry, following the train. Something on there, I suppose."

The train. Did the children board the train to escape? It would be a good idea, especially if they were being chased.

That would have to do. There was very little time left to investigate. If the children were on that train, he would have to hurry before Dave's men caught up with them. Maybe they had the wit and strength to evade him before it was too late.

# CHAPTER 16

The rocking of the train car had lulled William to sleep, but the sway only made Anna dizzy. She had managed to fold up her coat and move William's sleepy head from her lap to the coat without waking him up. The train car door slid mostly closed despite the rusty track that held it in place, but she kept it open to let in a silver streak of moonlight.

Her heart still pounded against her ribs, each beat heavy with fear and uncertainty. This train could be going anywhere. And how would they get back home? Neither of them had ever travelled on their own, and this was much rougher territory than Massachusetts.

Then there was Diamond Dave and his outlaws. They could still be following them, and it wouldn't take them long to find the train's destination, wherever that may be.

She hadn't realized that she still held the journal to her chest, despite her cold and shaking fingers. *Of course, the journal.* Everything that had happened tonight was because of that book. Somehow, Dave knew about the journal and the map, which meant he probably knew about why it was so important. She slipped it back into her apron pocket and curled around William where he slept beside her.

The rocking and lurching of the train car eventually put her into a fitful sleep, filled with dreams of gunshots and horses and a dark tunnel that breathed hate. At the end of that tunnel was a secret; she just knew it, but it was so black and frightening that she was afraid to take a single step. A cold wind brushed at her back, and she had the distinct impression that someone stood behind her. The space in the mine shaft gaped open to the entrance and filled with a shadow. Anna turned to see a man in silhouette against the entrance of the mine. He stood motionless and faced her in the dark of the tunnel. A halo surrounded him, a trick of the sunlight outside the shaft.

She knew she should be afraid of the tunnel now and the man standing there, but the way he stood there reminded her of someone.

It had to be her father. Everything in her gut told her that he stood there, watching from the entrance.

"Dad?" she said with a quiver in her voice. The sound didn't echo like she thought it would. The shadow never moved, never spoke, but only watched her.

The silhouette remained still as the darkness behind her crept and crawled with great black arms over the cut stone of the tunnel. It poured itself over the cart tracks and oozed over her boots, grasping at her ankles and crawling over the edges of her skirt. The panic in her chest built as the black crept up to her waist, leaving a frost-like chill on everything it touched. The dark enveloped her body like a blanket of ink, oozing up her neck, into her hair. Anna screamed, but the dark flowed into her mouth and choked out the sound.

The man in the light only watched her. He could do nothing; she knew that the moment she saw him standing there. He was only a specter, made of memories and hope. His form was the last thing she saw before the darkness took her vision.

Anna awoke with a start, and her eyes adjusted to the faint light in the sky. No more blackness or despair of the tunnel. The ghost of the man was gone, and they were alone in the swaying train car. She could have sworn she had been asleep for only a few minutes but the early morning light said otherwise. William still lay beside her, snoring a little with each breath.

Steadying herself against the wall of the car, she stood and stretched her legs. The cooler air here meant the train must be moving out of the desert. She peered from the gap in the door. The drawn out stretch of red and brown sand of New Mexico had given way to endless fields of green waving grass dotted by the occasional brush or solitary tree.

Just as she had thought. They must not be in New Mexico anymore. If it was already morning and the train was still going, they were far away from home.

She slid down to sit against the wall and gazed at the landscape racing by them. There was no way Mother was going to forgive her for this, for running so far away, especially with William. This was getting so much worse. The burning in her eyes threatened tears. *Not now. Please not now.* If William woke up and saw her crying, she would just die.

She brought her knees to her chest and felt the fullness of the journal in her apron again. The book slipped from the pocket, and she held it into the light, the morning sun glistening on the gold lettering on the cover: *Journal.* Years of use in her father's hands had faded the letters into just flakes of an embossed word in the leather.

Something else rolled out of her pocket, and she caught it just before it fell down her hip. The roll of coins. A small smile danced over her lips. At least they had some money, whatever it would be worth. Maybe enough to buy a ticket back to New Mexico, but she had no idea how much it would cost. What if it wasn't enough?

A lump formed in her throat. What if Diamond Dave was waiting for them to do just that? He might be just biding his time at the train station until she appeared there, ready to kill her and take the book. The burning started in her eyes again. Dave will never stop, not until he got what he came for.

The words her father had written came to her: *with this book, I have kept my map and notations. Without this journal, the map is useless, and the converse is true as well.*

Her family would never be safe. If she went back home, he would just show up again and kill them this time. She couldn't just give him the book. There's no way he would allow her to know its secrets and live.

She pressed her head back against the wall of the car, its swaying giving her a headache.

It wasn't the book or the map he actually wanted. Not really. Her eyes flew open. *Of course!* There was only one way to keep her family safe. She had to always know more than Dave did. Leverage. At least that's what she thought it was called. The journal was the key to everything that Dave wanted, to everything her father researched.

The book and the map were only the keys. The thing at the end of the map was the leverage she needed.

That meant she needed to study. She needed to know everything that her father knew.

She opened the journal and leafed to where she had left off reading.

Various markings riddled the top of the page, all marks that she recognized from her father's work in Sweden. Each symbol should be matched with an English letter or phrase: a code translator. She glanced through the codes, committing them to her memory. Then she read further down the page:

> *Limestone slab discovered by Olof Ohman.*
>
> *Inscription as follows:*
>
> *Eight Gotlanders and 22 Norwegians on this reclaiming/acquisition journey far to the west from Vinland. We had a camp by two shelters one day's journey north from this stone. We were fishing one day. After we came home, we found 10 men red with blood and death. Ave Maria. Save from evil.*

Anna glanced up from the book. She had seen enough of the map before Dave's men took it to know that marker #1 was the rune stone found in Kensington, Minnesota. According to her father, this stone would lead to the next clue. Of course, Dave had the map and would know to start in Kensington, but without the journal, he wouldn't know how to proceed or what he was looking for.

Her shoulders relaxed for the first time since she climbed aboard the train. Finally, she had a goal, something that she could focus on besides the possibility of getting a bullet in her brain.

She glanced through a few more pages, but they didn't make much sense. They would probably only be explained by following the map in an appropriate order, something she couldn't do without having it right in front of her. Unfortunately, she hadn't memorized enough of the map to remember what it had to do with these pages.

Her stomach grumbled with the growing light outside. Maria's dinner was the last thing she remembered eating, and each pop and gurgle in her stomach reminded her of that. She rose and tucked the book back into her apron. William still lay sound asleep against the wall. He would surely be okay if she left for just a few minutes. As the train lurched down the track, she slid open the front gate that provided access to the main cabins. The rush of air swirled around her as she crossed the plank to the next car and peered through the window.

Cargo car, packed with luggage.

Good. At least there was nobody here to question her on where she came from or how she got onto this train. She opened the door and stepped into the car, making her way down the center aisle between mounds of trunks and bags. She moved to the front and crossed over toward the next car.

Through the window, she saw a bunk car with a single aisle running down the right side of the car. The quarters were just like the train that her family had taken: individual closed rooms. The car maid walked down the aisle with her cart and provided the quarters with their breakfasts.

Anna watched and waited as the maid, her curly blonde hair tied up behind a black bonnet, and a white lacy apron over a long black dress stopped her cart and greeted those in the next room. The maid disappeared into the room and left her wheeled cart in the aisle. Alone and vulnerable to sticky fingers. Where was William when she needed something stolen?

Anna opened the car door and padded down the aisle, chewing at her fingernails as she listened for the maid in the quarters. The fragrance of fresh baked cinnamon scones and English tea wafted down the aisle as she approached the cart. A basket of hot, hard-boiled eggs steamed beside the scones, making her mouth water. How did William find stealing so easy? Her nerves were bound to give her away. Either that or the grumbling in her stomach. A quick grab and go. Just the way William would do it.

The maid smiled as she provided the cups of tea and plates of scones to the couple in the car, taking extra care not to spill a drop of the tea despite the swaying of the train car. With a nod of her head and a curtsy, she turned away and dusted the crumbs from her hands against her apron. She placed her fingers around the cart handle and stopped. Something was different as she gazed down at her cart. The ceramic tea pot and basket of scones was missing along with a handful of eggs, and among the crumbs were four shining silver coins.

Anna opened the door to their empty cargo car to find William still asleep. The car swayed and nearly threw her off balance with her arms full of breakfast. She steadied herself against the wall and smiled. She slammed the door closed hard enough to echo through the car. William's eyes opened, and he sat up.

"Wake up, King William," she said.

He rubbed the grit from his eyes and squinted into the morning light that poured from the open door. His tousled hair blew in the cool breeze.

Anna settled onto the floor next to him and placed the breakfast on the floor between them.

"I almost forgot what happened last night," he said, his voice croaking.

The smile fell from her lips. "Sorry. I wish I could say it didn't happen."

He turned away from the door and glanced down at the scones and eggs. "You got all of this by yourself?"

"Don't act so surprised." She tore the corner of one scone and placed the flaky pastry in her mouth. "And I didn't steal it."

He took a bite of his own scone and closed his eyes as he savored the cinnamon.

"Enjoy it now," Anna said. "I don't think it would be a good idea to try and get more. Trains like this don't look kindly on stowaways."

"Is that what we are? Stowaways?"

"Well, we didn't buy a ticket, so, yes."

"We were being chased—"

"They won't care. If we're discovered, we could be put in jail."

His eyes widened, and he stopped chewing.

"But probably not." She grasped a warm egg and peeled away the brown shell. "We can save some of the scones, but the eggs won't keep, so we need to finish them off."

William swallowed the bite of scone and took an egg for himself. "Where are we going?"

She shook her head. "I'm not sure."

His eyes turned down, and he just held the warm egg in his hand. "Why did this happen? Who were those guys?"

He had every right to know. After all, he was now just as much a part of this as was she, even if he had nothing to do with the mine and the discovery of the stash. She withdrew the journal from her apron pocket and placed it on the floor between them.

"It's all because of this. It's Father's journal."

William only looked at it as though he was afraid to touch it. "Why do you have it? I thought it went missing the night he died."

She took in a steady breath and let it out. Everything she was about to tell him had been her secret for so long. "You're not going to believe what I say, but I need you to listen." And she told him everything, from the moment she walked into the mine, to the discovery of the stash and their father's belongings, to meeting Dave on the street and his appearance on their doorstep. It was best to leave out the little part about Uncle John being Johnny Holiday. William didn't need to know that about him just yet.

"That's really Diamond Dave? The outlaw from your books?" he said and looked up at her with wrinkles forming between his eyebrows.

"How do you know about my books?"

He smiled. "I knew you were reading them, even if Mother didn't. I read them too after you just left them hiding in your room."

"You stole them from me? You little thief."

"So," he said and paused, working on formulating his next thought. "Why do they want this book anyway?"

"They believe that the journal and the map lead to a buried treasure."

The sunlight sparkled in his eyes, and the wrinkles between his eyebrows disappeared. "Father found a buried treasure?"

"Yes. Well, sort of. He found its location, but never actually saw the treasure."

Those wrinkles came back. "So, maybe there's no treasure at all."

The same thought had occurred to her. "Maybe. But Dave believes it, and that's why he came after us."

William still hadn't started to peel his egg but continued to just hold it. "I want to go home."

"I know. I do too, but if we go home now, those men will just come back."

"What are we gonna do?"

"Wherever this train ends up, I'll find a telegraph station and send a message back to mother. At least she can know we're safe."

"Do you even know how to send a telegram?" he asked.

She shrugged. "I watched father send one. It didn't look that hard."

"And then find a policeman or something," he said. "Maybe they can arrest those men when they come for us."

Anna smiled. "Good idea."

"And then Mother and Uncle John can come for us and take us home." He nodded and started to peel his egg.

"Okay. That's what we'll do." But she wasn't convinced that it would work. She had tried for days to find a sheriff back in New Mexico without success.

William swallowed and glanced down at the teapot. "No cups."

"I know. I couldn't risk taking everything. Just drink from the pot. It'll be just as good."

She finished her scone and drank the tea with her brother. The grumbling in her stomach had finally stopped, and she knew it wasn't just the breakfast. The secret she had held for so long was now out in the open. Finally telling someone else let the tension loose that had tied like a knot in her chest. Even if there was nothing she could do about it, at least it was not just her secret any more.

The train continued, and the sun moved on to the western horizon. They had not stopped all day, which meant that the train's destination was much farther away than Anna had anticipated. Twilight approached, and the train slowed. The roaring clack of the train wheels quieted, if only a little bit.

Anna peered out the open door to see the lights of a large town looming down the track. The steam horn sounded, sending white plumes bouncing along the length of the train. The chug-chug grew slower and the ground no longer whizzed by in a blur of fading colors.

"What do you see?" William asked from the center of the car.

"A city up ahead."

"A big one?"

"Yeah."

The tall edges of buildings shone against the horizon. More tracks appeared alongside their train. Wherever they were, this was a big station, and there were bound to be a lot of people.

She stepped away from the door and grasped William's hand. "We need to stay low."

"Why?" he asked as she pulled him into the shadowy corners of the car.

"Stowaways, remember?"

The color drained from his face, and he followed her. They slipped into the corner behind a few empty barrels.

The train slowed to a near-crawl as it approached the station. By now, the sun had set, leaving the station in a canopy of gas lamp light that flashed through the open door. Anna watched the lamp posts move past the open door, the first platform fast-approaching. The station sign came into view, and Anna craned her neck to read it: Kansas City, Missouri.

They really were far from home.

The squeal of metal-on-metal pierced into the night and echoed against the station walls as the train ground to a halt in a cloud of steam.

She grasped his hand. "Follow me and stay quiet."

He nodded and clutched her hand. She stood, and he followed her every footstep. Billows of steam clouded the platform. Somewhere in the mist, an attendant called out the station name to the passengers. Clatters of train cars opening rang out through the steam. Hazy figures of people standing in the steam looked like ghosts in the lamp light.

Plenty of people. Plenty of steam. Now was their chance to slip off the train and blend into the crowd, before the steam dissipated and the attendant could see them.

Anna readied her foot to jump out onto the platform but stopped when she saw the figures of three men wandering through the steam, surveying each car. Each of them wore a hat that shaded their faces and long coats that brushed against the spurred heels of their boots. One man smoked his hand-rolled cigarette and turned to toss away the butt when Anna saw the six-shooter holstered at his side. It was barely visible, but the gas lamps illuminated it well enough under his coat. This wasn't right. They were waiting for something . . . or someone.

When she didn't jump, William squeezed her hand. "What is it?" he whispered.

"We can't go this way," she said. "Come on. I have another idea."

She stood and led him through the front gate between the cars, the same route she took to find breakfast. The shadows cast between the cars would provide enough concealment, at least for a few seconds. She stepped around the plank and jumped down to the rails between the cars. William reached for her, and she helped him down as well. He found her hand again, and they crept around the dark side of the car, away from the platform.

The gas lamps cast hazy light through the steam, but the light was enough to see the other shadows along the alleyway that curved around the station. Another cloud of steam puffed along the cars and they used that moment to dash across the rails and around the far end of the platform. They plunged into the alley and ran until they emerged into the stone-paved streets of Kansas City.

She glanced back to the station as they continued a quick pace together. The train whistle blasted again, jangling her nerves. Nobody followed them. Thank heavens.

"Anna," William's voice called to her, drawing her attention.

His hand tugged against hers, and she stopped the moment she turned to look ahead of them. Those same men she had seen on the platform stood before them at the end of the dark and empty street, just feet from where she stopped. The one in the middle stepped forward, his face shadowed by his hat, and leaned down to face her. His breath reeked of whisky and cigarettes. He tipped back his hat with one finger, allowing the golden lamp light to shine against his left cheek.

"Well, well," he said, his voice as rough as gravel. "Looks like we found 'em boys. Now we wait. Dave's on his way."

# CHAPTER 17

Before Anna could scream, a hand covered her mouth and lifted her off the ground. William's hand slipped from hers as she plunged into darkness, away from the lamp light. The scent of stale tobacco filled her senses as it emanated from the hand that pressed so tight against her face. His other hand wrapped about her torso and held her firmly against his iron chest. She tried to kick at him, but his arm squeezed harder, and she couldn't breathe anymore.

Then his grip let her go, dropping her to the ground covered in smelly straw. She gasped, the familiar odor of barn and manure filling her nostrils. The smell of a stable. The man who had held her loomed over her. The other men approached, tossing William beside her.

She glanced up to the darkened rafters of a high-ceilinged barn. The faint light through the main door shone on the cross beams and pulleys far above her head. Cattle shifted in their stalls all around them with more mooing and baying of cows outside the barn.

The first man crouched down and looked at her. "No use calling for help. Nobody will hear you." He stood again and pulled back his coat to reveal the handle of his pistol at his hip. "Dave said to search 'em," he said to the men behind him. He pointed to her with a beefy finger. "He said this one would have a book that he needs."

Hands grabbed her from behind and pulled her upright. She gritted her teeth as his hands reached into her coat and then the pocket in her apron. As much as she wanted to fight and grab at the book when his fingers found it, she held back. There was no way she would win in that kind of a fight.

With a toothless smile, he raised the book high. "Found it."

Anna's heart sank as he took the journal away from her with dirty hands.

"I guess we won't be needing you two any longer," the man spoke and withdrew his pistol.

"Dave said to hold 'em," one of the younger men said as he sidled up next to the man with the gun.

"I don't give two bottles of whiskey about what Dave said. He's gonna get his book, and that's all he wanted," he said and cocked the hammer on the pistol. Then he muttered under his breath, "Dave, always tellin' me what I can and cannot do. Christ, he's like my momma."

The barrel of the pistol aimed at her head and she held her breath. That was twice now that she looked down the business end of a loaded gun in just a couple of days, and it didn't seem to get any easier. Her stomach twisted, and she bit the inside of her cheek. *What would it feel like when it entered the skull? Would it hurt much?*

William scrambled to his feet and rushed to her side, wrapping his arms around her waist, but her gaze never wavered from the end of the gun. Even through her coat, she felt the hammering of his heart against her skin.

When a gun fired, a flash usually erupted from the hammer, and she didn't want to see that happen because then she might cry out. She closed her eyes. Not going to flinch. Not going to give them the satisfaction of seeing her fear. Only she and Jesus knew how scared she was at this moment, and that would have to do. William didn't need to know. He was terrified enough right now for the both of them. She placed the palm of her hand over his exposed ear. Maybe it would muffle the sound of the shot for him, and he wouldn't jump too hard when it happened.

But the sound never came.

A heavy thud crashed down, trembling the floor boards at her feet. She jumped back, and her eyes flew open. Two sacks of cattle feed had swung from the pulleys overhead and collided against the man's chest. He tumbled back against another man behind him. They went careening with the sacks into a barrier wall and slumped, unconscious in a heap of wood and grain from a rupture in the sack.

Anna held William close to her as she backed away from the mayhem. The third man, with the journal still in his greasy fingers, stepped into the moonlight and pulled a pistol from his hip.

Another rope slung through an overhead pulley and zinged in the dark. A shadowy figure rode along that rope and travelled directly at him, striking him in the chest. He fell back hard into the wall of the barn.

William had buried his face against her waist, and he still clung tight to her with the chaos that had taken over the dark barn. Anna pulled him behind her and watched the figure leap from the rope and land without faltering like Peter Pan beside the fallen man. He stooped, grasped the pistol from the man's limp fingers, and turned to look at Anna and William.

In the faint silvery light, she saw the dirty face of a guy below the hat he wore. Maybe he wasn't just a kid; he didn't look much older than herself. He stood just a little taller though when he finally straightened his spine. He smiled, spun the barrel of the pistol in his index finger, and then shoved it into the pocket of the over-sized coat he wore.

"Let's get outta here," he spoke, his voice cracking just a little, and signaled them to follow him.

Anna's feet didn't want to move, but then, all three men that lay scattered about the barn stirred. William lifted his head and loosened his grip as he spied the kid standing in the moonlight.

"Unless you want to stay for them to wake up," the guy said.

She swallowed against a dry throat and shook her head. She forced herself to move forward, and William hurried with her. As she approached the door, she spied the journal lying in the dirt beside the fallen man who had taken it from her. She scooped it up and followed the stranger as he turned and moved into the shadows outside the barn.

The young man ducked through a gap in the wall of another building, and they entered a narrow corridor. It was too dark to see anything, but the smell of manure burned in her nostrils.

"Ugh, gross," William whispered behind her as they walked, each footfall squishing into a soft and spongy ground.

"Just a little further," the stranger said and moved faster ahead of them.

Clambering footfalls and shouts echoed behind them. The three men followed, and by the sound of it, they were angry. Of course, they would be. They just got attacked by a Robin Hood-type guy that dropped from the ceiling of the barn. And if they were as angry as they sounded, they wouldn't hesitate to shoot as soon as they caught them.

The air ahead of her changed and Anna saw the stranger turn sharply to the right. He squeezed under a heavy iron gate and then turned with a dirty hand held out to help her under as well. She took it and moved on her belly until she had come under the gate. Animals brayed and called, startled in the dark by the figures that had come into the corral. Anna stood to face several longhorn steers that stared at them from where they stood in the soft dirt and mud.

The stranger didn't wait for them to get oriented. He moved between the large beasts, and Anna followed him, slogging through the stinking mud with William clinging to her hand. The mud squeezed around her boot, rising above her ankles and grabbing her with each step. He led through the railings of the outer edge of the corral and into the shadow of an awning next to another barn. He crouched down and held out his arm to signal for Anna and William to hide behind him.

Anna fought to catch her breath and heard William trying to do the same thing. The stranger turned back and peered through the corral, quiet and still.

"We can't stay here," Anna whispered. "They're coming."

The kid waved his dirty hands at her to quiet her down, but he stayed still.

Shouts came from the men, ricocheting around them and against the buildings that surrounded the corral. Anna pressed her back against the wall. Those men were just on the other side the corral now, and it would only be seconds before they saw the three of them just sitting here and waiting. Waiting for what? To be shot?

The three men climbed through the fence and into the muddy corral. The kid slipped his hand into his pocket and removed the pistol. He cocked the hammer and aimed it up to the black sky.

The realization dawned on her in that split second before the shot rang out. She covered her ears just as it happened.

The flint struck in a quick spark as he pulled the trigger. The shot echoed as loud as a thunder clap. The steers jolted in shock, as did the men in the muddy corral. The terrified cattle went into a frenzy and rushed through their small confinement, crashing into fences, walls and anything else that remained upright.

Although she couldn't see it, Anna heard the screams and shouts of the men. And then everything went quiet except for the braying of the steers as they finally settled down.

The stranger shoved the gun into the belt of his pants and turned back to them, flashing a clever smile. Those men weren't going to track them any longer. Without a sound, he moved past Anna and William and signaled to follow him again.

So far, this kid had gotten them out of a pretty terrifying situation, so it might be okay to follow him a little longer. Staying in this maze of cattle stalls and barns wasn't likely to get them home. She stood, and with William at her side, they followed the stranger through dark alleys and stalls until they finally emerged into the open air of the street again.

She took in a deep breath, free of the heavy stink of a barnyard. The cobble stone street moved away from the vast labyrinth, and Anna glanced back to see a large wooden sign hanging above the entryway of the first barn: Kansas City Stockyards.

The kid walked with purpose ahead of them, turning down another street, winding his way toward some unknown destination without speaking. Occasionally, a street lamp revealed little things about him: his close-cut brown hair, the lace-up boots caked with mud from the stockyard, the way the hem of his pants was just a little too short for him. He just kept going and going, like he didn't care if they still followed him.

Anna wasn't too sure if she should be following him, anyway. He could be a pickpocket, a worse one than William. If he hadn't just saved them, she would have turned away and let him walk onward. But they were also stuck in a strange city with no other prospects at this time. And he was the only person they knew here who hadn't tried to kill them.

"Hey," Anna called out to him, but he just kept walking down the street and didn't turn back. "I said, 'hey.'"

"I heard you the first time," he finally spoke, but his pace never slowed.

"Well, then," she spoke and stopped, stomping her foot against the ground. "Please stop."

The kid halted and turned around to face her. His right eyebrow rose and a faintest grin curled at the edge of his lip. In this light, his eyes looked brown under the dirt that flecked across his skin.

"What?" he said and cocked his head to the side.

Anna flushed as he looked at her. He was cuter than she had first suspected, now that she could see him in the light. She squared her shoulders. "First of all, thank you for saving us."

"Is that it?" The slight grin broadened.

"Who are you?" William spoke up and let go of Anna's hand.

The grin disappeared, and he took a step back, his mouth slightly agape, as though he were confused that anybody would bother to ask. He stood taller, one hand on his lapel, and cleared his throat. "Jackson T. Belford."

"Good to meet you, Jackson. I am William Holloway, and this is my sister, Anna."

Jackson nodded and turned away from them. "All right. Now that's over, keep moving." He started back to his same pace again.

His rudeness made Anna's cheeks burn. She rushed to keep up with him.

"Excuse me, Jackson, but where are we going?"

"To my hideout," he said as he ducked into the shadows of another alley. "Those three guys are not the only ones following you. The train station was full of 'em, like hornets in a nest. So, if you want them to find you, then let's stand around and talk some more."

Anna almost stumbled, and her mouth dropped open. This kid may not have been one for many words, but he was smart. Okay. No more questions. Just follow him and get to his hideout.

The alley opened onto another street covered in cobblestones and lined on either side by a boardwalk. The horn of the train rang out again, and it was so close that Anna surmised they must have made a half-circle through the city from where they had gotten off the train. So many people walked the street and stood along the boardwalk. Music and laughter rose from the saloons, boarding houses and hotels down the length of the street. Gas lamps lit the boardwalks, but most were painted red or covered in red handkerchiefs. Jackson continued down this street as though he didn't even notice the men and women along the walk watching and calling out to them with rude comments.

Anna slowed and kept William close. "Where are you taking us? This place is . . . it's not proper."

Jackson glanced back at them and laughed. "Don't worry. We'll be fine here."

She rushed up to him and grasped the arm of his coat. He stopped and looked at her, the red glow from the lamps eerie against his skin.

Anna lowered her voice and leaned toward him. "But this is a red-light district." She tried to give him a knowing look, something that would be beyond William's understanding, but Jackson just laughed again.

"I know." He turned back toward his destination and continued walking.

She grasped William's hand tightly. Even if William had stolen and read some of her books, hopefully, he hadn't read about stuff like this. The red lights were a signal that this was an undesirable and bawdy area of town, a place that her mother would call 'a den of questionable morality;' whatever that meant. The saloons here would be loud and the women even more so. And Jackson had no problem walking straight into this place. She worried that his so-called "hideout" would be right in the middle of the red-light district.

Anna rushed to catch up to him. At least if he knew where he was going, she wanted to stay as close to him as possible.

Jackson turned off the main street and entered a back alley of a boarding house. He approached a dark door and gave three distinct knocks.

The door barely opened, and a pair of blue eyes on a feminine face peered out.

"It's me," Jackson said.

"Who is that with you?" the woman asked.

"Friends who need some help."

The door closed, and for a moment, Anna's shoulders fell. Nobody could help them. But then a chain rattled on the other side of the door. It swung open, and a young woman stood there, her curly blonde hair tied up into a clean bun. Anna wanted to place her hand over William's eyes when she saw the woman's cleavage just above the low-cut white bodice. The woman didn't seem to mind that she only wore her white bloomers and no dress to cover her undergarments.

Anna blushed for her. The lady stepped aside and allowed them into the dimly lit corridor of the boarding house.

Anna inhaled the heady scent of lilac perfume floating from the woman's skin as she walked past her. That fragrance mixed with the smell of cigar smoke and whiskey the further they walked into the establishment.

The woman moved out in front of them as she led the group down the hall. Piano music lilted through the red wallpapered corridor, stenciled in gold and white flowers. Little lamps with dangling crystals set in the wall lit the hallway in intervals.

Ahead of Anna and William, the woman chatted with Jackson in tones that Anna couldn't hear. Jackson nodded about something and then glanced back at them. The woman flashed a quick look back as well, her siren eyes gazing under curtains of thick black eyelashes. They were obviously familiar with one another, Jackson and this woman. A knotted twinge started first in Anna's chest, and her cheeks warmed. She dug her nails into the palms of her hands. Was this jealousy? Of this woman, who apparently had enough experience in this world to know what beautiful looked like. The way she swayed her hips as she walked and how her bottom looked so much like a perfect heart.

She glanced down at her own dress, covered with the apron, now stained with mud and rust, probably from the door of the train. And her face must have been a mess. She hadn't washed in a couple of days. Her eyes had never looked like that woman's, and neither had her bottom, and she definitely didn't look like that now.

Jackson and the woman turned and faced forward again until they turned the corner. They stepped out onto a balcony that overlooked a grand ballroom. The music and smoke and liquor was so much stronger here, as was the laughter and sounds of gaming. William let go of Anna's hand as he stepped up to the railing and gazed with wide eyes down to the spectacle below.

The blonde trained her eyesight onto another woman in the ballroom and ticked her head to the side when she finally looked up. The woman downstairs wore a tight-fitting red dress and white hat decorated with a dark feather that announced her long before she entered a room. Anna didn't have to know much about her to understand that she probably ran this place. She looked to be in her 50's, her long, dark hair lightly peppered with faint hints of gray. The fake smile she wore faded when her eyes fell on Jackson, and Anna didn't fail to notice his hands tighten around the railing.

The older woman excused herself from the company downstairs and headed toward the staircase, her hands in black lace gloves holding up the edge of her long red skirt. She ascended to the upper landing and faced them. From here, Anna could see the thick black eyeliner that enhanced her soft brown eyes. Wrinkles set at the outside corners of her eyes and mouth spoke of the thousand smiles this woman offered her customers.

"Thanks, Sophie," the older woman said to the blonde as she marched toward them. Her eyes set sternly upon Jackson.

"Boy," she said to him. "Where have you been? It has been three days. You know, I thought you were dead."

She placed a hand on his head and sighed. Jackson's eyes fell to his feet. "You are a mess," she said with the faintest hint of a smile in her eyes. "Come here." She pulled him into an embrace, and he hugged her back in return.

"Sorry, Kate," he said as she released him. "Lost track of time."

"Are you his mother?" William piped up. Anna nudged him with a sharp poke of her elbow. It wasn't proper to speak like that out of turn, and he knew it.

"Oh, heaven's no, dear," she said and glanced at both of them. "I ain't nobody's mamma. I just take care of him like I am. Somebody needs to."

She extended her hand out to Anna and William. "Name's Katherine Higgins, but everybody here calls me Kate. This is my home and my business. Are y'all friends of Jackson, here?"

"This is Anna and William," Jackson said. "Some awful types grabbed them at the train station, but I took care of it."

"I bet you did," Kate said and gave him a scowling eye as she pulled the silver pistol she had spied from his coat. "Any idea who those men were?"

"Yes, ma'am," Anna spoke and averted her gaze. She was not up to talking about the details of her father's secret. But maybe this woman could help. In the least, perhaps she could guide them to a telegraph. "I believe these men work for Dave Thibodaux."

Kate laughed a throaty and sharp sound. "Diamond Dave, that's a name I ain't heard in a while."

"You know of him?" Anna asked.

"Of course. He and his gang used to hang out in my saloon every time they passed through town. Rowdy bunch. Would shoot out the windows after they been drinking too much. I've had to replace just about every pane of glass in this place five times over because of them. Well, however you crossed his path it's best to just stay away."

When she waved her hand, the smile left her face for only a moment, a look that prodded at Anna as though to say, how do you know Diamond Dave? She didn't push the issue, though.

"You two from around here?" Kate asked.

William spoke first. "No, ma'am, we're not from here. From New Mexico. We just want to get back home."

"Travelling alone?" Kate shot that same look at Anna again.

"Yes, ma'am."

Kate finally glanced away. "Well, I know there isn't another train to New Mexico for about three more days. You're welcome to stay here until then."

Kate turned once again to Jackson. "And you," she said as she took his dirty coat off of him, revealing his white button-down shirt and suspenders. "Get yourself upstairs. All y'all smell like the stockyards. We'll get you fresh baths and fresh clothes."

She motioned for Sophie to lead them upstairs but Anna interjected. "Um, Ms. Kate. I was wondering if you could tell me where I might find the nearest telegraph station? To get a message back home?"

Kate smiled. "Just Kate, my dear. And the telegraph won't be open for about three more days as well. It's a weekend, and the operator just refuses to work then. Sorry."

Anna nodded, but the burning started in her eyes again. She looked away from Kate and tried to breathe through the tears that threatened to come. Kate patted her shoulder.

"It'll be all right, dear. Kate will take good care of you until then."

Sophie led them upstairs to the corridor of boarding rooms. Just as Kate had promised, the maids drew a hot bath in the steel-basin tub in the shared wash room located halfway down the hallway. Both Jackson and William were kind enough to allow Anna to go first.

The steam of the water drifted into her nose as she washed her skin. The rose fragrance from the castile soap relaxed her muscles. As she lay back in the basin, she gazed up at the ceiling and closed her eyes.

Three days. Three days to wait here just to send a telegram. Three days to get on the train back to New Mexico. Mother would be worried sick by then. Behind her eyelids, she still saw flashing images of her mother crying over Uncle John. Then came the sound of her voice as she shouted after her not to leave the house.

The shudder started in her shoulders first. It was okay; nobody would see it now. She let the tears fall, and she placed her wet hands over her face as she cried. Best to get it out now before she had to go back out there and face William. He didn't need to know that she had no idea how to fix this problem.

# CHAPTER 18

It might have been the long trip or all the anxiety of being nearly shot twice. Or perhaps it was the warm bath, but Anna had fallen asleep as soon as she lay down. It was only the knock at the door the next morning that stirred her.

She stood and smoothed out the white linen nightgown that Sophie had given her the night before. She padded to the door and unlocked it to see Kate standing there holding a tray of breakfast.

"Morning," Kate said. "Thought you might be hungry."

Anna stepped aside and let the woman in. She no longer wore the gaudy red dress from last night. Instead, she wore a simple dark gray dress with white ruffles at the end of the sleeves and the collar. She carried the tray into her room, set it on the side table and opened the curtains to let in a stream of bright sunlight.

The delicious fragrance of bacon and coffee drifted in her wake as she lifted the cover on the tray of food.

Anna's mouth watered. She hadn't eaten anything since the breakfast she had taken on the train. "Thank you so much, ma'am."

"Dig in," Kate said with a wave of her hand. "No use waiting on my account."

Anna sat at the single chair and bit into a crispy strip of bacon. She sipped at the hot coffee as Kate moved to the bed, arranging the linens.

"So, do you have a momma back home?" Kate asked as she smoothed out the quilt.

"Yes, ma'am," Anna said.

"Well, you are far too polite and educated to be originally from New Mexico. Where did you actually come from?"

Anna swallowed a bite from a jam-covered biscuit. "Boston. We just moved to New Mexico recently."

"I figured. Met a lot of people from Boston. Why come out west? This place is too rough for a couple of kids."

Anna cleared her throat. "My father died, and we left Boston to live with my uncle."

Kate's eyes softened. "I'm sorry, dear. Well, I'm sure your family will be relieved to have you and your brother back home in a few days."

The older woman turned to depart the room, but Anna spoke. "Pardon me, ma'am, but I was wondering if it would be possible to have ink and paper? If it's not too much trouble."

"Of course," she said and smiled.

"And," Anna said again before the woman left the room, "thank you for taking us in."

"It's my way of giving back. Look at Jackson; that boy would be nothing but trouble if it weren't for us. He was just an ignorant orphan when I found him in Tennessee. Now if he would just stop running off. This last time was because I tried to get him a job."

She laughed, and Anna smiled.

Kate clasped her hands before her. "Just let me know if you need anything else." She slipped through the door and closed it behind her, leaving Anna to finish her breakfast alone.

The biscuits were hot and fresh, and she could have eaten twenty of them. Unfortunately, there were only two, and they disappeared quickly. With her stomach full, she changed out of the nightgown and pulled on the dress that Sophie gave her last night. She buttoned up the bodice and looked at herself in the full-length mirror at the end of the room. It wasn't fancy like Kate's dress, and it didn't reveal a cleavage like Sophie's, but it was clean, and it fit.

Now, if she could get her hair under control. She ran her fingers through the long locks over her shoulder, still damp from her bath last night.

A knock sounded at the door again, and she turned, hoping that it was another tray of biscuits and bacon. But the air caught in her throat when she opened the door.

"Morning," Jackson said from where he leaned against the threshold.

Her cheeks flushed, and she stopped combing her fingers through her hair. In the morning light, he looked taller. And cleaner, which must have been a benefit of having a bath last night as well. He gave a crooked grin.

"Did you sleep okay?" he asked.

"I guess so," she said. Her eyebrow raised against her will. "Can I help you with something?" That came out more annoyed than she meant it.

He glanced down the hall as if he scanned for anybody else that might listen in on their conversation. Then he faced her again.

"So, William told me what happened to you two."

Her brother stepped out from behind him and bit his lip. He moved through the door and planted himself right on top of her bed as she watched him.

"What?" she said and shot a glare at her brother. "You told him?"

"What's the big deal? He's our friend now," William said with a shrug of his shoulders.

Jackson sidled into the room and closed the door. "So why do they want that book? What is it anyway?"

At least William hadn't told him everything. She sighed. "It's my father's journal. Those men took the map that went with it, and together I believe they hold clues that lead to a buried treasure."

Jackson leaned back against the door with his arms folded across his chest. "How do you figure?"

"Just trust me, okay? I know enough about my father and his work to understand what he was doing. And somehow these men know about it too, and they're coming for the book."

Jackson dropped his arms and shoved his hands in his pockets. "But the map doesn't work without the book, right?"

Anna nodded.

"Then just destroy the journal."

She shook her head. "Won't work. They know where we live. They came to our home. They'll just come back, and something worse could happen."

"You need to find what is at the end of the map. Then you will have something to bargain with."

That is exactly what she had been thinking since they escaped those men yesterday. It wasn't truly the map or the journal that was important, but what was at the end of it all.

"So, do you know where the next clue is?" Jackson asked.

William leaned forward on the bed, the wood frame creaking with the movement. She hadn't shared even this much with her little brother. They were supposed to be going home, not further down the trail of a mysterious buried treasure. A trail that got their father killed.

"Well?" William asked.

Anna folded her arms and looked away from both of the boys. "I do. Minnesota."

"All right," Jackson said and clapped his hands. "There's a ferry that docks here at the Missouri River and heads up north. It stops at Sioux City and then we just go on North to Minnesota from there."

"Wait. There is no 'we,'" Anna said.

"Hey, you need me, and I gotta get out of this town." His eyebrows rose as he pleaded with her, making his brown eyes twinkle. "This place is killing me. I can hunt. I can build a fire and shelter. And, my apologies, but neither of you seem to be the type that can do that."

"I never said we were going anywhere. We need to find a sheriff or someone who can arrest Dave and his men when they get here. And then we're going home."

The sparkle in Jackson's eyes faded and his shoulders fell. "I know about Diamond Dave, and a lawman hasn't been able to jail him in over twenty years. Hell, he's got men all over the West that he pays to give him information. How do you think those men found you at the train station? Chances are good that he has a sheriff or two on his payroll too."

*Damn.* She hadn't thought of that. Maybe she couldn't trust anybody.

"You can keep your family safe by staying ahead of him." His voice dropped, and he stepped close enough now that she could smell the soap on his skin. "And imagine if you found the treasure. That's one hell of a bargaining chip."

Anna swallowed against a dry throat. "Let me think about it." But looking into Jackson's eyes and the desperation in his voice, it was difficult not to take him seriously. She glanced once to William, his hopeful eyes staring up at her. His life was at risk too if she undertook this adventure.

"Okay," Jackson said and stepped back. "Just don't take too long."

Flashes of lightning on the dark horizon burst through the tall windows looking into Kate's saloon. The piano music continued, however, the player appeared oblivious to the coming storm. Poker games and Faro progressed with eager customers sitting among the tables, hoping to win big tonight. Sophie stood beside her, leaning on the bar, in a dress of dark blue silk and black lace.

The tall double wood and glass pane doors opened, and a swirl of wind and leaves blew into the saloon with the cool chill of the storm. The breeze danced across the saloon floor and to the bar, where Kate felt the chill rise up the back of her legs. She stopped wiping the glass she held in her hand and turned to face the figure standing in the doorway.

A man stepped through the doorway with an entourage behind him. He tilted back his hat with one finger, and his handsome blue eyes scanned the room.

Kate's grip on the glass tightened. "You have got to be kidding me," she said under her breath.

# CHAPTER 19

He stepped through the threshold and slipped the hat from his head, leaving his shoulder-length blonde hair in a tousled mess.

"Well, Kate," he said with a wicked smile. "Long time, no see."

"If it isn't Diamond Dave Thibodaux," she said.

Kate forced a smile and leaned toward Sophie. "You go hide those kids right now," she whispered.

Sophie put on her best demure face and stepped away from Kate, her slender fingers dancing along the bar until she moved up the stairs to the boarding house.

Dave sidled up to the bar. The strong musk of a sweaty horse followed with him as did the other men that had come with him.

"What'll it be?" she asked, the smile still painted across her face.

"I believe it'll be whiskey all around," he said and slapped a hand on the bar. The men laughed and stepped about the saloon, examining the tables and the few patrons that remained near the fireplace.

She set the glasses across the bar and filled them with the amber liquid. "Where have y'all been hiding? I ain't seen you in a dog's age," she said.

"Under a rock," he smiled and took his glass. With a single swallow, he downed the whiskey and placed the glass before her.

She filled the glass once more. "It's been too long."

He drank. "Well, I have purpose in my life again."

"I'll bet you do," she said, and her eye wandered up the boarding house stairway.

Sophie rushed into Anna's room without a knock, the scent of her perfume swirling around her. The letter Anna wrote was almost done, but she jumped when the woman entered and smudged the ink a bit on the last word.

"He's here," the woman said, breathless. "You need to hide."

Anna almost dropped the pen. How did he find them already?

"Get William," Anna said, trying to control the shaking in her hands. Sophie nodded and disappeared from the room again. With the pen still in her hand, she finished the letter, folded the paper before the ink had completely dried, and then sealed it with the wax stick Kate had given her.

Sophie returned with William, his eyes wide and he grasped her hand as soon as he was in the room. Jackson had come with her.

"What do we do?" Anna said as she held William at her side.

"Hide in the closet," Jackson said, glancing back down the hall to see if anyone was coming.

"And then what?"

He stepped inside the room and placed a hand on her shoulder. "I'll come get you when it's safe." Jackson grasped Sophie's arm, and they left the room, closing the door behind them.

Anna took in a deep breath and gathered the letter and her father's journal. She moved with William to the closet but took one last look in the room when she spied her coat lying across the end of the bed. There couldn't be any sign of them in the room, not if Dave showed up to look for them. She grasped the coat and scrambled into the closet and gazed through the narrow gap between the closet doors into the quiet room.

The sound of her heart pounding in her ears was enough to deafen her, but nothing else moved outside the room. The hallway remained quiet except the few jingles of laughter from the women that wandered the corridors. Even William, who was always so restless and fidgety, sat still beside her, his breathing quiet and even. His eyes stared wide out through the gap, the light of the lamp on the table casting a gold glow across his face.

The sound of raucous laughter and singing was enough to normally bring the nostalgia of her saloon back, but not tonight. Tension kept Kate's spine rigid as she watched Dave lean back in the velvet-upholstered chair in front of the fireplace. His loud voice sang off-key with the piano that still pounded out the songs from twenty years ago.

*Those poor kids.* Whatever they had done to cross him, it was unfortunate because Dave could be relentless.

But so could she.

She pulled the cork on another bottle of whiskey. The good stuff, not the usual watered-down drink she served most of her patrons. This was from the case she kept in the basement. Even the fumes coming from the lip of the bottle were enough to get someone tipsy. And Dave loved his drinking.

So, she would keep it coming, even this stuff that poured like oil into the glass she had just polished. When the whiskey had filled to the brim, she nodded to Sophie, who palmed the glass and walked it to Dave. She smiled and swung her hips with each step, the ruffles in her long skirt accentuating her form. Her fingers slipped behind his neck as she moved into Dave's lap and handed him the strong drink.

A faint grin formed on Kate's lips. Dave drank the whiskey, one after another, as Sophie continued to bring him each glass. Kate's other girls that worked in the boarding house soon joined in, helping to distribute the liquor to Dave's men. The girls always helped to sell more from the bar, and this was the most important night ever.

Most of the other patrons had departed for the night, but Dave and his men had grown louder.

Dave stood from the chair, staggered and fell to the ground in drunken laughter. Sophie crouched beside him

"What happened?" he said, his words slurred and his eyes half open. He looked up from his place on the ground to the other men in the saloon. Most of them had fallen asleep at the poker tables or sat beside the piano, singing.

"Looks like you and your boys have had enough," Kate said from the bar. "Time to head out."

Sophie helped Dave to his feet, and he threw his arm around her shoulders. She walked him toward the door.

"No," he said. "I wanna stay here tonight. You know I love this place, Kate." He shoved away from Sophie and tripped toward the stairs.

Kate shot a quick glance to Sophie, who rushed to his side. The bastard headed toward the boarding house. He pulled himself up along the railing and put his arm around Sophie again. "I've always liked it here." He leaned closer to Sophie. "And I really like her."

He staggered to the upper landing and walked as he leaned against the wall.

"How about you sleep it off in one of the rooms at the end of the hall?" Kate said, following them. Sophie glanced at her and then nodded behind Dave's back to the first door on the left.

That was Anna's room, and Sophie must have had the kids hiding there.

Another door opened down the hallway, and Jackson stepped out. For a moment he hesitated, his face pale and his jaw tight. Kate shook her head. Dave would pay him no mind as long as he didn't draw any attention to where their new guests were hiding. Jackson placed his hands in his pockets, put his head down, and just walked down the hall past them. As far as Dave would know, Jackson was just another guest at the boarding house.

"I don't think I can walk that far," Dave said, pushing away from them toward the first door on the left, dragging Sophie with him.

The girl almost gasped as he forced the door open. Kate held her breath and stood at the doorway. Dave stumbled into the room and collapsed onto the bed. The scent of whiskey trailed after him. He groaned as he rolled onto his back and closed his eyes against the lamp light.

Sophie stood frozen at the door with Kate at her side. Without saying a word, Sophie shifted her glance to the closet, and Kate knew where the kids were hiding. Snoring arose from Dave's sleeping body, echoing down the corridor.

Jackson appeared at Kate's side and gazed into the bedroom.

*What do we do?* he mouthed silently.

She placed a finger against her lips to silence him further.

Anna's heart rattled against her ribs with thunderous beats as soon as the door opened. She smelled the whisky before she saw Dave stumble into the room and fall onto the bed. The wooden frame of the bed argued with a loud creak when he collapsed on its mattress. Anna placed a hand over her mouth, afraid that her breathing would give them away.

Then the snoring started. He was out cold, probably drunk thanks to libations from Kate's bar. William trembled beside her, and the hand she had around his shoulders squeezed him closer to her. The bedroom door remained open, and Kate and Sophie filled the threshold, their faces as pale as hers probably was.

Kate's eyes wandered to the closet. Sophie must have told her where they were hiding. And then Jackson appeared, his coat and hat on as though he was ready to run.

Everyone just stood there for a minute, glancing back and forth from Dave to the closet. Anna's legs ached as she tried to keep them still. The journal almost burned in her hand. A movement caught her eye, and she spied Kate signaling to her from the door. It was time to go. Anna nodded, not sure if Kate saw her or not.

She moved her hand from her mouth and pushed against the closet door. It opened with a soft click, but even that sound jangled in her fingers, and she paused, shooting a glance toward Dave. He didn't move, but the lamp light glistened on the diamond-studded gun at his hip, just evident beneath the opening of his coat. With William's hand clutched in hers, she forced her legs to stand. The ache worsened in her knees and threatened to drop her to the ground, but she pulled herself upright and padded toward the door.

A deep exhale sounded from the corner of the room, and she stopped. Dave turned his head and smacked his lips, but his eyes remained closed, just like a giant in the fairy tales, and she was Jack with a pocket full of magic beans. He stilled once again, and she started to take another step when William pulled his hand out of hers.

She glared at him with wide eyes, but that didn't stop him from tiptoeing away from her and straight to the bed where the sleeping giant lay. A faint gasp came from Kate and Anna heard the pounding of her heart so loud in her ears. What was he doing? She was going to kill him for this unless Dave killed them all first.

William moved silent and stealthy toward Dave, his eyes trained on the pockets of his long duster coat. When he was close enough, his small hands fished into the first pocket and then another. Dave slept through it all, his breathing even and slow. William moved faster, more desperate, as he came up empty with each pocket.

Anna's fingers clenched tight when she knew what he was doing. The map. He looked for the map, but Dave must have put it somewhere else.

Then William stopped, and his hand moved to something at Dave's throat. From the door, Anna barely saw the glint of iron there. William worked the cord until it came free. Another deep breath escaped Dave's lips, and William froze for a moment. One wrong slip from her brother could put everyone in that room in jeopardy. William stood, every joint moving slow and deliberate like the little professional thief that he was.

Her brother turned away from Dave and padded across the room to Anna. He held out the thing he had just taken: her father's pendant. The outlaw had taken it from her back in New Mexico, and William had just risked his life to get it back for her. He dropped it into her hand and then hurried to Kate and Sophie. Anna forgot to move for a second as she stared at the pendant. William had actually understood what it meant to her, and she never thought he had payed attention to things like that.

Kate motioned to her again, her eyes wide and reproving. Anna pocketed the pendant in her apron and stepped to the door. Kate closed the door with the quietest of latches once she was in the corridor with the rest of them. Without a word, Kate turned and quickly led them down the hall and toward the back exit where Jackson had brought them into the boarding house the other night.

"All right," Kate said and gathered them together. Her gaze fixed onto Jackson. "Get them out of here and keep them safe."

"Yes, ma'am," he said with a nod.

She grabbed him and pulled him close, planting a kiss on his cheek. "Boy, you stay safe too. If anything happens to you, I swear—"

"I'll be fine, Kate," he said, his voice muffled against her.

She finally released her grip, and he stepped back, straightening his hat. Kate opened the door just as a crack of thunder broke through the night. Jackson stepped out, and William followed him. But Anna stopped at the threshold and withdrew the letter from her pocket. She faced Kate and handed it to her.

"If you happen to see Johnny Holiday come in here, can you please give this to him?"

Kate accepted it with knits of lines drawn across her forehead. "Little girl, what are you doing mixed up with these outlaws?"

"It's a very long story," she said with a faint smile.

"All right," Kate said, but she still looked at her with suspicion. "I will, but I expect an answer one day."

"One day, hopefully, I can give you one." Anna moved to step away, but she turned back to Kate. "And thank you, for everything."

The woman nodded to her, but just then a movement in the corridor behind her caught Anna's attention. One of Dave's men, someone she had seen chasing them to the train station, stumbled into the corridor and leaned against the wall as he stared out toward them. The dirty lines in his face straightened out, and his eyes grew wide when he saw Anna standing there. He pushed away from the wall, and his drunken fingers scrambled for the gun at his hip.

"Hey!" he shouted back down toward the gaming hall. "They're here! I got 'em!"

"Go now," Kate said, her hand wrapped on the door knob.

Anna leaped down the steps to the alleyway just as Jackson gave one final glance back to Kate before she shut the door. Then he turned and bolted into the dark. There wasn't time for him to look back and make sure Anna and William kept up with him. She would just have to make sure that they did.

They ran into the darkened street as a clatter of men's voices shouted out into the night behind them. There would be no escape through the stockyards this time. They had to keep ahead of the outlaws, or they were going to die.

William found her hand again as they ran. Anna kept Jackson in her line of sight and ducked with him into another alleyway. He stopped and crouched behind a stack of crates behind another saloon, craning his neck around the building to survey their escape. She took this small moment in time to catch her breath.

"So where do you want to go? The ferry will take us to Minnesota. The train could take you back home." Jackson said and glanced back at her. Through the dark, he looked at her with a stern gaze.

William looked up at her and didn't say a word. Everything in his eyes told her that whatever she chose, he trusted her. Flutters in her stomach turned her insides to jelly, but she had made her decision hours ago. Hopefully, it was the right one.

"To the ferry."

Jackson smiled. "Of course. Your wish is my command."

He took off in a run around the crates. Anna stood and raced after him with William at her side. Another flash of lightning and crash of thunder rumbled the streets of Kansas City. The night air stagnated and stilled with the coming storm. A fishy odor soon filled the humid night as they neared the banks and docks of the Missouri River.

The docks looked almost like the platform of the train station, with lights and a boardwalk extending to the great ship where it sat on the water. Passengers loaded down the floating ramp toward the boat, its lights sparkling in the shimmering black waters of the river. Two great smoke stacks loomed over the top of the ship like lighthouses. A long ramp descended from the side of the ferry to the docks where an attendant stood to take tickets.

They would only have seconds to board before Dave's men saw them. Anna rushed up to the ticket booth at the front of the pier as she pulled silver coins from her apron. Yes, this money wasn't hers, but she had no guilt in spending it this time. The attendant gave her the tickets and the three of them hurried into the crowd of passengers that moved toward the boat.

A policeman stood along the dock and eyed them as they moved. They must have looked odd, three kids boarding a ferry without an adult. For a moment, she wondered if he was one of the men that Dave paid to look out for them. But then he looked away, keeping his eye on the passengers as a whole.

William clutched her hand tighter as they stepped up onto the ramp and ascended into the main level of the ferry. Even Jackson now grasped her hand. She glanced at him, and he smiled with victory. Her heart danced in her chest, and she bit her lip. They made it!

They stopped at the railing at she looked out across the docks. Dave's men had stopped at the edge of the pier. Their eyes met, the touch of wickedness creeping into her brain. Perhaps it existed in everyone, but she definitely summoned it tonight as she glared at them, daring them to come after her.

As the last of the passengers climbed aboard, the attendant removed the plank, and the ship gave a final blast of the steam horn before it pushed away from the dock. The men stood there, some pacing the docks like hunting dogs that couldn't reach their prey.

A small smile played at the corners of her mouth, and she waved an irreverent goodbye while they watched the ferry travel up the Missouri River.

# CHAPTER 20

"These are almost as good as Kate's," Jackson said, his mouth full of bacon.

Anna sipped at the breakfast tea. William didn't say much as he ate his stacks of bacon and eggs.

"Well, at least we paid for the trip this time," she said and winked at William.

"Not stowaways," he said and smiled.

"And the beds are nice, too," Anna said. "Much better than the train accommodations we had." No more dirty cargo car and sleeping on the floor.

"Get any more reading done last night?" Jackson said, his mouth still full.

"A little," she said and pulled the journal from her apron. She opened it to the last pages she had reviewed. "But it doesn't make a lick of sense. I'm hoping it will when we get to the first marker, though." The last few pages had been just symbols and notations along the edges. Her confidence waned, wondering if she needed the map after all.

"Let's just get to Kensington and see what's there," he said and put a huge grin on his face that left a dimple in his chin, the kind of smile that made her laugh against her will.

Two days on the ferry was enough to make her sick of being on the water, but sunny skies and warm weather greeted them when the boat finally made dock in Sioux City. The town was small, just a trader stop, but Jackson maneuvered his way through it as though he had been here before.

Anna and William waited outside a mercantile and watched the many people milling around the street as they exited the boat. Jackson had disappeared into the shop and said he would take care of things, whatever that meant. Several minutes ticked by with men and women walking past them down the street, eyeing them with indifference.

"All done," Jackson said, startling Anna from her daze in the summer heat.

He sat next to them and placed a burlap bag of his purchased supplies across his lap. "Good news. There's a wagon train headed up to St. Paul this afternoon. Kensington will be almost on the way."

"Almost?" Anna asked. That didn't sound very good.

"Well, we're gonna have to leave them part way to make it up to Kensington. That's what this stuff is for."

He pulled out a scouting map, a flint, two canteens, dried meats and crackers, and fishing line. "I can get us there. Don't worry."

They had gone this far, and it was too late to not trust him.

"Okay," she said.

XXX

Kate swept the last of the leaves across the saloon floor. With the storm, the wind blew everything into the place the night before. That, and the ruckus from Dave's men when they bolted out of the place to follow the kids. And they had never come back. Word from the dock master was that the kids had boarded a ferry headed north, and she could only assume that Dave and his gang had gone the same way.

The doors opened with a long and slow creak, and a pair of boots stepped with heavy thuds on the wood floor.

She didn't bother to look up. The night had been too long for her to worry about trivial things today. "Sorry, we're closed until sunset," she said and drew the broom across the floor again.

"That's unfortunate," the familiar voice echoed through the empty saloon. "I was hoping for the best drink in town."

Kate raised her head and turned to face him with a genuine smile. He stood in the door, silhouetted by the morning backlight. A long brown leather duster extended down to his boot heels and a dark hat shaded his eyes, but she recognized his scruffy but handsome face and his ruddy brown hair.

"I don't believe it," she said. "Johnny Holiday, in the flesh."

"Kate, it's good to see you. It's been too long."

"Not long enough," she said as her smile faded. She knew better than to tell him too much. After all, she remembered days past when he was the rowdiest drunk in the saloon. But he had never been mean, unlike Dave. She glanced down to the letter tucked behind the bar. She shook her head and spoke, despite her better judgment. "That girl knew you would be coming through here, but I didn't believe it."

John perked up and stepped toward her. "You've seen the children, then? Rumor is spreading through town that Dave was here as well."

She set aside her broom and stepped behind the bar. "It's true," she sighed and reached for the envelope.

"I shouldn't do this, but," she said and handed the letter to him, "the girl said to give this to you should you be passing through."

John peeled open the letter, tearing the red wax seal on the back. The rumors he had heard about two kids coming off the train a few days ago led him to Kate's saloon, and he was right to follow his gut. They had been here, and now he held Anna's words in his hand.

She had begun the letter initially with tender words to her mother, but it was evident that she had been interrupted. Then in a rushed and anxious script, she had printed only four words at the end: Kensington, Minnesota. Ohman farm.

This was clearly meant for him. A breadcrumb in a trail to find them.

"They took the ferry north, but Dave and his men are hot on their heels. He can't be too far behind."

This was all he needed, and he knew what to do. John fit his hat low above his eyes again, gave her a quick smile, and headed back out into the sunlight.

$$\times\times\times$$

Two days in the wagon train wasn't nearly enough. When twilight came again, and the lead wagon marked their road to Kensington, Anna felt her knees go weak, and the pit in her stomach grow. This is where they would leave them, out in the middle of a dark field and no end in sight. Jackson didn't look too worried, though. The wagon master left them a skin of water and a satchel of hard tack before they parted ways.

So many people had helped them during the short days that they had been with the wagon train. Even other girls her age rode with the wagons, going to unknown and hopeful places. Anna wanted to have that same optimism, but she traveled a different road with a different destiny.

And now she stood on the trail and watched the wagon train drive away into the dusk.

"Come on," Jackson called out to her. "We need to find a place to camp soon."

She didn't turn away from the last of the wagons until it wended down a hill and out of sight. They were gone--the singing and conversation and civilization. The hollow space in her stomach widened when she finally started down the trail toward Jackson.

They continued onward until Jackson veered off the main road and into a copse of trees far from the trail.

"What are you doing?" Anna said, stepping over the grass as high as her waist. "I thought we needed to take the road?"

"It's getting dark," he said. "And we don't want to be on the main road at night. Dave and his gang could find us pretty easy that way. And not to mention others who might try to rob us."

Her stomach dropped, and she glanced back to the road. The thought of people sneaking up on them sent chills down her arms, and she shivered. With William at her side, she quickened her pace to catch up to Jackson.

The grove of trees thickened the deeper they went until Jackson finally stopped. With his hands on his hips, he surveyed the space around them. "We can camp here tonight. I'll get a fire started if you could collect some pine boughs," he said to Anna and then looked at William, "and you find me some fire wood."

She started off into the trees, finding what she could in the dark. William hurried around her, picking up whatever sticks and twigs littered the ground until they both had full arms. It didn't take long for Jackson to have a small fire started and the boughs set around the flames for beds softer than the ground.

With the orange flames licking into the air, Anna pulled her coat tighter around her and nibbled at the strips of dried venison that Jackson had purchased at the mercantile. Jackson stretched out on his make-shift bed and sipped water from his canteen. William had curled up under his coat and already fallen asleep, but nothing about this place made her sleepy. She was tired, yes, and her feet and legs ached from the last two days of walking with the wagon train, but she was more awake than she had ever been.

Snatches of songs and poems still danced through her head from the talk that the girls in the wagon train had left with her. A thin smile fell on her lips when the songs lilted against her silent lips.

"What are you thinking?" Jackson said.

She still gazed into the fire. "Just songs and other things."

"What other things?"

The smile slipped from her face when she remembered her father's voice, reciting a poem that had once amazed and terrified her.

"By a route obscure and lonely, haunted by ill-angels only," she said.

He sat up, his brow creased. "What's that?"

"Edgar Allan Poe. 'Dreamland.'"

"Never heard of him. Sounds creepy."

The orange fire had darkened to a glow of red embers. Jackson leaned over the coals to add more kindling.

"Thank you for helping us," Anna said.

Jackson smiled. "No problem."

"Can I ask you something?" Anna said. He nodded and settled back down to lean on one elbow. "How old are you?"

She could see the wrinkle in his forehead. It was not meant to be a difficult question, but she could see that he struggled. "Seventeen next month, I think."

"You think? You mean you don't know for sure?"

He shook his head. "Nah. I never had much use for birthdays."

"So, you don't even know your birthday?"

"Nope. Kate just gave me a birthdate and told me how old she thought I was."

"Where are you from? I mean before Kate's."

"Arkansas."

"Do you still have any family there?"

Jackson was quiet for a moment. "I don't think so. My pa died a long time ago. Momma said it was because he was involved as a cavalryman during the western Indian war and just couldn't take it anymore. And then she took to drinkin' too. She'd rather be drinkin' all day than bother with what I was ever doing. So, one day I struck out on my own. Was on my own for a while until Kate found me up in Tennessee."

A twinge of guilt crept into her thoughts. She shouldn't be prying. Mother would say that it wasn't lady-like.

"I really liked Kate. She seems to be a very good person."

"She is," he said. He rested his head back against the boughs and gazed up to the stars. "But I wasn't destined to stay there."

Anna cleared her throat, but only in order to organize her thoughts. "Even with Sophie there?"

"Sophie?" he asked and glanced at her. "What do you mean?"

"Well, you and her seemed awful . . . close."

He let out a small laugh. "No way. I just taught her to read and stuff. She's like a sister to me."

Anna's shoulders relaxed. Somehow, she had gotten all knotted up and let her spine loosen. "Oh, okay."

She laid back against the boughs, the heat of the fire warming her. "How long do you think until we get to Kensington?"

"Couple days probably."

The stars brightened overhead with the complete darkening of the night. A single streak of light moved across the heavens, and she heard Jackson shift to his side.

"Hey," he whispered. "Do you know any more of that Edgar Poe stuff?"

She smiled. "In each nook most melancholy, There the traveler meets aghast, Sheeted memories of the Past, Shrouded forms that start and sigh, As they pass the wanderer by."

"Beautiful," he said. "Good night."

"Good night." She closed her eyes, the images of ghosts wandering in the forest zipping through her mind. The sounds of the woods came alive around her: the rustling of the trees, the occasional chittering of an animal among the ground brush. A scream sounded in the dark; probably just an owl. She hoped it was only an owl. She kept her eyes closed just in case it wasn't and she stayed that way until she finally fell asleep.

# CHAPTER 21

The edges of a farm came into view along the worn trail. The day had grown hot and humid, but a bank of clouds had obscured the sun, if for only a few minutes. Even in this heat, a man worked along the fence line, straightening a single post with his shovel.

They had to be getting close to Kensington, especially according to Jackson's map.

"This guy might know," he said to Anna and hurried toward him.

"Excuse me," he said, and the farmer looked up at him, his brow sweaty and the scent coming from him strong enough to kill a horse. He eyed Anna and William as they approached. "Are we close to Kensington?"

The man nodded. "Just over the hill."

"We're looking for the Ohman farm," Anna said.

He laughed and looked down to the spade. "Are you, now. I wouldn't bother with them."

"Why?" William asked.

"Well, son, they're a crazy lot. If you all are looking for work, try the Schrader farm over east of town."

A lump formed in Anna's throat and she wanted to argue with him, but Jackson spoke before she could.

"The Ohman farm would be just fine for us," he said.

"Well," the man said and wiped his brow. "About two miles north of town. But don't come back here looking for something, because I warned you."

He turned his back on them and continued digging at the base of the post. Jackson frowned at him but stepped back onto the trail.

"That was odd," he whispered to them and continued. Anna glanced back one last time to see the farmer shoot her a glare before he went back to digging.

They found the small town of Kensington and then continued north just as the farmer's directions indicated until they approached another farm. By this time, twilight descended on the horizon. Wheat and cornfields stretched out from all sides of the main house, a building with a single floor and soft glowing light through its windows. To the west stood a barn encircled by weather-worn fencing enclosing a corral. A sleepy horse rested against the fence, his eyes drifting half-closed.

This had to be the place. Otherwise, Anna thought she might just collapse in their field and make camp. She was too exhausted to continue onward tonight. But as the house loomed closer, flutters started in her gut. They had come all this way to find the farm, and she didn't know what she would do if the Ohmans really were crazy. She pulled the sleeve of her coat over her hand and wiped the thin coat of dust and sweat from her face. Locks of knotted and dirty hair fell over her shoulders. She pulled it back and rolled it into a bun at the back of her head.

"What are you doing?" Jackson whispered to her.

"These are strangers," she said. "I need to look presentable." Mother would be so disappointed if she didn't at least try.

"I think you look pretty," he said. "You don't need to fix anything."

Her cheeks flushed, and she glanced away from him, the flutters growing into a swarm. She turned away from him and stepped up to the porch. "Okay, let me do the talking." She knocked on the door and then stepped back.

Floorboards creaked from inside the house. Shuffling boots sounded behind the door, and soon, the door creaked open. A pair of timid eyes, the corners wrinkled by sunlight and age, peered out at her.

"Who's calling?" a gruff man's voice called out to her.

"I am sorry about the late hour, sir—" she started.

"Who are you? A reporter?" he asked, his voice laced with an accent that she recognized from her time in Sweden.

"No, sir. We're only children."

The man staring out to them hesitated for a moment, and the door opened wider. He stood tall before them, his head almost to the top of the door, his once-blonde hair now almost white. His aged blue eyes squinted at the three of them as he studied their faces. A small round pouch of a belly hung over his dark slacks and bulged his suspenders. He scanned the space behind them, and William glanced back, curious at what the man could be looking at.

"You kids out here by yourselves?" he asked.

"Yes, sir," Anna responded.

"What are you all doing out here alone?"

Another female voice came from within the house. "Who is it, Olof?"

"I'm sorry, Mr. Ohman," Anna spoke. "We have come a very long way to ask something of you. My name is Anna Holloway. I believe you met my father, Thomas Holloway."

The creases around his eyes vanished and his mouth opened into an O. "Oh, God help us. Come in, come in."

He ushered them inside. Anna stepped across the threshold to the scent of fresh baked bread and the crackling of a fire in the hearth. He opened his hand out and indicated for them to sit in the rocking chairs scattered around the room.

"Forgive me for my rudeness," he said. "I cannot trust anyone these days. I get so many reporters or vandals who try to egg my house, or something else equally as ridiculous."

"I see," Anna said, but none of that made much sense to her.

"What can I do for you?" he asked as he settled into his plush arm chair beside a table with a glowing oil lamp.

She withdrew the journal from her pocket. "I'm here because of my father's work."

"Well, Dr. Holloway is one of the few men I do trust, and any who work in his name I will accommodate. How is the good professor doing these days?"

Anna and William shot a glance at each other. He didn't know.

"What is it?" he said, leaning forward with an elbow on his knee. "Is he not well?"

"Mr. Ohman, my father was murdered. Shot in the back and it all happened after he came to see you."

His complexion paled. "I am so sorry."

"That's why we are here. We've traveled a very long way to speak with you. My father wrote about a stone you found on your property. It had an ancient writing on it—"

Olof stood, brow furrowing deeply and his voice louder. "After I found that cursed stone, nobody believed me. Everybody said I falsified everything. This is not true. I found it in the ground, just as I told your father, tangled among the roots of a tree. And only your father believed me. The rest of the folks in this town treat me like a laughing stock."

"He found other stones like it," Anna said. "Proof that you were telling the truth. And it was because of this that someone took his life. He kept a secret about that stone. Mr. Ohman, I need to see it, just once. If I can inspect it, I can see what he was keeping secret."

Olof remained silent for a moment. The creases in his face softened. His stern eyes turned to her, but he hesitated to speak. Finally, he let out a deep sigh.

"Very well, come with me, but only you," he said and signaled to Anna as he lifted his lamp. "My wife will prepare dinner, and you may stay the night after you have a look. It's a long walk back from wherever you came."

Anna stood and followed him as he stepped out of the room. She gripped the journal tighter and glanced back to Jackson and William. The boys watched her go, but William was almost in tears. He didn't want to let her out of his sight, but this had to be done.

The sky had grown darker as she followed him into the night, trekking across the grounds toward the barn. Leaves rustled in the faint breeze drifting through the dark night. Only the light from Olaf's lamp illuminated a small circle around his feet. Anna kept close enough to him in order to see their path, but she didn't want to get too close. This man was a little jumpy already, and it made her even more nervous.

He opened the side door to the barn, and the rusty hinges creaked on their pivot. With the darkness and the shadows cast by the lantern spread across the mysterious room they were about to enter, Anna couldn't help feel that this must be what it was like when the earliest explorers opened the ancient tombs of Egypt. She imagined the walls lined in hieroglyphs and gold-leaf treasures. They entered the dark space of the barn, and a dusty draft wafted out like a breath from deep inside a tomb.

Just as the archeologists had before her, she stepped into the vast open room, and Mr. Ohman approached a broad, wooden table set along the far wall. The light of the lantern cast an ethereal golden glow across a dirty linen sheet draped over the object set atop the table.

Yes, very much like the cavernous spaces under the great pyramids, just without a gross and dusty mummy. At least she hoped there would not be a mummy under there. What if there was? She ran through her escape plan in her brain just in case. Below that sheet, though, was something ancient and special. Probably not a mummy, but much more incredible. That's what her father thought, and it was enough for her.

As they approached the table, Anna's knees trembled. The air around the sheet thickened, something so tangible that she could nearly feel it spilling off the table in a cold fog.

Mr. Ohman grasped the cloth in his meaty hand and pulled it free, finally revealing a stone slab, three inches thick with clumps of dried mud clinging to its edges. The smooth surface had been wiped clean to reveal its face, covered in engravings much like a tombstone.

Anna hadn't realized she held her breath from the moment they had walked into the barn. She let it out slowly as she stepped up to the table with him. Mr. Ohman drew the lantern in closer. As the light moved, small shadows played across the flat surface of the stone and spilled into the shallow rune carvings.

"This is what I found," he said, running his hand over the surface.

The writings were carved in nine straight rows. She recognized some of the symbols because her father had scrawled them in his journal. And then she saw it: the unusual X. Just as her father had described it. This was the first symbol that meant something to him that made this stone so important and authentic.

In her awe of the stone, she nearly forgot the journal in her hand. She drew it out into the light and opened up the pages to the section titled *"Marker #1" again*:

*. . . Further directions are plotted on God's corner of the stone . . .*

God's corner. She had heard her father say that before to her. To be on God's corner meant the "upper right hand" because to be with God would be at his right hand.

She scanned the face of the rune stone, but there was nothing else in addition to the rows of runes that covered the surface, which her father had already translated and put into the journal. No, there had to be something more.

She stepped back a few paces. This was something her father had pressed her to do on many occasions. When the task at hand seemed difficult or impossible, one must simply step back from the problem and often the solution would reveal itself.

Of course, she thought, as she gazed at the stone in a broader sense. The stone was about three to four inches thick. She craned her neck into the lantern-lit side of the stone and noticed writing inscribed on the sides of the stone as well. It appeared to be another three rows of the same carved runes.

She glanced back to the journal and noticed something she had skimmed over previously. At the time, it had made no sense. Her father had written on the side of the page. She turned the book on its side. He must have translated the runes on the edge of the stone:

*There are 10 men by the inland sea to look after our ships fourteen days' journey from this peninsula. Year 1362.*

Then she saw a smaller inscription in the upper right corner of the runes, but there was no corresponding journal translation. She flipped through more pages, but there was nothing to translate these other runes. Were these more directions?

"Mr. Ohman, do you have something with which to write?"

"Of course," he said and drew over a stack of parchment paper and pencil. "I've been making rubbings of the stone."

She smiled and placed the parchment over the final carvings and created a rubbing of her own. These symbols were exactly what the journal wanted her to find. The fluttering intensified in her chest with each stroke of the pencil across the paper. *Finally!* The first marker found, and it was so much more than she had expected.

After a dinner of cabbage stew, rye bread and fresh milk, the Ohmans invited them to sit before the fire in the front room. Mrs. Ohman sat beside the lamp and worked on knitting while Olaf smoked his pipe and lay his head back in his chair. Anna had once seen her grandfather do the same thing, and fall asleep with the pipe hanging from his mouth, spilling ashes onto his lap.

Anna felt a little uneasy about pulling out the journal in front of them, but Mr. Ohman possessed one of the markers. He was already in the middle of this, even if he didn't know it. And so far, they hadn't asked too many questions about why three kids were in the middle of Minnesota with no adults.

She sat on the knotted-rag rug before the fire and paged through the journal. Jackson sidled up next to her and peered across her arm at the pages.

"What did you find in the barn?" he said, keeping his voice low enough to not disturb the Ohmans.

"It was beautiful," she whispered. "And I saw these." She ran her finger over a page of symbols. "These were carved onto the stone. My father had translated everything." A wide grin spread across her face as she unfolded the rubbing she made of the stone.

Jackson moved closer and spread out the rubbing across their laps. He was so close now that she felt the heat from his leg cross through the fabric of her dress. Together they perused the journal code and matched the rune carvings in the rubbing. Jackson whispered out each symbol as he matched it, and Anna wrote along the edge of the journal.

When Jackson had no more symbols to read to her, Anna lifted up her head. "Father was brilliant."

"Why? What does it say?"

"It doesn't say anything."

He screwed up his face and looked at her. She smiled at him. "It's not a sentence. They're map coordinates." Her finger moved down the page, to her father's small scrawl like a footnote. "Here lies the second marker. He translated this to longitude and latitude, the directions to the next clue. Can I see the map you got in Sioux City?"

Jackson reached into the burlap bag and withdrew the map. They unfurled it across the rug. She gave him the longitude, and she scanned the edge for latitude until they both intersected. Anna placed her finger on the map and looked up to him. The fire light danced in his wide eyes.

"That's where the next marker is."

# CHAPTER 22

The morning sunlight poured through the window of the washroom, lighting Anna's long brown hair. Mrs. Ohman had lent her the comb that she drew through each strand. After she wound it into a long braid that would hopefully stay put through the day, she straightened her dress and the apron around her waist. The morning light shone onto the pocket, and she gazed down, catching a glimpse of the thing she had almost forgotten.

She pulled the pendant from her pocket and held it into the light. The iron curved in the palm of her hand. It wasn't a delicate piece of woman's jewelry, but it was so much more important to her. After Dave had taken it, a piece of her heart went with it until William had retrieved it for her at the risk of his own life. She kissed the pendant, a simple prayer placed into its iron curves, and then tied it around her neck. Her fingers smoothed it against her chest as she gazed at it in the mirror.

A deep breath to calm the nerves. With a new destination, this might be the last time she would look in a mirror for a while.

The heady smell of cooking bacon and fresh bread drew her from the washroom. The boys had already settled at the table when she approached.

Mrs. Ohman turned from the wood stove with a towel in her hand, ready to take the tray of bread from the oven. "Miss Anna, please have a seat. Fill up for your trip."

Jackson stood, his knees knocking the table and rattling the silverware. He looked at her with a smile. "Good morning."

She almost laughed as William gave him an odd look and stepped around the table while Mrs. Ohman filled their plates with sizzling bacon.

"So, Mr. Belford tells me you will be travelling onward," Olaf said as he tore into his slice of bread.

"Yes, sir," she said. "Back to New England."

William shot her a look with his mouth full of bacon. She hadn't had the chance to tell him everything, and he had slept right through their discovery last night.

"Well, you can catch a train in Kensington. That can take you on to Minneapolis, and you can connect from there. Trains from all over the country go in and out of there."

"Thank you, sir."

"I hope you like apples and biscuits," Mrs. Ohman interjected. "I have a basket of goodies for you to take on your journey."

"Thank you for your hospitality," Anna said. She dipped her hand into her apron pocket and withdrew a piece of parchment, something she had torn from the corner of the rubbing she had made. Another bread crumb that she had written for Uncle John. "I would like to ask a favor." She slid the folded paper toward Olaf. "If my uncle should come looking, could you please give this to him?"

Olaf's beefy fingers scooped up the paper and stuffed it into his shirt pocket. "Of course, dear. Anything for Professor Holloway's family."

Breakfast continued with little conversation, and then the three of them collected their things. Mrs. Ohman passed around her wide grandmotherly hugs, and they departed into the cool morning Minnesota air. Anna glanced back once to where they still stood on the porch, watching them disappear across the farm.


Kensington remained quiet in the morning except for the small train station that murmured with the sounds of people waiting for the 10 o'clock train to Minneapolis. Anna purchased their tickets for three seats together.

The boys hadn't said much until the train started moving and the people around them had settled in to reading books or newspapers.

William leaned toward her and kept his voice low. "When are you going to tell me where we are headed?"

Jackson leaned forward on his knees from where he sat in the seats facing them. "We deciphered the code on the stone."

Anna smiled. "The next clue is in Rhode Island. Newport, Rhode Island. Looking at the train routes, we can connect from Minneapolis to Chicago, and then straight on to Rhode Island, but we'll probably need to get a boat to Newport."

"So what's in Newport?" William asked.

She shrugged. "I don't know. That's just where the first marker is leading us."

William glanced back and forth between her and Jackson. "Do you think the treasure is there?"

"I'm not sure." She realized how silly this was starting to sound. They headed off across the country, to a city by the sea but they had no idea what they were going to do when they got there or what they were looking for. She wondered if she was going to need the map that Diamond Dave had taken from her.

William's shoulders drooped, and he looked at the ground.

"What's wrong?" she said and placed a hand on his back.

"I want to find the treasure," he said. "But I also want to go home. I miss Mother."

Anna shot a glance to Jackson, who now lost his smile. She turned back to William. "I know. I do too. But we need to keep going, stay ahead of Dave and his gang."

"I know."

"Hey," she said and patted his back. "Just lay back and get some rest for now. Let me study Father's journal a little more and see if I can find any more answers. Okay?"

He nodded and leaned against his seat as he gazed out the window.

William tried to hold back tears. Anna could recognize that little twitch in the corner of his mouth every time he did it. She bit the inside of her cheek, and that did the trick to stop any welling in her own eyes. She had to be strong for him. Any sign of weakness and he could crumble into a heap of worry and fear.

She cleared the lump from her throat and sat back with the journal in her lap. Jackson's warm hand moved to hers where she held the book.

"We'll be just fine," he said. "Newport. Just a few days' travel, I reckon. Then we go from there, wherever it takes us."

"Thanks," she said and smiled at him.

"So," he said and averted his gaze, but not before she saw his cheeks redden. He moved his hand and nodded toward the book. "What's the next clue?"

Anna opened the book and paged through to the next section she hadn't yet had a chance to review. Jackson leaned over and gazed at the book as she read her father's familiar script:

*Should you find this place, you must know it to be the prime meridian for the Knights as they settled in the New World. From here, the various inscriptions, runes, and alignments could guide a Templar to various land claims made by their fellow Knights and lead them to safety. Even from this place, the coordinates could lead one to Kensington.*

*I believe this location to have been created by one Prince Henry Sinclair, who was the Grand Master of the Scottish Rite of Freemasons. He had come from a long line of Viking ancestry, the very people who arrived to the New World years in advance. He would have known the best sailing course to the New World as passed down by his ancestors.*

*Many Templars who fled the horrors of October 13th in France came to Scotland and fought with King Robert the*

*Bruce and Prince Henry Sinclair's grandfather. Prince Henry, therefore, grew up as a Templar.*

*Prince Henry likely sailed secretly to the New World and brought with him monks who were also closely tied to the Templars and traveled from Gotland in Sweden. Together they created this location.*

*These monks of Gotland worked closely with Templars. Now, I believe strongly in their hand of creation within this location for the monks of Gotland revered the Virgin Mary and other women in their worship. And thus, we find references to Venus, a common sign of goddess worship through many ancient cultures.*

*At this very spot, the monks utilized the architectures such that, given the precise moment, one can interpret with the solar and lunar alignments the symbols for the coordinates of various Templar locations.*

*This, in fact, may be a compass.*

"A compass?" Jackson said, a knit forming between his eyebrows. "Is the next marker a compass?"

Her eyes wandered across the next few pages of symbols sketched by her father. "I'm not sure. These markings are probably on the compass, but it doesn't say where it's located. Maybe it's on the map, I don't know."

"Solar and lunar alignments? What does that even mean?"

She re-read the segment again. "Probably something astronomical. According to this, it probably has something to do with Venus."

"The planet?"

"Maybe."

He sat back, his face a puzzle of concentration. "May I read it?"

She handed the journal over to him as he perused it and studied the symbols. He stayed that way for most of the trip to Minneapolis, flipping through pages and then back again.

The train arrived in Minneapolis, and the connecting train didn't arrive for another few hours while they waited in the sweltering summer heat of Minnesota. Thankfully, they had Mrs. Ohman's meal she had prepared for them. They boarded the next train, but not until late in the day, and the sun had readied to set.

Anna sat next to the window this time and bunched her coat up against the glass to use as a pillow to rest her head. In the fading twilight of the moving train, the green of the leafy trees turned to dark, inky splashes over the branches. A small town occasionally zoomed by, but they were few as they got further from home.

The rocking and sway of the car lulled her to sleep, but the rest was uneasy, and she awakened whenever the squeal of the wheels on the rail screamed loud enough. During the moments when she did sleep, nightmares of a gunshot in the dark from a diamond-studded pistol startled her awake.

A blast of the train's horn woke her, and she lifted her head to see the morning light stream through the windows. She squinted and gazed out the window to the grand city that lay just outside.

"We're in Chicago," Jackson said from where he sat beside her.

The train chugged into the main station, a huge building in the center of the city. So many people walked the streets outside the rail, women with parasols in hand and men with tall hats. The city surrounded the station and rose high above the puffs of steam from the locomotive.

William held onto Anna's hand as they walked onto the platform and into the station, its white walls and great columns reminiscent of a Greek temple. Panels of windows opened out to the city. Large doors opened out to the street, and Anna gazed out into the expanse.

An enormous Ferris wheel down another block turned and took patrons on a view of the city. Thousands of people flocked along the streets decorated with electric lights, colored streamers, and banners. Music floated along the fountains that spurted and gurgled along the main street.

"Welcome to the World's Fair," a man's booming voice spoke to her from the doorway.

"The what?" she said and approached him.

"The World's Fair," he said, his eyebrow raised. "You haven't heard of the Fair yet?"

Anna shook her head, and he tipped his tall hat to her. His coat must have been hot on this summer morning, but his dapper white shirt stayed in place as did his gloves.

"The Fair introduces the world to the greatest achievements in Science and Industry, my dear lady and gentlemen." He nodded to Jackson, who also looked out through the windows with a slackened jaw. "Come see the moving walkway and a fully functional electric kitchen. Enjoy the culinary delights and music of Chicago while you visit."

"We're not staying," William said.

"Well, young sir, you should reconsider staying for just a few days to enjoy our great city," he said, like the salesman that Anna had suspected he was.

"Yes, do," another man said and stepped up to them, almost obscuring the man announcing the Fair to them. He tipped his bowler hat and smiled below his bushy mustache. He bowed to them and took Anna's hand, placing a kiss on the back of it.

Jackson's hand hooked into the bend of her elbow, and he moved in close to her as the man nodded to him.

"Welcome to the Windy City," he said. "Consider staying in our city. I am the proprietor of a hotel just down the block, within walking distance of the Fair. You can even see our lovely Ferris Wheel from your window."

Jackson tugged on her arm. "No, thank you. We need to be on our way."

The pressure from his hand made her look over at him. Jackson's jaw had gone tight, and the more he tugged on her, the more she wanted to step away from this man.

"Thank you," Anna smiled and nodded.

"Of course," the man tipped his hat again. "If you come this way again, please consider the hotel. Dr. Holmes is my name. Henry Holmes, and I look forward to a future visit from you."

He turned away and stepped through the open doors toward the center of Chicago. Jackson pulled on her arm again.

"What is wrong with you?" Anna said when she turned to him.

"That guy was creepy," he said, his eyes still following the man as he walked out the door. "Let's just get our tickets and get out of here."

She tried not to roll her eyes, but Jackson still held onto her arm and glanced back occasionally to the door. So far, he had not put them in any danger, and she trusted Jackson to help them when needed. Maybe this was one of those times she needed to listen to him.

After navigating through the crowds, she found the ticket counter. She pulled more silver coins from the roll in her apron and stepped up to desk, where a man with gold-rimmed spectacles and a handle-bar mustache looked at her through iron bars.

"Three tickets to Rhode Island," she said and slid the coins across the counter.

With a reproving look and nothing more, he accepted the money, handed her the tickets and her change.

"The train departs at 2 p.m.," he said, without glancing up from his register. "Please be aboard at least 20 minutes prior to departure. At platform 3." His fat finger pointed down the long corridor.

She took the tickets and stepped away from the counter, heading down the east wing.


The ticket master lifted his gold-rimmed spectacles and gazed at the silver in the palm of his hand. Maybe he wasn't seeing it right. It couldn't be. What was the chance that he would actually come across these very coins? When his boss told him to keep a sharp eye out for silver Washington Mint coins dated 1882, he thought it would be impossible, but here it was.

He craned his neck and pressed his face up against the iron bars as he let his glasses fall back down again. The girl who had given these to him was just a kid and not what he had expected. But she had disappeared into the crowd. Where did she say she was going? Rhode Island?

No time to waste. He rose and walked to the boss's office across the terminal. With a sharp rap on the door, he waited until Mr. Payson opened the door, standing there in his fine tweed suit and pepper-gray hair.

"I thought I told you no interruptions," Mr. Payson spoke, his breath smelling of cigar smoke and coffee.

"Yes, sir," the cashier stammered. "But you wanted to be notified about these." He held out the coins for his inspection.

Payson took them and held them under a monocle that he produced from his waistcoat. His jaw fell slack, and the color drained from his face.

"Where did you get these?" he asked and pulled the monocle from his eye.

"Three children, booking tickets to Narragansett, Rhode Island." He pointed to the corridor to Platform 3.

"Very good," Payson spoke and stepped from his office, pushing the cashier aside. *Very good, indeed.* He thought it strange that Thibodaux was so anxious to have these coins examined but, whatever the boss wanted, he got. And Dave paid well. There was no other reason he could last so long in hiding as he did.

Just one simple telegraph message to Thibodaux's men and his job would be complete. The telegraph office loomed down the block, and he would send any information that he knew about those kids to Dave. It would be best to be out of Dave's debt for good.

# CHAPTER 23

ohn removed his hat before he stepped onto the porch. His horse pawed at the ground where he had tied it and bent its head low to nibble at some grass beside the hitching post. This had to be the Ohman farm, from the best directions he could get from the not-so-helpful mercantile owner in Kensington. He straightened his hair and then rapped his knuckles on the door.

Someone shuffled on the other side.

"Who is calling?" a woman's voice called out through the closed door.

He cleared his throat. "Ma'am, my name is John Holloway—"

Before he could finish, the door opened, and a plump woman with her white hair pulled back into a bun stood there. Her bright eyes smiled on him, and her hands reached out before he could say anything else.

"Please, come in," she said and ushered him into the house

He stumbled across the threshold and almost dropped his hat. "Ma'am, this may seem strange, but I have reason to believe that my niece and nephew came around these parts."

She clasped her hands together. "Oh, how wonderful!" She closed the door behind him. "Miss Anna said you might come."

"So they were here?" he spoke, the fatigue in his body melting away.

"Of course," she said as she returned to the kitchen and withdrew a canister from the cupboard. From inside she fished out a folded paper and held it out to him. "She asked me to give this to you should you come this way."

He opened the parchment. Scrawled in Anna's script were three simple words: Newport, Rhode Island.

John smiled; another breadcrumb. "Thank you, ma'am." He turned to leave.

"Those children need help," she said, and he stopped. "Please find them as soon as you can. They didn't say much, but I know they went on to the train station in Kensington. They were planning on connecting in Minneapolis."

John nodded and replaced his hat over his tousled hair. "I will, and thank you for watching out for them."

XXX

The train whistle blasted its final signal for boarding, but Anna had already led the boys to the proper car and cabin. As soon as she opened the door, she smiled. A bed. Two beds actually, bunks. They hadn't slept in real beds since the boarding house in Kansas City.

William ran past her and leaped onto the upper bed. "This is just like the train we took from Boston."

"Except we're one bed short," Anna said and wrinkled her nose.

Jackson stepped up beside her and winked. "I guess someone's going to have to share."

"Ha," she said and shoved him back with a laugh. "Be careful, then. William tends to snore, and he moves so much that he might kick you in the head."

Another whistle blew. The departure call; and the wheels whistled against the track as the train jolted forward. Anna caught herself against the wall of the small cabin before the next jolt. The platform moved, slowly at first, passing the many people as they walked to their boarding stations.

For a second, she thought she saw the man who had sold her the tickets, standing on the platform and watching the train depart. His gold-rimmed glasses framed his eyes and a flash of light blinded the glass inside the frames. Then he was gone.

The car swayed, and the door rattled as the train picked up speed. The station disappeared, and soon did the city of Chicago, with its World's Fair, or whatever the barker had called it. Such a grand party. Anna peered out the window at the Ferris Wheel as it grew smaller and smaller with distance. The yearn of the celebration gnawed at her gut. Someday she wanted to be a part of it, with all those pretty women and their lovely dresses and a man on their arm.

"This is amazing," Jackson said just over her shoulder.

Startled, she pulled back from the window to find him gazing out as well. "What? The city?"

"No. The train. I've never seen anything this fancy." He stepped back and sat on the edge of the bed. "Travelling so fast around the country."

"I guess so. It's just a train."

"But these places. Chicago." He opened his arms wide as if presenting a gift.

"You travel around all the time though," Anna said.

"Yeah, but just to places like Missouri, Arkansas, Tennessee. I've never been to New England. And I always travel alone. It's a lot better with company."

"I wish it was under better circumstances."

"I like these circumstances just fine." He smiled, and Anna's heart jumped around for a second.

"Me too," William said from the top bunk.

She wished that he could be off running around and exploring, just for a little while, at least for right now.

Jackson laughed and looked up at him. "Looks like we're sharing a bunk. Which one do you want?"

"Top," he said quickly.

"All right. Top it is."

He stood and presented the bottom bed to her. "Looks like you have the bottom."

She nodded and sat on the bed and removed her coat. She rolled it up and lay back with the coat as a pillow. The car swayed with increasing speed. William jumped down and ran to the window to watch the landscape move past them with Jackson looking over his head.

Her brother chattered to him, but she disregarded him as her fingers found the pendant at her neck. She held it up to the sunlight streaming through the window. It caught the light in a bright flash that left a ghost of blinding white in her vision.

*I'm always two steps to your right.*

In that blinding light, she saw her father's eyes the day he gave it to her and said those very words.

She wished that were true.

# CHAPTER 24

Anna awoke with a start, the burn of the pendant's reflection just a memory. The train car rocked and jostled her from where she lay. She sat upright, the cabin dark, the sun long set along the horizon.

How long had she slept? She sat upright and let her eyes adjust to the dim twilight that streamed through the window. The cabin was quiet except for the squeal of the wheels. She stood and glanced at the upper bunk, but it was empty.

That woke her up quickly. Her hand felt over the linens, and there was nothing. Not even a warm spot where William or Jackson might have been sitting or sleeping. Her stomach dropped, a sickening lurch that left her mouth dry. Where were they?

The car rocked again as she moved to the cabin door, and she stumbled. She stepped out into the hall, now lit with lamps along the walls. She steadied herself as she made her way forward to the lead cars. Maybe they had gone to one of the coach cars since she had fallen asleep. The niggle of uncertainty eased when she thought of it. That would have been kind of them to let her sleep, but they should have left a note or something.

She crossed the connection bridge to the next car and opened the door. The scent of roast beef and boiled rosemary potatoes filled the room. The dining car, with its bright lights and wonderful fragrances. She moved into the car and down the center aisle, past dining tables filled with men and women, some families, who ate as the car swayed down the track. At the furthest table on the left, she spied the two as they ate.

William perked up when he saw her and gave a little wave and a smile. She moved to the table and sat beside Jackson.

"You scared the life out of me," she whispered under her breath as she slid into the seat.

"Sorry," William said with a mouthful of stew. "You looked like you needed the sleep. We didn't want to wake you."

"It was my idea," Jackson said. "I told him we should leave you in peace for a while. I should have thought—"

"It's okay." She took in a calming breath and smelled the food on the table. "I was just worried."

"Here. We got you some soup in case you slept through dinner." He pushed a silver bowl of soup toward her. The scent made her stomach growl.

The salty broth tasted perfect, as though she hadn't eaten in a month. Jackson talked through the rest of dinner, regaling William with tales of his travels through Missouri. William laughed at most of it and stared with silent and quiet breath through the intense parts. She was sure that he made up some of it. Nobody could have seen that much in seventeen short years.

She finished the soup and two rolls that Jackson had saved for her and sat back and listened to more of Jackson's stories until he turned to her.

He shot a sideways glance to William. "Should we show her?"

William smiled and nodded.

"Show me what?"

"We went on a little adventure while you slept," Jackson said, a half-grin forming on his mouth. "Do you want to go on one?"

"I guess," she said with a raised eyebrow.

William looked like he was ready to burst when Jackson took her hand and stood from the table. Her brother took the lead as he walked out the front door of the dining car. They walked across the connecting bridge and into the next car, a coach car. They moved through it, down the center aisle, swift and agile. The feel of Jackson's hand in hers as they moved faster made her heart race. The sway of the car and the quickness at which they moved sent pulsations of excitement into her veins until her ears rang.

Another cross bridge. Another car. They moved, and she almost ran behind them. William opened another door, and they stepped out onto a bridge that stood wider than the others. The sound of the steam engine roared, and puffs of white that were still warm and damp blew past them. William stopped and held onto the railing as he gazed out into the vast dark. Anna and Jackson did the same. The air moved so fast now, swirling William's hair on his head.

Her pulse still pounded and didn't give up with the exhilaration of the fast-moving air and the loud engine. The steam engine puffed furiously with the rhythmic chug of the pistons. A partial moon cast a dim silvery blanket over the vast empty and black fields around them. This is what it felt like to be alive and so awake. The speed of the train. The cool and clean breeze. She closed her eyes and inhaled deeply, the fresh air filling her lungs.

"What is that?" William called out over the roar of the engine.

Anna opened her eyes and followed his pointing finger into the dark far ahead of the train. Somewhere down the track, sparkles of light danced in the night. Not enough to be a town or even a farm in the distance. And they moved along the track and through the field.

Jackson grasped her hand with an iron fist. "We need to go. Now."

"Why?" Anna said and turned to him. His jaw tensed, and a knit of concern wrinkled between his eyes. "What is it?"

He pulled her back, and William stepped away with them. "Run."

The train's brakes grabbed the wheels, and the locomotive squealed in protest. The car jolted, and Anna fell into Jackson, but he kept going, faster and faster. She grasped William's hand as well, and they plunged into the next car. The giant train bounded down the track, and the brakes screamed again. The blast of the train's horn sounded in a deafening wail.

They moved into the dining car as passengers stood and peered out the windows to see what was happening. The train wasn't scheduled to stop until tomorrow, so it shouldn't be slowing down or screaming its whistle. A volley of gunshots rang out in the dark somewhere outside, and the brakes grabbed again. Voices in the cabin rose in panic, but Jackson moved without hesitation. Anna glanced back through the window to see firelight moving along the slowing train.

"What's going on?" Anna called out to Jackson.

"This is what a train robbery looks like," he said. "And my bet is that it's Dave and his men."

Her gaze shot back through the windows and a woman screamed. Men on horses rode next to the car as it slowed even further.

Jackson pulled them out onto the connection bridge to the cabin car when another volley of gunshots rang out into the night. The train had slowed enough that she could hear the beating sound of horse hooves. Men's voices called out in hollers of victory. They had to be climbing onto the train now.

Anna followed Jackson into the cabin car. Their cabin was only five doors down. They needed to make it. Lock the door and hide inside and hope that Dave couldn't find them. It had to work.

The door of the cabin car behind them flew open, and a tall silhouette stood in the gaping space, shotgun in hand. A handkerchief covered his face with eyes shadowed under a broad hat.

Jackson didn't stop but ran harder toward their cabin.

"Hey!" the man shouted and took off after them.

Jackson bolted to the room and shoved them through just as the man raced to the door. He pulled it closed and slid the lock into place. The door rattled with each pound of the shotgun against the door.

Anna's heart screamed in her ears with the shaking door. Jackson placed himself between the door and her.

"How did they find us?" she said, breathless.

"I don't know." Jackson jumped a little as the man pounded on the door again.

However they found them, she knew what they wanted. She placed a hand on the pocket of her apron, where she always kept the journal and the folded rubbing of the stone.

A cock of the shotgun on the other side of the door echoed, and everything else went silent in that fraction of a second after the sound. Jackson turned, grabbed Anna's and William's arms and pulled them to the ground. The blast of the shotgun roared in the dark. A shower of a thousand wood splinters rained down on them.

The smell of the gunpowder filled her nose with the settling of the wood fragments. The man filled the missing upper half of the door. He reached inside, slid the lock out and forced the rest of the door open.

"Get up," he said, his voice deep and graveled. "Dave's waiting on us."

Jackson met her gaze from where they crouched together. This was the first time she had seen him truly worried. Not when they were running through the stockyard in Kansas City. He had everything together and knew what his next move would be. But now his face had grown pale, and his eyes watched her with desperate loss.

She swallowed and stood on shaking knees, her arms up before her. As soon as she had stepped close enough to the man, he grasped her arm and shoved her out into the corridor. He then trained the shotgun on Jackson and William.

"You too. Get up."

The boys stood up behind her, and the man shoved them all into the corridor. With the gun at their backs, Anna led the way down the length of the train, through the cargo car and into the dining car. The train had ground to a halt, and when Anna stepped into the dining car, the sounds of crying and men shouting assaulted her ears. Two other gunmen stood among the people, who now cowered on the ground.

"Found 'em," the man with the shotgun said through the handkerchief covering his face. Jackson stumbled into William as he shoved the gun into his back and pushed them forward.

"Well, looks like we can get goin'," another man said. The others hurried through the crowd, taking pocket watches from the men and jewelry from the women in the car.

Anna stepped down the center aisle. Eyes watched her the entire time, and it didn't take a genius to know what these people thought:

*thank the Lord I am not those poor children.* She stepped out into the cool night air interrupted by the smell of burning torches. The firelight danced around the tracks, each one held into the darkness by a man on a horse. The animals skittered among the brush, terrified by the occasional gunshot into the night.

"Well, well," a voice called out to them. The thick Louisiana drawl told her it was Dave behind the handkerchief that covered his face. "You kids gave us a run for our money. I'll give you that." He rode into the center of the gang. The torches that surrounded him cast shadows from the brim of his hat, leaving his face in a shade of black. The light glittered on the diamond-handled pistols just evident at the edge of his coat.

The man with the shotgun shoved them forward, and Anna stepped down the small iron ladder to the tracks. Bile burned in the back of her throat. There was no getting out of this now, not with all these men and all those guns. She was pretty sure that even Jackson had no escape route figured out this time.

"Looks like we are going on a nice trip together," Dave said. Another gunman sidled up beside Anna. "Get on." Dave glanced to the back of his saddle.

The ground almost dropped out from under her. He expected her to ride with him, and the boys to get on horses with the other men. The thought of riding that close to him made her sick, but it didn't look like he gave her any other choice.

The man beside her hoisted her up on the horse, forcing her to sit against Dave. The heavy smell of whiskey and tobacco wafted from his coat collar, stirring the queasiness in her stomach. But the worst part wasn't having to share a saddle with him. It was seeing William placed with another one of these scoundrels, and the way his lip quivered when he looked at her through the torchlight. She searched through the faces hidden behind handkerchiefs and found Jackson as well, hidden behind a mountain of a man atop his horse and a rifle in his hand.

Don't do anything foolish. At least that's what she thought he tried to tell her with the desperate gaze he had fixed on her.

"Better hold on, honey," Dave said. "And don't think about doing something stupid. Things just got real serious for you three." He half turned back and spoke only to her. "The book. Now."

Pressure seized her heart like a vice. She couldn't bear to part with the journal again, especially into the hands of a vicious killer like Dave. But that's exactly what he was. Cold and brutal. He would take it out of her dead hands if she didn't give it to him.

She reached into her apron and found the leather spine of the book, but her fingers didn't want to let it go. She had to do it, or he would kill her. Or worse, kill William or Jackson and make her watch. She pulled the journal from her pocket and placed it in his open palm.

"Good girl," he said and placed it inside a leather bag hung over the saddle horn. He turned away from her and spurred his horse. It started off into the dark with the posse and their torches following in a line toward some unknown destination in the wild.

# CHAPTER 25

John led his horse down the sloped plank from the train's livery car and onto the station terminal. The city of Chicago bustled with too many sounds and a cacophony of smells since he had last been here. The World's Fair had turned the city into a beehive of activity, and John didn't enjoy it in the least. Too many faces that could possibly recognize him. That was the best thing about his isolated farm in New Mexico: few people and even fewer distractions.

He pulled the brim of his hat low and kept his head down as he walked his horse toward the stables. He tied the horse to a hitching post and drew water into the trough.

The shrill voice of a boy whose voice had just begun to change caught his attention. He craned his head around the body of the horse until he spotting the lad across the street from the stable. The kid called out to anyone who would listen. The newspaper he held in his hand stretched out from his body as a banner to those who walked past him on the street.

"Train bound from Chicago to Rhode Island hijacked by bandits" he called to the crowd. "Read all about it!"

That couldn't be a coincidence, and those bandits knew exactly which train to stop. He marched across the street, dropped a coin into the boy's hand and scooped up the paper. The story was printed across the front page, accompanied by drawings depicting the horrific act.

*Gang of highwaymen rob locomotive bound for Rhode Island*

*The unfortunate citizens aboard the train robbed of their precious possessions*

*The dastardly deed was performed by masked gunslingers bearing torches that burned of the devil's fire.*

John skimmed through the flowery poetry describing last night's robbery, but it sounded like very little was actually stolen. A few trinkets from women's finger's and necks. Men's cuff links and watches. Nothing significant. His finger traced the body of the article, and then he stopped.

*Three youngsters were forcibly removed by these agents of evil in the center of purgatory in Northern Ohio. They consisted of a young lady, a young man and a boy, may the angels be with them. Despite the best efforts of the bravest of constables aboard the train, the bandits escaped into the night with the stolen goods as well as the three children.*

Sure. The constable did everything he could to stop them. But it told him everything he needed to know: Northern Ohio. It had been a long time since John visited the homestead in Ohio, but he would always remember the trail that took him there. He could still find it even in the dark. No doubt that the gang would seek shelter and take his prisoners there to keep out of the public eye for a short while. Dave was smart enough to know that his little hijacking of a passenger locomotive would draw attention.

He glanced back at his horse, who sloshed water from the edges of the watering trough as it drank. The last thing he wanted to do was to get back onto a train. But if he was to get ahead of Dave, that's what he needed to do. Cleveland would be the closest and taking the train could buy him enough time to prepare.

Anna awoke with a start and leaned back as soon as she realized she had fallen asleep with her head resting on Dave's shoulder.

"Rise and shine," he said to her with a laugh laced with too many hand-rolled cigarettes.

The horse plodded forward, but its step quickened with the coming morning light and with its destination in sight. The sun hadn't peaked over the edge of the world yet, but the faintest outlines of crumbling fences lined both sides of the wagon trail. She peered over Dave's shoulder to find buildings scattered ahead of them, the ancient ruins of a farm. The remains of an old red barn stood just beyond the fence line, its roof long-since caved in, and the faded red paint dangling off the walls like autumn leaves.

Heavy tree growth had nearly swallowed the perimeter of the farm and obscured the small farm house until the horse rounded the gap in the fence line. The roof was intact, unlike the barn, but patches of moss collected across it and curled over the eaves. Shuttered windows looked out into the vast wild, and some of the panels hung at odd angles on broken hinges. White peeling paint fell from the walls to the porch. Leaves blew across the porch with the faintest breeze like whispers from those boarded windows.

In this dark and empty place, no morning larks warbled, and no insects whirred in the grass. Everything here had gone dead and silent a long time ago.

Her fingers had clutched the back of Dave's coat, and when the ache started in her knuckles, she released her grip. Prickles of goose flesh brushed over her forearms, and she looked away from the house. It looked haunted, and if it wasn't, then it probably held some terrible secrets.

The horse approached the house, and Dave reigned it to a stop. The rest of his posse stopped with them, and everybody dismounted. One man stepped up to Dave's horse and helped Anna to the ground.

The ache in her thighs and knees left her legs wobbly. Someone helped William to the ground, and he moved to run to her, but a hand to the back of his shirt stopped him.

"It's okay," Anna said to him and then found Jackson. The dark circles under his eyes meant that he had stayed vigilant all night, unlike her. She had allowed herself to fall asleep, but he had kept watch. He forced a tired smile. At least he was okay. For now.

Dave stepped onto the porch, every board complaining with his steps that plodded toward the ancient door. He said nothing to them, and it only seemed best to follow him. There was nowhere else to go, and a gang of outlaws hovered behind her with Jackson and William in their hands. She stepped onto the porch behind him with the boards under her feet bowing with dry rot.

He shoved open the door, and a waft of musty air breathed out from inside the house.

"Welcome to our humble abode," Dave said and stretched out his arms to present it to her. "It's not a fancy hotel, but it keeps us away from Johnny Law."

They really do say that. She had thought it was just an expression used in her penny novels.

William wrinkled his nose. "What's that smell?"

"Oh," Dave said and made himself comfortable on an old wood chair by the empty fireplace. "It's probably fifty years of animal nesting. Wanna see the best part?" he asked and jumped to his feet again.

The round hand-tied rug that stretched across the floor flipped over easily with a swipe of Dave's boot, exposing an iron ring clasp on a hatch door. He lifted the door, and a cool puff of stagnant air drifted up into the main room. The cellar stairs plunged into a well of darkness below the house.

"Your room," Dave said with a grin.

"What?" Anna had meant to only think it, but it came out against her will. The musty, damp air drifted up from the dark hole and under the edge of her skirt.

The pistol appeared in his hand, and he pointed the barrel at her. "Go on." The silver metal glinted in the light as he waved it between her and the hole in the floor. "Get on down there before we have a problem."

It was the same smile, the same swish of the gun that she had seen the night he and his men forced their way into Uncle John's house. And it was the same gnawing pit that formed in her gut now. She glanced back at William and Jackson, who stood behind her with Dave's filthy men surrounding them. Jackson's jaw clenched tight, his eyes fixed on her. *Just do it.*

She turned away from them, lifted her skirt above her ankles and stepped down the cellar stairs. The clomping of the boys' boots close behind her echoed in the dank space below the stairs. The dark blinded her at first, but her eyes adjusted as soon as her boot landed on the hard dirt floor. The hatch door slammed shut, and she almost stumbled in the dark with her heart pounding at the sound. William tripped at the last step and fell into Anna. Though he didn't say much, his wiry body trembled in her arms.

Something scooted across the floor overhead. Dust sprinkled down through the slats between the floorboards where thin strips of daylight shone down into their prison. The boards creaked with a rhythmic sound: a rocking chair placed over the hatch door.

Jackson moved beside her in the dark. "Well, we're still alive."

"What do you think they're gonna do to us?" William asked, still wrapped in Anna's arms and leaning against her.

"I have no idea. I think he just wants Father's journal."

"But he already has it. Why didn't he just let us go?" William said and turned to face her in the dark.

This was the question she was afraid to ask. *Why, indeed.*

"He still needs us," Jackson said, but even in the dark, she saw his knowing gaze toward her.

Anna reached her hand out to the dark until she found the wall and then slid down to sit on the cold earth. William and Jackson sat on either side of her, and William rested his head on her shoulder. Despite the occasional noises overhead, William fell asleep beside her. But her body stayed vigilant. Whatever happened up there could spill into the cellar at any time. She wasn't about to fall asleep again and let them get the drop on her. Jackson held his breath any time the voices rose, and the footfalls quickened. This went on for hours, the daylight that skimmed through the slats fading as evening approached.

Shouts started, and something fell, maybe it was the rocking chair. Jackson stiffened, and his hand moved to hers. His fingers quaked, but he squeezed her hand, and his eyes sparkled with the fading evening light that shone down through the slats.

"What's happening?" she whispered.

"Dunno," he said, his eyes still fixed on the faint light above them. "Argument probably. Maybe it's about us."

"Maybe it's about Father's journal," Anna said. "He might have it, but I'm sure he can't understand half of what's written in there."

"Yeah," he said, and she heard the smile in his voice. "Probably dumb as a stump."

"Dumb Dave Thibodaux."

He laughed and leaned closer to her. "And those probably aren't real diamonds anyway."

The shouting continued, most of it muffled through the floor. A shot rang out, and she jumped. Jackson's hand gripped hers tighter, and William startled next to her. Then silence. The only thing she heard was the pounding of her heart in her ears. William sat still, his fingers grasping the arm of her coat.

A voice spoke from upstairs, firm and demanding. It had to be Dave, but she couldn't make out what he said.

The cellar door opened and cast a bright beam of lantern light down the stairs. Heavy boots descended the steps, and one of Dave's men peeked down at them.

"Dave wants to talk to you," he said and pointed to her.

*What if he heard them making fun of him?* She was sure that jokes at his expense wouldn't set well with him.

Her mouth had gone dry. She moved to stand up, but Jackson's hand gripped hers and pulled her back down.

"I have to go," she whispered to him.

"I know," he said, his eyes desperate and fixed on her. He moved quickly before she knew what he was doing. His rough fingers grasped her face, and he pulled her in with a swift kiss. Her head spun, and her ears rang, and for a moment she forgot all about Dave's man standing on the stairs.

The look of surprise on Jackson's face must have mirrored her own.

"What was that?" Anna asked.

"I don't know. I'm sorry. It just felt like the right thing to do."

Anna smiled, the ringing in her ears still making her head spin. "I think it was."

The man on the stairs cleared his throat, but Anna didn't want to let go of Jackson's hand.

"Dave ain't gonna wait all day," the man said.

"I really need to go," Anna whispered.

"Everything will be okay," Jackson said, the worry around his eyes now faded into a faint grin.

"I know." She pulled her hand free and stood on shaking knees. She faced the staircase and the imposing shadow of the man cast down from the lantern light.

*It'll be okay. Just remember the kiss.*

She turned back and looked at him again. The grin had fallen from his face with each step she took up to the house. Her boot caught the edge of the next stair, and she almost tripped. *Need to focus. The man was right.* Dave wasn't going to wait forever, and a shot had already gone off upstairs. It wouldn't do her any good to provoke him any further.

But her lips still buzzed and her cheeks flushed when she thought of what had just happened.

# CHAPTER 26

Anna emerged onto the main floor, the bright lanterns a stark contrast to the dark cellar she had sat in for hours. Dave sat at the kitchen table, the journal and map spread out before him.

His other men were scattered about, some sitting like a bunch of lazy dogs in the chairs before the fireplace. Others sat out on the porch while one man sat on a rocking chair strumming an old guitar.

"Why don't you join me," Dave said and motioned her toward the table.

She stepped toward him, the man who had summoned her kept in her peripheral vision. This pit of vipers surrounded her on all sides, but she wasn't about to let any of them surprise her with anything.

Dave leaned back in his chair, one arm resting on the table. His blonde hair looked like a mess of long straw in the orange glow of the lanterns. The dancing flames cast shadows across his face and made his eyes sink into his head like the way a grim reaper appeared in her father's old medieval books. He held his hand open to the chair across the table. She settled into it, her fingers clenched together on her lap.

"I believe you can understand this book." His fingers tapped the journal, opened to the page about the Kensington rune stone cipher.

She glared at him. Of course, she understood it. She had spent years learning right beside her father, absorbing everything he had to teach her. And Dave was the last person on earth with whom she was going to share it.

Dave snorted, and a half grin spread over his lips. He reached to his hip and drew his gun, but instead of pointing it at her, he rested it on the table. The barrel looked at her while the diamonds twinkled in the light.

"Weren't you taught to respect your elders? Answer me."

She clenched her jaw but forced the words out. "Yes, I can understand it."

A wicked smile formed over his lips. "Well, I suspected that, Miss Anna. Now, you and I can come to an agreement. Something that will benefit the both of us. I believe that there is something you need from me, and I am willing to give it to you in exchange for a service you could provide for me."

The outlaw's smile made her hate him even more. She knew what he was getting at, but what could she possibly need from him?

"At least one of those young men downstairs is your brother. I believe it was the boy we snatched from John's house. Now he's looking up to you for protection, and I am just the man to give you all that and more."

Oh, he was good, too good. But he didn't become the most dangerous outlaw and train robber in the West without being that cunning.

"I'll even give y'all three square meals and use of the outhouse. I just need one thing from you. You can help me interpret these maps and this book," he said and tapped the journal again. "Plus, as a bonus, none of y'all will get shot. I really don't like shootin' kids, and it would be best if you didn't make me. Sound like a fair deal?"

Anna swallowed the dry lump in her throat. Of course, she would have to help him. That was exactly why the three of them were even still alive. He needed her help, and she had suspected it this whole time.

She nodded, and he clapped his hands in mock victory.

"Very good," he said. "Now let's get started." He leaned back and called out to his man standing behind her. "Get those boys some stew."

The man responded and moved about in the kitchen where she could no longer see him from the corner of her eye. He then carried two steaming bowls of soup down the cellar stairs. At least Dave kept his word on this subject.

He turned the journal around and slid it across the table toward her. "Tell me what you know so far."

She glanced over the open pages, markers that she had memorized leading up to Kensington and the stone at the Ohman farm. If these were the pages he had been reading, he was so far behind, but did he even realize it?

"This mark here," he said, his dirty finger pointing to the sketches at the top of the page. "This is the same as this." He indicated the location in Kensington.

Maybe he wasn't as dumb as she had suspected. Yes, he trailed behind them, but if she lied and guided him that way, she would put the Ohmans in his way. They had been too good to them, and they were innocent in all of this.

"It's the same mark, but we already have the coordinates beyond it," she said, her gaze turning back down to the book. She couldn't bear to see the satisfaction in his face.

"All right. Where to next?"

She turned the page and pointed out the next marker, and aimed him toward the site indicated on the map: Rhode Island.

He looked down at the map and shook his head with a smile. "You can actually do it. And do you know where in Rhode Island?"

"Newport."

"What exactly are we looking for over there?"

"It'll probably be another stone. And according to this," she pointed to markings in the journal that continued onto the map, "it should be in plain sight."

"So, is that gonna be the treasure?"

"I don't think so. It will probably be another clue to another marker."

The lines around his eyes reappeared. "Why in the world can't they just say 'here's the treasure, boys' instead of sending us runnin' all over the country?"

"Because that's the point of a hidden treasure," she said and felt the poison on her tongue when she said.

His eyes narrowed as he looked at her. "I like you. You got that . . . spark or whatever. It'll keep you alive longer."

Then he turned the journal and flipped through the pages. "Can't you just look through this thing and find out what the clues are so we can cut straight to it?"

"It doesn't work that way. These are only deciphering tools. I have to see the actual markers—the stones—to see the code. Then I can use the book to interpret the clue. Without the markers, it's useless."

He rested back against his chair and looked into the lantern. "Fine, then. Sounds like we're heading to Rhode Island at first light. You'd better get some rest. It's gonna be a long day tomorrow." He signaled to his men to take her back downstairs.

She stood, but her knees still shook. All she needed was just one chance. "You have us under your boot. We aren't going anywhere, but if I could study the journal then maybe the codes will be easier to interpret. It may make it faster to get where you want to go."

He leaned back in his chair and watched the lantern light. "That's fine." He turned to his men. "Get her a lantern and some stew as well."

Before Dave could change his mind, she grasped the journal and held it to her chest. She turned away from him and followed his man down to the cellar again, this time with a light to guide her down the stairs.

Jackson stood as soon as she came into his view. The rush of blood into her cheeks warmed her face. For only a moment, she had been distracted from their brief kiss to deal with Dave, but now she had returned. The man left them with a slam of the floor hatch. She settled back against the wall between the boys.

William leaned close to her as soon as the door had closed. "What did he want?"

She held the journal up to the light.

William eyed the book in her hands. "He just gave you back the journal?"

"That's it?" Jackson said. The tension in his neck left his muscles straining under the collar of his shirt.

She put a finger to her lips and then glanced up at the floorboards. The boys looked up as well, and they all waited until the noise settled above their heads.

"Looks like we are riding out tomorrow for Rhode Island. He wants me to help him find the treasure," she whispered.

Jackson scrunched his face like he tasted something terrible. "What? We're not gonna help him."

"Well, it doesn't look like we have much of a choice. We're outnumbered and definitely out-gunned. I have to do it. He gave me his word that we would be safe."

"But what happens when we find it? How safe are we gonna be then?" Jackson said, and the flicker of worry returned to his eyes.

"I'll try to find a way to get us out before then," she said, but she had no idea what she was going to do. It would take a miracle to escape Dave's posse, and even if they could escape, she was sure he could catch up to them again.

Her stomach grumbled, and she glanced down at the bowl of stew in her lap. Even if it belonged to Dave, she had to eat. She had to sleep. They all needed to if they were going to make the long trip tomorrow.

"Why don't you guys try to get some sleep. I need to make sense of this book before tomorrow."

"I'll help you," Jackson said.

"I can do it. Just get some rest."

"I know you can do it." He grasped her hand again. "So let me help you. There's a lot to do tonight."

His hand was warm in the cold cellar. "Okay. We'll do it together."

William had settled next to her while she ate and poured over the book. The symbols from the Kensington stone still burned in her memory, and she reviewed these with the cipher. She was sure she had it right.

"What do these mean?" Jackson whispered and pointed to the row of symbols.

She shook her head. "I'm not sure. These will be dedicated to whatever is in Rhode Island, but they don't make any sense at all. Maybe they will when we see the next marker, but they don't right now."

She paged further on. So many unusual drawings, more codes. One page caught her attention.

"Do you see something?" he asked.

"I think so." Her father's script detailed the interpretations of several columns of symbols. Her finger ran across the word at the top.

"Astrolabe," she said.

"What's an astrolabe?"

She smiled, her memory stirring back to the dusty shelves and recesses of the university museum astronomy lab where her father would sometimes perform consulting work. She had once wandered the corridors and rooms as a child while he talked to some stuffy old professor.

"It's a device used in astronomy." She remembered seeing one among a room filled with telescopes and star maps. "It's usually small, maybe five inches wide. It has a dial and an etched plate of symbols. Medieval sailors used to use them with the stars at night for navigation."

"Do you think we'll find this in Rhode Island?"

She shrugged. "I've only ever seen them locked away in a museum. I'm not sure what this has to do with anything."

She turned through more pages and found more of her father's own words on the page near the end of the journal. With her voice low, she read it to Jackson. *"Description discovered on rune stones at Spirit Pond in Maine. Appears to be instructions regarding the setting and neutralizing of certain traps. Of most interest is the final text of a very specific trap. It appears to be a water trap of some kind; the water symbol is always engraved with this description."*

Below his writing, her father had sketched the simple engraving of four wavy horizontal lines in parallel.

"That must be the water symbol," Jackson said, running his finger over the print.

She read the next statement—

*"According to the inscription, when the trap is triggered this will set a series of gears in motion to open a channel and flood the area to be protected. This was a common medieval trap to protect valuables underground. The trigger would be known only to those in the highest circle of knowledge regarding the valuables. This stone appears to be an instruction manual to those in that highest circle."*

"There's another stone," Jackson said, his glistening eyes now wide as he looked up at her.

"And a trap, apparently. Some sort of water trap."

"A trap to hide the treasure. Do you know what this means?" He smiled, looking almost as excited as the moment just before he had kissed her. "We're getting closer."

She glanced up to the floorboards. "And so is Dave."

# CHAPTER 27

The next morning went as Anna had expected and Dave stuck to his word. He provided a simple breakfast of venison and biscuits and even allowed them to wash up in the nearby creek before they departed as a group, due east.

They kept to the forests, no doubt because Dave hoped to avoid the local law enforcement. He also insisted that Anna and the boys ride directly behind him.

The trail wound on for hours through the deep green forests of Ohio and eventually Pennsylvania. They stopped as the sun set low and dusk approached. No farmhouses with a roof overhead, no tents to provide shelter. They just set out bed rolls under the stars with a fire at the center of their meager camp.

Dave set out two men for watch, one to the north and the other south, and they would trade off throughout the night. He didn't miss anything. And there wasn't much discussion after dark.

Sleep was nearly impossible on the hard, bumpy ground. A few times she awoke to the sound of an owl or the trees rustling.

Morning came and, much like the previous day, they ate breakfast and started out on their horses. But after riding until midday, they soon came to the edges of a town. It had seemed so long since Anna had seen civilization.

Dave stopped the group and sent one of his men into town. From what she could tell, he was sent out to obtain train passage for them.

Sure enough, the man was able to get tickets for them and their horses in the cargo cars, but he didn't have enough money for all of them. This would mean, if Anna assumed correctly, that only four other men would accompany them and Dave. Those were better odds if they were to ever escape.

Dave stood with them on the train platform. The last of the occupants from the previous trip departed from the cars. He eyed the attendants, his hand always just inches away from his guns. Anna and Jackson stood shoulder-to-shoulder, crowded in by Dave's men. William waited in front of Anna with her hands around his chest. There was no calling for help among all these people. Dave had them corralled and wouldn't hesitate to shoot anybody that tried to lend them aid.

The attendants emptied the last of the cars, and Dave turned toward her. "Now this train is gonna take us right into Rhode Island. I don't want any funny business. You keep your heads down and mouths shut. You got it? I see any of y'all trying to cause problems, then somebody's gonna get a bullet in the back." He stooped and grasped William's elbow. Her brother stayed quiet as the outlaw pulled him to his side and out of Anna's reach. "Just an insurance policy for now."

William glanced back at her, his eyes pleading. Anna nodded, but the tightening in her throat made it hard to breathe.

The attendant on their platform announced the boarding call, and they moved as a group toward the car. The horses came with them, which meant another long ride in a stinking livery car. They spread out among the benches, Jackson and Anna sitting as far away from Dave as possible.

William watched her from where Dave held him across the car. The door slammed shut, and it made her jump. The train's whistle blasted three times, and the locomotive jerked forward. Wheels squealed against the track, pushing the cars along and gained speed until they no longer spun, metal against metal.

Dave leaned toward William and whispered something in his ear. He tapped his finger against the boy's shoulder. William jumped up and hurried over to Anna.

He settled next to her, his body rigid and cold.

"You okay?" Anna said and shot a glance at Dave, who now leaned back with a smile and pulled a flask from inside his jacket.

"Yeah," William nodded.

"What did he say to you?"

William kept his eyes to the floor. "He said to make sure you do as he says and he won't kill us."

The car swayed in a rhythmic dance for hours and miles. Air rushed through the side windows, thankfully dissipating the smell of the horses. At least they didn't have to ride the animals this whole way. That much time on a horse and with these men would have been unbearable.

Anna leaned toward Jackson, who rested his head against the car wall, his eyes closed. But the rise and fall of his chest was too agitated for him to be asleep.

She nudged him until he opened his eyes and peered at her from the corner of his vision. "What are you going to do when this is all over?" she asked.

"I dunno. Haven't thought that far ahead. Just hoping I make it out of this."

"Would you go back to Kate's?"

"If I did, I wouldn't stay there."

"Maybe," she started, but the rest of the words didn't want to come. "Maybe you could come see New Mexico."

He turned to look at her and smiled. "You want me to come to New Mexico?"

She smoothed out the apron over her skirt, her fingers brushing over the edge of the journal in her pocket. He didn't used to make her nervous, but now he had to go and change all of that.

"Well, only if you want to come. There's lots of work to be had there. It's a good place to make an honest living," she said.

He crossed his arms over his chest and gazed up at the ceiling. "I'll consider it, but it depends."

"Depends on what?"

"Depends on if you tell me the truth."

"Truth about what?"

He looked at her again. "You tell me if that was the best kiss you ever had."

"Gross, you guys," William said and scrunched up his nose.

Anna's cheeks flushed, and her ears rang. "Jackson Belford—"

"Jackson T. Belford," he said with a smile.

Her eyes widened. "It is not polite conversation to have right now."

"She's never been kissed before," William said.

That little brat. "William!" she said through gritted teeth. She would smack him upside the head right now if Dave wasn't watching them.

"Well, it's true," he said. "Mother always had a chaperone around when you had a gentleman caller."

*This can't be happening.*

"You have gentleman callers?" Jackson whispered and leaned closer.

She put her head in her hands. "I'm not going to talk about this anymore."

"Oh yeah," William said. "The last one, what was his name? William Gibbons, I think. Dark hair. Really tall. But his family was rich."

"William, please shut up," Anna said and raised her head.

"Rich, huh?" Jackson said and looked away, the smile slipping from his face.

The squeeze of regret wrapped around her chest. "My mother arranged it. I didn't like him at all. And this was in Boston, before my father . . . " She couldn't finish it.

"That's okay," he said. The grip he had around his chest tightened. "Just good to know."

Anna sighed. This hadn't gone well at all. Not only did she have to be leery of Dave and his men, sitting next to her brother and her friend just became awkward.

She licked her lips. Why did they always have to be so dry when she needed to say something important? She leaned toward Jackson. "The kiss was fine," she whispered, low enough so that hopefully William couldn't hear.

With all of this, she hadn't heard Dave approach them. A little kick to William's boot caught her attention, and she looked up at him as he stood before them. He had removed his hat and his coat, leaving his hair blowing about in the circulating air of the car.

He smiled at William. "You ever shot a gun, boy?"

William slumped next to Anna. "No, sir."

A stone of anger boiled in her stomach. Her nails bit into the heels of her hands from her clenched fists.

Anna's eyes narrowed, and she looked up at Dave. "He doesn't want to talk to you."

Dave smiled and crouched down. "Is that true, boy?"

William nodded.

"Well you ain't got nothin' to be afraid of, so long as big sister here does what she's supposed to do. What's your name, kid?"

"William Holloway, sir."

Then his eyes shifted to Jackson. Dave stood taller and broadened his shoulders, his left hand resting onto the handle of his gun. "And you; you're not one of them, are you?"

Jackson stiffened next to her. "No, sir."

"No, you're street smart. You're your own man," he said. "You remind me of myself. You ever shoot a gun?"

Anna was not in the least surprised when Jackson nodded.

"You ever shoot a man?"

Now, she was surprised when he nodded again. "Shot my uncle in the foot with a .22." Jackson's gaze hardened. "He was a lot like you."

The stone in her stomach softened, and she wanted to smile.

Dave grinned, and Anna imagined a tongue flicking between his lips like a pit viper. "Oh, I guarantee there ain't nobody out there like me. Y'all know who I am?"

This time she was going to stop his intimidation. "I know who you are, Diamond Dave. I know the things you've done."

His eyes turned back to her. "Your Uncle John tell you about me?"

"No, sir. I can read."

"Well, then, did he tell you about himself?"

She only bit her lip. In fact, no he had not. She had to learn it the hard way by discovering his stash in the silver mine. This was something she hadn't yet revealed to William, and now the niggle of worry rose into the back of her throat.

"Ol' Johnny Holiday. He and I used to be best friends, you know. Met each other in Tombstone. Hit it right off. He was the best gunslinger I ever did know. Hands were steady like nothin' I ever seen. We knocked over maybe twenty banks together."

"Good for you," Anna said and glanced down to her feet. She clenched her hands together. They wanted to strike him so badly.

"You don't know much about your Uncle Johnny, do you?" he said. "Well, I didn't know much about y'all. Never talked much about his family. I never actually thought he had any. One train robbery and he disappeared on me. I'd been looking for him for years. He'd been gone a long time, and I run into him one day a coupla years ago. He's all drunk and starts tellin' tales of a brother of his. Some smart professor type in Boston. Tells me about something 'amazing' he found. If it were true, it would be the biggest stash we ever seen. He was goin' on about ancient treasures and gold and jewels."

"Then why didn't you just go find it right then?" she asked.

"I wanted to, but the next day he sobered up and wouldn't talk about it anymore. Says he musta been drunk and made the whole thing up. He skedaddled outta town and I ain't seen him after that. Didn't know where he'd run off to. But I knew Johnny better than he thought. I found that brother up in Boston. I got to talkin' to him at that fancy university up there, and that was when I knew that Johnny was not tellin' tales outta school. I tried to make him a deal, and that's what makes you kids smarter than he ever was."

A hole of desperation opened in the center of her chest. It was a great dark pit where she tried to hide her sadness, but now it just gaped open like a mouth with teeth. Tears welled in her eyes; she knew what he was going to say next. It was going to happen no matter how much she willed it to go away.

"Please, stop," she said, the tears rolling down her cheeks.

"No, that man would not accept a deal," he continued like the braggart he was. "I tried to negotiate with him best I could. 'Take me to the treasure or die,' I says. I did the only thing that was left to do. I shot him square in the back while he was running away. And I believe that you kids know better than that. Deals will keep you alive, and we both benefit."

Anna hated him, now more than ever.

Dave placed his hat back on his head, smiled, and then stepped back to his corner of the car. He had done all the damage he had come to do.

William turned to her, his eyes welling in tears. "Is that true? Did he shoot Father?"

Hate was the only thing that she could feel for Dave. Her eyes burned with tears and, as he walked away, she whispered to her brother, "Yes, he did, and I'm going to kill him."

# CHAPTER 28

Anna tried to get William to talk, but he didn't say much after that. And the train travelled for at least another day, stopping only a few times to exchange passengers—everyone, except for them, of course. Even though twilight had fallen, the familiar scent of ocean danced upon the breeze, a scent she recognized from her days living in Boston. They had to be getting close to Rhode Island.

The train whistled as they approached a station, their final destination on this rail.

The locomotive ground to a halt not long after she first detected the Atlantic air. The posse filed out onto the platform, horses and all, as they stepped onto the ground that no longer swayed back and forth. Dave moved them through the station at Newport.

The group rode from the train station and headed east. The map indicated that the marker was on an island, and all islands would be in the ocean to the east.

The docks came into view. Anna wished she could be happy to see the ocean again, but it also meant that they were so far from home. Dave stopped the posse just before the docking stations.

"We'll get ourselves a boat," he said. "The rest of you boys stay here until we get back."

"I'm going with you," Jackson interjected from where he sat on his horse.

"Like hell, you are, boy," Dave said with a laugh. "You will stay here with the rest of 'em, for good luck." He winked at Anna.

She glanced back at Jackson, his hands tight on the reigns of the horse. She knew what he was trying to do, but he needed to stop, or it was bound to get him shot. "It's okay. We'll just go find the second marker and be back soon."

Anna and Dave dismounted, and he approached the docking station where he arranged a small steamer boat to take them to the island. Dave didn't have to pull her inside the boat or force her to stay. His men had William and Jackson. He knew what he was doing when he made them stay behind.

The boat rocked on the sloshing waves that slapped the water-swollen wood. There was only a partial moon, which left the water like thick black oil, stretching out around them. The captain guided them into the dark, and he must have known where to go because the horizon had disappeared. Ocean spray curled over the keel with each slap of the waves. Anna clutched tighter to the journal in her apron pocket for fear of losing it over the edge of the boat should it pitch with the increasing height of the water spray.

A strip of black land dotted with occasional lights in the windows of the few homes residing there appeared in the dark. The steamer slowed, and the lights enlarged as they neared. The captain docked, and Dave left enough coins for the him to wait for them, no matter how long this would take.

They stood on the dock, and Dave lit his lantern. He reached into the coat of his pocket and withdrew the map. The light fell on the lines and symbols drawn across the surface.

"Well, where do we go from here?" he asked and peered into the dark.

She searched the map and the island details. "Looks like maybe the eastern side, a few hundred yards that way," she said. She nodded her head to a worn path that skirted the island just beyond the docks.

Dave stepped from the dock with only his lantern light to guide them in the dark. Waves crashed against rock somewhere in the night around them, and the mist sprayed into the air, dusting her cheeks.

She couldn't help but remember *Treasure Island*. It had been one of her favorite books, and now here she was with a nasty pirate in search of buried treasure. The stone that had settled in her gut lightened a bit as her imagination took off. Anything to get her mind off the fact that Dave held her friend and her brother hostage. What if she couldn't find it? And what if she could, and then the markings didn't make any sense?

A silhouette of black against black rose at the edge of the island, a structure that seemed out of place compared to the few houses that scattered this location. Dave glanced down to the map. That had to be it. Her footsteps slowed, and Dave glanced back to her.

"What is that?" he asked.

She shrugged. "How should I know?"

"You'd better know."

He held up his lantern as they approached.

The gold light fell onto the weathered remains of stone bricks covered in black and green lichen. Like an ancient Greek ruin, the structure loomed upon an isolated patch of grass. In a bygone era, it must have been a great tower, but time and weather had proven themselves to be a formidable force. The closer they got, the larger the tower grew.

A simple two-board picket fence surrounded it. Someone understood that this tower held some significance and hoped to keep out troublemakers. They stopped at the edge of the fence, and the light illuminated more of the tower. The remains of the structure held at least two stories, if not more. Eight columns composed the base level, separated by perfect and evenly spaced archways. Above that level were occasional niche and rectangle openings.

"This has got to be what we're looking for," he said and stepped over the fence.

She glanced around the dark as the lantern light walked away from her. There had to be someone out here who cared that he had climbed over the fence. But she was alone. With Diamond Dave. And nobody came to stop him.

Her shoulders slumped. She lifted the edge of her skirt and climbed over the fence as well. The structure towered over her the closer she got. Her fingers splayed open, and she touched the column. This was where her father once stood, perhaps doing the same thing. Maybe he was right beside her, even if she couldn't see him, and his hand was on hers and reading the stone.

"Come on," Dave's voice startled her.

He slipped through an archway and into the tower. She followed and entered into his little space of lantern light. Her mouth gaped open when she gazed upwards to the inner walls of the tower.

Symbols and hieroglyphs decorated the inner aspect of the archways and to the upper level of the tower.

"Oh yeah, I'd say that we found it," Dave said.

Someone like Dave had no ability to understand how amazing this structure really was. This tower was ancient, more so than anyone living on this island probably realized. She could spend days just standing here and studying the writing on its walls.

"So what does this all mean? What's the next clue?" he said and raised the lantern above his head.

Too many symbols. Hundreds. Maybe thousands. "I don't know."

"Don't tell me that, girl."

"Just give me a moment." She scanned the lower arches. None of them looked at all familiar.

It had to be here. Just one of them. That's all she needed.

Then she saw it. The very thing that brought her father to this place. It was so subtle, so random, that she almost missed it.

The ~~hooked~~ X, carved into a brick blackened with lichen and time.

This was the place her father had called "the Prime Meridian of the Knights Templar." This was the linking place where the Knights would come and get coordinates to any of the other destinations or safe places. Perhaps, even to their treasure. This was their compass.

Her heart pounded against her ribs. She opened the journal and turned toward the light to read it better.

"What is it? You found something, didn't you?" Dave leaned in and looked down at the pages as well.

The pages opened under the golden light, and she ran her finger down to a statement that she had read, but at the time didn't make sense. Now it all came into focus.

"What's it say?"

She read the passage aloud to him. "At this very spot, the monks utilized the architectures such that, given the precise moment, one can interpret, with the solar and lunar alignments, the symbols for the coordinates of various Templar locations."

"So what does that mean?"

"It means that somewhere among all these random symbols is the code for the next location." According to her father, it required the sun and moon to work at the precise moment. When was that moment?

"Okay, so where is it?" Dave asked.

She searched the pages of various codes and symbols, but her father had written nothing about the moment when this would happen. There had to be something. He wouldn't have just left out this most important step. She glanced back up to the carvings in the stone. Then, a glint in the rock caught her eye, something crystalline set in the stone and aimed eastward toward the ocean. But it was too high for her to see well. Bile formed at the back of her mouth when she thought of what she would have to do.

"I need a boost," she said and pointed up to the area where she saw the sparkle.

He cupped his hand, and she placed her boot there. She stood on his hands, her palms steady on his shoulders until she reached a hand-hold in the stone. The smell of whisky and tobacco coming from him almost made her gag, but she focused on the glint in the rock as she pulled herself up.

When she stood high enough, she saw a beveled quartz stone set in a rectangular space within the wall. Polished, it was almost as clear as a window gazing out to the east. She smoothed her fingers over its edges where it blended in with the granite bricks.

"Okay," she said, glancing down at him. He helped her down, his hands a little too grabby around her bottom as she stepped to the ground. She pushed away from him as fast as she could and groaned as he smiled at her.

She looked away from him and back to the symbols on the opposite wall. Anything to get her mind off of him and how awful he really was. The carvings appeared so random, no patterns or repeats at all. But her gaze stopped at one, something she hadn't seen before. And there was nothing random about it. The mark was carved in the exact same location as the crystal but on the opposite side of the tower. The lantern cast shadows across the brick and distorted the image, but it was clear enough.

A carving of a sun, its rays reflecting on water.

Sunrise. Of course. The crystal pointed due east, where the sun would rise. At that precise moment, the answer would be revealed.

"Hmm," she said and put her hands on her hips. "We wait until sunrise."

"What for?"

"Not exactly sure, but that's when we will know what to do next."

"Well, I reckon that's about an hour."

And that hour would be like an eternity, having to share the same space as Dave. He settled down on the ground with his back against the wall, and she sat as far away from him in that circle of light as possible.

Minutes ticked by. What if she was wrong? This marker wasn't as clear as the stone in Kensington. She opened the journal again and scanned the pages and pages of symbols that her father had sketched. Each of them a symbol carved into the tower somewhere. But this time he hadn't provided interpretations like he had with the Kensington stone.

One of the marks caught her attention though. She tilted the book to the side, and a series of symbols now had meaning. They didn't need interpretations because she had seen these particular marks before, in the astronomy exhibit at the museum. Taurus the Bull, Pisces. Cancer. They were all probably here if she searched hard enough.

"It's getting close," Dave's voice stirred her from the pages.

She glanced up to see the first hues of pink and orange stretching across the sky. She rose to her feet and gazed out across the sparkling ocean and pulled the charcoal pencil from the journal's spine. Dave had gone quiet again, ready for anything. Good. She didn't need him talking and distracting her when the sun rose.

The intense yellow brightened on the horizon, and Anna stepped back, glancing up to the crystal facing to the east. The first snatch of light broke over the ocean, and it glinted into the quartz. Anna held her breath and watched it, but there was nothing impressive about it. Crashing waves sounded in loud echoes within the tower, like heralding angels of the coming morning. Ocean spray danced through the open arches, and the light sparkled in the quartz.

The sun inched higher, and just when she let out a disappointed breath, the crystal exploded into an array of light that cast beams across the western wall of the tower.

She turned on her heel to face the wall. For that moment, she forgot about Dave and the quest for buried treasure and everything that had happened in the last few weeks. Her eyes widened with the shimmers of light against the tower's array of symbols. To anyone else, the light would appear random and erratic. But she knew better. There was nothing random here, not if the Templars built this tower.

She opened the book and sketched the symbols illuminated by each beam of light. Never before had she willed the sunrise to slow down, but she did now as the beams began to fade. The marks didn't make sense yet, but she couldn't even remember which one she had sketched as she moved on to the next one. The crystal shimmered one last time, and then the light blinked out as the sun rose higher above the water.

When she had been in school, she had run a race with other girls in a contest to see who was fastest. Her heart beat now just like it had then when she reached the end and realized she had won. No wonder her father had loved his work. That was the most amazing thing she had ever seen, this centuries-old marvel of architecture and light.

"Did you get it?" Dave said and stirred her from her thoughts.

She swallowed down the last of her excitement. "I think so."

"What does it say? What's the clue?" Dave asked.

She glanced down at the page. She had been sketching so fast that she hadn't had time to really look.

Emptiness settled into her gut as she glanced at the symbols.

"It doesn't say anything," she said in disbelief.

*No, that cannot be right. The monks of Gotland would not have created something so incredible to be gibberish.*

"What do you mean?"

"They're not words at all," she said. "They are all astrological symbols. See," she pointed to them in order. "Leo, Pisces, Aquarius, and so forth. They're not words."

"This can't be right." He shoved the book back into her hands. "It must say something."

With his yelling and her frustration, tears welled in her eyes. "I don't know what it means."

She could feel the world crumble around her as he continued to yell. It had to mean something. For her sake and for the sake of her brother and Jackson, it just had to. After all, the Kensington stone had coordinates. But how could astrological symbols be coordinates?

Her eyes drifted back down to the book, the pages open in her hands. Through the tears, she could almost make out her father's inked sketch marks.

Of course. He wouldn't have just left it like this. It had to mean something.

She wiped the tears away and opened to the sketches he had drawn, pages that hadn't made sense before now.

"It's an astrolabe," she blurted out.

He turned, his forehead wrinkled. "A what?"

"An astrolabe. It's a really old navigation tool used by sailors in the Middle Ages. Back then, the Templars—the monks—anybody sailing here would have used an astrolabe. It has a dial and a plate with a bunch of symbols, and each one was unique. They had astrological symbols on them to create the coordinates. There are six symbols here that the light pointed to, three for latitude and three for longitude."

She almost laughed. That is why her father drew the astrolabe. "Where do we find one?"

Oh. This is where things get hard again. She shook her head as the smile faded. "It would be a very specific astrolabe. The journal said they found it in Maine. But I have no idea where it is now. The book doesn't say."

His eyes darkened despite the sunlight. He grabbed her arms, shoved her back against the wall, and she cried out. "No more games. Where do you think it would be?"

The tears flooded her eyes again. "I—I'm not sure. There were a lot at the museum in Boston. Maybe 25 or so. Maybe it's there. But there are hundreds, thousands, in museums around the world. It could be anywhere."

"You had better hope it's in Boston."

She knew what he meant by that. Their hourglasses just started running, and if they were empty before they could find an astrolabe, then that would be the end of them.

# CHAPTER 29

Anna leaned over the edge of the boat despite the spray that hit her face with each wave slapping against the vessel. She didn't usually get seasick, but this morning was different. Ever since Dave threw her into the wall, her stomach wouldn't settle, and the uneven ride back to the mainland made it so much worse.

"Get it all out now," Dave said over the roar of the steam engine. "There won't be time for weeping and wailing once we're back on the trail."

She closed her eyes and took in a deep breath, but the fishy smell that had soaked into the wood of the ship nauseated her more. Or maybe it was the sound of Dave's voice.

The bay came into view, and the boat slowed. The captain pulled it into the main dock and lashed it to the post. Dave stepped out onto the dock and leaned back to give her hand up, but she stepped up around him and marched ahead despite the rocking in her brain that still made her dizzy. The last thing she wanted to do was hold his dirty hand. She didn't need him to lead the way to know where she had to meet up with his posse.

Just as arranged, the group of outlaws waited on the outskirts of town with their own small camp and fire. William sat beside Jackson on a log away from the main group of men, but as soon as he saw her, William jumped to his feet.

Her pace quickened, mostly to get away from Dave, who still walked several feet behind her. William rushed to her as she neared the camp and threw his arms around her waist.

"Everything okay?" he asked.

Jackson stepped up behind him, his hands stuffed in his pockets. He kicked at the dirt with his boot, but Anna still saw the tension in his shoulders and the worry around his eyes.

"Yes," she said. She forced a smiled down to William, but Jackson didn't smile back at her. He was smart enough to know by now when she lied. "We found it."

"And the next clue?" Jackson asked.

The smile on her face slipped. "Yes. We got the next clue."

"And?" he said, his eyebrows raised, but the skeptical tone in his voice made her stomach drop.

"And looks like we're headed for Boston," Dave interrupted.

Anna couldn't look back at him but kept her gaze on Jackson and her arms around William. The way Dave riled up his men, telling them how he found the clues, made her sick. And at some point, she would have to tell Jackson that she had no idea what to do next, even if they made it to Boston.

Dave's men finished saddling the horses, and they were on the trail within the hour. He kept them to the forested trails off the main roads. Not a surprise, especially since the law was probably looking for him after robbing that train. But the way he barked orders this morning made her nervous. Her penny novels had exaggerated his handsomeness and his ability for a quick gun draw, but they failed to describe his mean streak and violent tempers, which now brewed like a thunderstorm on the horizon.

Anna watched Dave from the corner of her eye but brought her horse back alongside Jackson's. He glanced back to the other men that rode behind them, and thankfully, they didn't pay much attention. She motioned to William, who rode beside Jackson, and he sidled his horse closer to them.

Jackson leaned against his saddle and whispered. "Something's up. What's going on?"

Anna glanced back to the men as well and then turned to Jackson. "We need to start coming up with a plan to get away. And soon."

"How do you expect us to do that?" His voice rose, and she shushed him.

"I don't know. But you gotta help me come up with something."

"Why?" William's small voice interjected. "What did you find out there?"

Anna glanced to Dave again. The outlaw had taken his horse several paces ahead. There was no way he could hear them.

"Maybe a dead end," she whispered. "But it's taking us back to Boston. That may be our shot. We know the city. We know how to hide where maybe he can't find us. And maybe we can get a message back to Mother and Uncle John."

"How much time do we have?" William asked.

"I bet we'll be there by tomorrow, so we need to come up with a plan long before we get there," she said.

"Okay," Jackson said, his brown eyes piercing into her. "I'll work on something, but you just gotta keep Dave distracted."

"How am I supposed to do that?" It was so hard to keep her voice low.

"You're the only one that can. He needs you more than he needs us."

That's what worried her the most. She sighed. "Okay. I'll do what I can."

"Hey," he said and placed a hand on her forearm. "We'll get out of this. I promise. You still got the journal?"

Her hand moved to the book in the pocket of her apron. "Yeah. But he still has the map."

"That's okay. Remember, he can't do anything without both of them. We can do this."

She nodded, but the racing of her heart spoke of nerves and anxiety. He released her arm, and she nudged her horse forward again, back to her rightful place in the line behind Dave's horse. The animal trudged along, following blindly within the pack. Its even sway calmed her nerves a little, but her fingers found the pendant at her neck and rubbed the smooth metal surface. If there was ever a time when she needed the most luck possible, this was it. Rubbing the charm for luck was probably just a superstition, but she wasn't about to drop the last ounce of belief she had in it.

Yes, Dave knew where Uncle John lived, and if they escaped and ran back there, he would know where to find them. But they had run out of time and options. They needed to break free of his grasp as soon as possible. Before he realized that there was no astrolabe and no way to find the next clue.

Now, more than ever, she wished she had never gone into that silver mine.

The posse followed the trail that meandered through thicker and thicker woods. Frogs croaked from a nearby river that gurgled somewhere beyond the brush. Pollen from flowering trees drifted like fairies across the path, sometimes catching in her hair. The heavy perfume from the flowering trees following the wisps of pollen hung in the air and reminded her of verbena and lilacs.

The day had grown hot and still, and even though the mid-afternoon sun burned brightly, the leafy canopy overhead wouldn't allow the light to penetrate to the trail. Dave still rode ahead of her and around the bend of the trail as it curved along the edge of the river, the banks getting ever closer to their path. On the opposite border of the trail, the trees sprinkled over a hill that sloped into the darker underbrush.

Through that dark, a bright flash of silver winked into her eye. She squinted against the sudden burst of light that had come out of nowhere. She held up her hand to the light and glanced into the underbrush. Sunlight must have caught the edge of a spur or a saddle button, but it wasn't possible, not with Dave so far ahead of her. It still flickered in her eyes, and she squinted toward the darkened hillside where only slips of sunlight fell through the trees. She searched the brush as the light still glinted at her.

For only a second, the flicker darkened and her eyes focused into the dark of the shrubbery. In the shadows of the trees, a figure crouched under the brush. His familiar brown eyes gazed out at her from under a hat. Ruddy brown hair shone under the hat and brushed the collar of his long duster coat. Uncle John lowered the edge of his gun, the handle with the bright silver plating that had caught the sun and reflected into her eyes.

She wanted to jump off that horse and run to him. He must have seen it too because he placed a finger to his lips to keep her quiet. Anna couldn't stop the little creep of a grin that started on her lips, and she gave him a brief nod.

He did it. He had followed every clue she left for him. And now he had come to save them.

Her fingers clenched around the reins, and she let out a steady breath. She glanced back to William and Jackson, who had no idea what was going on. William looked up at her, and she shot a deliberate glance to the trees. At first, he just squinched his eyes and nose, confused. And then the lines smoothed and his eyes brightened. Even Jackson saw it, though he didn't know who crouched in the dark.

She turned back around, her veins pulsing hard and fast. A real ambush, not the embellished versions she once read about in her penny novels. It was about to happen. She bit her lip and glanced back to the brush, but the dark was empty. John had vanished somewhere in the shadows. Oh, please don't go.

Whatever was about to happen, she just had to run for it. Grab William and run.

The beat of her heart pounded so loud in her ears that someone must have heard it. Dave turned in his saddle and looked back at her. Did he suspect something?

"Hey, keep that horse up here," he said.

Her ride had drifted back. The mare must have seen Uncle John, her ears perked and her eyes wandering into the trees. She had slowed down enough that it brought too much distance between her and Dave's horse. Anna nudged the mare and pulled her head to look down the trail. The mare quickened her pace and closed the distance between herself and the lead horse.

Maybe Dave didn't suspect a thing.

Anna's eyes shifted back into the darkened hillside, and a subtle movement caught her attention. Dull gray metal protruded through the brush at the top of the hill. Double barrels of a shotgun.

*Oh, Jesus, Mary and Joseph.* Her hands clutched the reins tight. The blast would likely scare the tar out of the horses. Every single one of them. Her tongue dried up, and she licked her lip.

A click sounded ahead of her and Dave's horse tripped on a rock. It stumbled forward, and Dave lurched just a little onto the mare's neck at the moment the gunshot rang out. The shot struck the top of his hat, right where the center of his head had been only a half second prior.

The sound of the shot ricocheted through the canyon, and the horses all jumped in unanimous fright. Dave's horse reared back, throwing him to the ground. Anna's mare skittered sideways, but she clenched her thighs around its belly and pulled the reins to control it. She veered the horse around to see Jackson and William, their animals both scrambling around the trail.

"Go now! Run!" she shouted to them. "Back down the trail!"

Jackson immediately turned his horse and kicked it into a full run. William did the same, his small legs wrapping tight into the stirrups. Another shot rang out from the trees, and one of Dave's men fell back off his horse. Jackson charged his horse in a gallop around the men and back down the trail. He glanced back once, satisfied that William was close behind him. The other three men reached for their guns and tried to control their horses at the same time, each animal jumping and screeching at the sound of the second shot.

The trail was clear, at least for this second as the posse and their horses scrambled in confusion. She raised her heel, ready to drop it into the mare's flank. A hand grabbed her foot and pulled with such force that she couldn't grasp the saddle horn. She fell to the ground, and her horse skittered to the side, pulling the reins free from her hands. The impact of the hard earth against her back knocked the wind from her lungs, and then the grip on her foot moved to her leg.

Adrenaline pounded in her veins. She pushed herself up to her elbows and scrambled back from him. His hat had fallen into the wind with the gunshot, and it left his blonde hair to fall wildly over his eyes. He still had one hand on her leg and yanked her toward him, but he also had his other hand on the reins of his horse, trying to keep control of the animal in the fray.

He was desperate and raging. There was no way he could keep both her and the animal under his control, not under these circumstances. His horse yanked against its restraints again. This was it. There might not be another opportunity before he had a better hold of them both. She pulled back her free leg and kicked out toward him. Her boot struck him in the chest. She pulled back quick and landed another powerful kick to his face. His grip on her leg loosened for only a second. That was all she needed.

She scrambled to her feet and doubled back. Dave lay on the ground, grasping at his bleeding nose with the horse fighting against his grip. She yanked the reins from his hand and jumped onto the stirrup as the animal stamped sideways. She pulled herself onto the saddle and kicked the horse into a full gallop. Dave shouted at her, his hand skimming her boot again just as the horse took off.

A shot rang out behind her, a different sound than the shotgun from the trees. The sound of it whistled past her ear, leaving a wake of hot air that brushed her cheek. She held her breath in that second. That was a pistol shot. And it had been aimed in her direction. That diamond-studded pistol had five more shots. Dave wouldn't miss again.

She prodded her heel harder into the horse's flank. The animal bounded down the trail. Another shotgun blast echoed through the canyon, and a volley of gunfire erupted behind her. Any of those shots could be directed her way. *Can't look back. Can't slow down.*

The hoofbeats underneath her pounded in a cadence that kept her focused. The mare's heart thrummed just under her body, the animal probably terrified of the gunshots behind them. She crouched low in the saddle, keeping her spine down and her head almost against the animal's neck. The hooves hit the dirt in rapid succession. *Have to focus on that, not the gunshots.*

Another set of hoofbeats offset against the sound of her own horse. The mare's ears perked, aware that something else moved just beyond the brush outside of the trail. They're coming. Faster than her own horse. She pressed her feet into the stirrups and squeezed her knees into the horse's side.

A shadow moved in her peripheral vision, just beyond the edge of the brush. The mare shied to the side of the trail and away from something that emerged into the sunlight. The rider kept stride with her, his long buckskin duster flying behind him like a cape. Shotgun in hand, Uncle John rode beside her.

Another pistol shot rang out and whistled between them. John glanced back, but Anna kept her gaze forward and her stance low and even with the horse. She didn't dare look back there. She would lose her balance, and then it would all be over.

"Keep going," John shouted out to her, and then he pulled his horse back and spun around.

The shotgun blasted from behind her. She gripped the reins closer to the horse's neck, and the animal bounded up a gentle slope and around a curve in the trail. Only the single sound of her horse's hoofbeats sounded in her ears now. John was still back there, the sound of his shotgun still echoing through the gulch. The mare breathed hard, but she kept going, pounding down the trail.

Everything in the forest had gone silent since the last shot from Uncle John's gun. At least several seconds had passed and nothing. The horse panted hard, the edges of its mouth foaming, but it kept going at its frantic pace. She loosened her knees and pulled back on the reins, gentle and steady. But the animal didn't respond.

"Whoa!" She called out to the mare again and pulled the reins even harder, but it jerked its head and almost ran off the trail.

A spooked horse is a deadly horse. That's what Maria once said to her. And this horse was unreasonable and erratic. If Dave didn't kill her, this horse might just do the job now.

*Please, oh please. Just stop.*

She clenched her teeth and pulled back on the reins again.

*Don't let me die like this.*

A movement to her right made the horse skitter to the side. It was so quick, at first, she wasn't sure what happened. The heat of another horse galloped beside her, and Uncle John's gloved hand grabbed her horse's rein. The two animals ran together for a moment, and then John slowed his horse. Her mare slowed with it.

"Hey, easy now," he said, his voice steady and calm.

The mare came in step with John's horse, and they both slowed to a trot. He pulled them both off the trail and onto a clearing over the hill. The horse's ribs flared and shrank so quickly that Anna thought it might collapse in the grass. She released her grip on the rein that John held and clutched her shaking fingers around the saddle horn. The animal slowed to a walk and sauntered over the edge of the hill. Its ears perked when it saw two other horses and their riders waiting at the top.

Jackson, atop this horse, held the reins of William's horse, keeping them calm and centered in the clearing. Her horse slowed to a stop beside them, and John and the boys dismounted. Her knees trembled, and she moved to step down from her horse, but her legs wouldn't hold her upright. She stumbled back, and Jackson rushed to her, catching her before she fell into the grass.

"I got you," he said. He pulled her to her feet.

She turned around and stepped away from him, her whole body shaking now. There was no stopping what came next, no matter how hard she tried. Tears burned in her eyes, and she gasped for breath. Her throat tightened, and the sobs erupted from her throat. Everything that she had held in since the day she discovered the silver mine came out in hot tears and clenched teeth. It wracked her body, and her spine shook with the water that poured from her eyes.

Jackson stepped closer to her, and she held a hand out to push him away. It caught his chest, and he brushed it aside, pulling her into him.

There was no point hiding it. He had finally seen her break down. She buried her face in his neck and wrapped her arms around him.

"You okay?" Uncle John said.

"No!" she said and lifted her head from Jackson's shoulder. "I'm not okay." She stepped back from Jackson, sniffed and wiped her fingers across her cheeks. "None of this is okay."

William rushed to her side and wrapped his arms around her. She placed a hand on his back.

"I meant, are you hurt?" John said, his voice calm and low.

She sniffed again. "I know what you meant. I think I'm okay." Her breathing came out in shaking catches, and she fought to slow it down. "I'm sorry I yelled at you."

John smiled from under his hat. "It's all right." He glanced back down the trail. "It won't take long for Dave to pick himself up out of the dirt and come after us. That is, after he stops bleeding. I think you broke his nose with that kick you planted on him." He flashed her a grin.

She couldn't help but smile when she thought of her boot heel landing against his face.

"Let's get you all back home," John said. He shifted his horse around and then his steely gaze landed on Jackson. "I don't believe we've met."

Jackson stood straighter and grasped his fingers behind him. His face had gone pale as John fixed him with his stare. "Jackson T. Belford, sir."

"He's with us," Anna said as John stepped toward him. Jackson swallowed and shifted his stance, ready to step back from him.

"Is he now?" John said. His voice changed, firm and low.

"Yes, he is. Jackson, this is my Uncle John," Anna said and stepped in front of John. "Jackson helped us out in Kansas City. He was living at Kate's."

John stopped, and the hard lines around his eyes softened. His mouth curved into an instant grin. "One of Kate's boys. Well, hell, why didn't you say so?" He turned away and mounted his horse. "All right, mount up. Time to head home. You coming with us, Jackson?"

"Yes, sir," Jackson said. Anna turned around to face him and saw the grin that had formed on his face. "I got nowhere else to go."

She smiled, and the flitters of butterflies started in her chest. She turned away from him and approached the mare. The animal had calmed enough to control her breathing, but the slick of sweat on her body would take a while to dry. She handled the reins and readied to put her foot in the stirrup when her eyes fell on the saddle bag. The silver button latch lifted easily, and she found the edges of the map inside.

They had everything they needed now. The journal. The map.

That should have been enough to make her happy. But she knew better.

"We can't go back home, not yet." She turned around to face Uncle John, who turned his horse around to face her. The boys stopped their horses as well, and they all looked down on her.

"Anna," John said with a sigh. "No more of this. Your mother is worried sick."

"I know, but if we go now, he'll come back for us. We'll always wonder when he'll come back. But I know where he's going right now."

"That's right," William said. "He was headed to Boston."

John shot a glance to each of them. "How is this a good thing?"

"Because if I know exactly where he's going to be, then I can notify the Boston sheriff. They can stop him for good. Put him in jail where he belongs."

John sat on his horse, his face shaded by the brim of his hat. She couldn't tell if he was considering her strategy or getting ready to haul them all home.

He removed his hat and dusted off the edge as he turned his face toward the sun. He shook his head. *Oh, no. He was going to force them all back to New Mexico.*

"This is crazy," he said and looked back down at her. "But it's a good idea. If we do this, you kids have to listen to me. Do what I say when I say it. Understood?"

Her stomach did somersaults. This was really going to happen. "Yes, sir."

"But I gotta stay low too. Otherwise, the sheriff will be hauling me in just the same as Dave." He said and shot a glance to each of them. Anna gave a half smile. "I know exactly where we can hide."

# CHAPTER 30

Storm clouds had collected over the harbor as evening approached. The Boston skyline came into view, with its hundreds of lights sparkling on the water's edge. From where they looked upon it at the fringe of the city, the place was beautiful despite the occasional flashes of lightning on the horizon. Anything better than the last few nights sleeping under the sky on a hard ground and no campfire.

"There it is," Anna said as her horse shuffled under her. John gazed out over the city with her.

"Looks a bit crowded," he said.

"It'll be all right." She nudged the horse and took over lead as the front rider. This was no longer Uncle John's wild west. Boston was her town, and she knew it well.

By nightfall, the rain had descended as they wound their way through the cobblestone streets. John kept the collar of his coat up and the brim of his hat low, but nobody bothered to look up at them. Gas lamps lit the streets, guiding their way down familiar roads among houses with iron fences and eaves that towered high above the paths. She guided her horse down the road until they approached a home with dark windows that rose high above the leafy trees that surrounded the property.

She led them around through the back gate and to the servant's entrance by the carriage house. The horse stopped, and she dismounted to gaze up to the third-floor windows that looked out to the harbor.

Jackson stepped up next to her. "This was your house?" he said over the downpour of rain that soaked them.

"My home."

"Wow." His hand shielded his eyes from the rain as he followed her gaze to the top. "I've never seen such a big house."

"Come on," she said and jumped over a puddle toward the back porch. She stood on her tip-toes and reached up to the upper door frame. If everything was as they had left it, the key should still be here. Her fingers found the cold iron, and she pulled it free. The door unlocked with ease and they stepped inside.

Rain pattered against the windows, but everything inside was dry if not a bit cool. Then the smell hit her nose, the same closed-up dampness that she remembered from deep inside the silver mine. Stagnant and heavy.

The porch opened into the kitchen. Except for the dim light through the windows, everything was dark and still. Their things were in their places as if just waiting for the family to return from holiday. Copper-bottomed pots and iron skillets hung from a rack in the center island of the kitchen. Barrels of flour, rice and wheat waited at the far corner of the kitchen next to the empty hearth.

William stepped beside her. "Looks just like we left yesterday."

John stepped inside, the water from his coat pooling at his feet on the stone floor.

She pulled her coat off and called out to all of them. "You can hang your things in the porch. It'll dry so much better there."

John drew off his duster and hung his hat on a hook, but then he just gazed out at everything around him as though he stood in awe of what he saw and didn't dare touch a thing. He took deliberate and careful steps through the kitchen. His eyes had gone wide, examining the windows and shelves.

Anna stepped up beside him and led him into the parlor. Furniture covered in white linens stood sentry throughout the room and, in the gaslight that shone through the windows, appeared like ghosts standing still against the walls. John stopped, his eyes wandering to the grand stairway with its dark oak banisters that rose to the second floor.

"Everything okay?" she whispered to him.

"Not sure," he said and approached the first step.

"That goes to the bedrooms and father's study on the third floor."

The lines around his mouth softened, and his eyes glistened in the faint light. "I never came to see him here."

He paused, and Anna wasn't sure if she should say something.

"He lived here, had a family. I had a niece and a nephew. And I never came to see my brother."

"It's okay," she said. "I think he understood—"

"No, it's not okay. I left everyone behind, including him." He turned toward her, and his voice dropped even lower. "I'll do right by him. I will."

He blinked his eyes quickly and turned away from her.

She cleared the lump that had formed in her throat and looked out across the room. William had already pulled a sheet from the lounger.

"Okay, make yourselves comfortable. I'll head out and find a constable and be right back."

"You're not going out there alone," John said.

"I'll be okay," she said and straightened her shoulders. "There's always a policeman at the harbor. I'll just tell him that Dave is planning on breaking into the museum and be back in about twenty minutes."

"I'll go with you," Jackson said and stepped around John.

"Like hell, you will. The two of you together without a chaperone? Your mother would kill me."

Anna tilted her head and grinned. "We haven't had a chaperone for long time now. I think we will be just fine."

John's eyebrow rose and shot her a pointed look.

"Not that I would ever speak of these things with you anyway, but nothing happened. I'm just saying that you don't have anything to worry about."

He slipped his thumbs into his belt buckle and shifted his weight. "Fine. Just be careful and get back here as soon as possible."

"We will."

Anna turned, and Jackson stayed close as they left through the back porch, their wet coats back on. Thunder cracked overhead as they stepped out into the rain. She could have done this just fine without anyone following her, but with the storm outside, it was nice to have Jackson there.

"Is your uncle really Johnny Holiday?" he finally said as they crossed the street and headed for the harbor.

She laughed. "Yeah. I think he is."

"A real-life outlaw!"

"Diamond Dave is a real-life outlaw, and he's not that impressive."

"I know, but at least your uncle's nice."

"I guess he is," she said. In fact, he had been so great the whole time, and she hadn't even recognized it. He really did take care of his brother's family, just like the telegram he had sent to the house said he would. This whole time, he had watched out for them. He knew Dave was a threat to them, and he had tried to keep them safe. And he would have if she hadn't found the silver mine.

Just as she had suspected, a policeman patrolled the docks. She and Jackson relayed a tale of a suspicious man that would likely try to break into the museum. Though he looked at them with skepticism, he said he would investigate.

And that was it. She had done what she came here to do. She and Jackson hurried back to the house, but she checked the dark and rainy streets behind them as they went. The house wouldn't be a good hiding place if the policeman—or anyone else—followed them home.

By the time they had returned, John and William had removed the rest of the sheets and then sat down to a dinner of dried fruits and jerky from John's saddle packs. Not long after they had all settled down to eat, William laid down on his side and rested his head on Anna's lap.

"Don't you be falling asleep there," John said over the yellow glow of his lantern. "Not when there are perfectly good beds upstairs."

"Okay," William said and yawned. He pulled himself to his feet.

"I'll come with you," Anna said and stood with him. John handed the lantern to her, and they wandered up the stairs.

Though William shuffled up the stairs, he went straight to his old bedroom as soon as he got to the upper landing. A white sheet covered his bed, just like everything else. She yanked it free to find the blankets still intact.

He moved to climb onto the bed, but she placed a hand on his shoulder.

"Not with those wet socks."

He groaned and pulled off his socks.

"And your trousers. Just get down to your underthings."

"Fine," he fussed and pulled his shirt off. Finally, he was down to his underwear and crawled under the covers.

She collected his damp clothes. If she could get them hanging over the bannister, they might dry out by morning. She turned to leave the room, but William's voice stopped her.

"Are we really heading out to New Mexico tomorrow?"

"Sure are."

He yawned. "Good. This doesn't feel like our home anymore. I thought I missed it, but I don't."

She smiled. "Me too."

William rolled to his side, and it only took a few seconds before his breathing slowed. She pulled the door closed with a soft click. With the damp clothes draped over the bannister, she started for the stairs again, but she stopped at the landing and gazed up the second stairway to the study. The landing was so dark, and only shadows, twisted by the occasional flash of lightning, crawled around up there. That was the last place she visited before they had moved away from here for good.

Just one last look. The very last one.

She raised the lantern and padded up the stairs. The heavy wooden door opened with ease, and she stepped inside. Like the rest of the house, it smelled like it had been closed up for far too long. But it also held the heavy scent of books, like a vast library. The mahogany desk, also covered in a white sheet, sat vacant across the room. The faintest tang of India ink danced in the air. Thick red velvet drapes covered the windows, allowing very little outside light into the room.

The lantern light illuminated her way around the overstuffed chair and cast a gloomy shadow into the fireplace that faced the desk from across the room. She grasped the sheet and pulled it from the desk. There were far too many of these things all over the house. It made the whole place look like a funeral home, and she wouldn't have her father's study remind her of death.

She set the lantern down on the desk and settled into the chair where her father had spent so many working hours. The leather creaked under her body. She had never sat here before, and it felt like blasphemy. But she leaned back, her head resting against the back of the chair. From here, she remembered the crackling of the fire in the hearth as she had played at the foot of the desk when she was little. And from this seat, his large portrait looked down on her from above the barren fireplace.

His eyes watched her with a kind of knowing and playful gaze where he sat, his right arm outstretched on the arm of the chair and his other hand grasping the lapel of his black jacket. Forever lost within the oil paint that adorned the canvas.

The latch of the door clicked and startled her gaze away from the painting. Uncle John filled the doorway, his head without a hat and his hair mussed. His brown suspender contrasted with his brick-red shirt, sleeves rolled up to his elbows.

"Everything okay?" he said. "You were gone a while. I searched the whole house for you."

"It's fine. Just needed to be in here."

He entered the room, and his eyes turned up to the painting. "It's a good likeness. He was always a little arrogant about his hair. I guess he shoulda been. Ladies always liked him."

The way he stood there, looking up at the painting, was uncanny. It was as though her father was in the room with her—except for the suspenders and dirty brown trousers, which her father never would have worn; he looked just like him.

"I never knew he had this done," he said as he stared at the painting.

She looked up at her father's face again. They were brothers, but they almost could have been twins. The faintest hint of a smile on her father's face was so similar to the look Uncle John sometimes had. The similarities even went down to their hands, captured in the picture where her father's hand lay gently open.

"I hadn't seen him in so long," John spoke, his voice dropping. "I never got along well with our parents. It was never a surprise that I found Dave—or he found me. That's why we never spoke. Who wants a bank robber for a brother?"

He turned to her, his hands resting on his hips. "It was the Bulwark train job that did it. We got the biggest load we had ever seen, and I got a bullet. One inch to the left and I would have lost my life. That was it. I told Dave I was done, and I couldn't believe he was okay with it. Thought maybe he got a little spooked too. We both had close calls with that train job."

"Was it just the bullet that changed your perspective?" she asked.

"Not at all. I didn't need all that money, but I wanted to finally be respectable. Laid low for a little while, then bought a farm in New Mexico. Worked it myself for a while. Then some Mexicans needed some work, and there you go. Had a fully functioning farm and I was an employer. I had people depending on me. It took a few years, but I was finally happy with what I'd done except for one thing."

"Your family," Anna said as she stared at her father's picture.

"Yes. I wanted to reconcile with my family. I found my brother here in Boston, but I was afraid of what he might think, coming back after all these years, but he was there for me. Welcomed me back with open arms. I hung around for a few weeks, and he started telling me about this great project he was working on. He went on and on about Templars and the treasure. I was happy for him. He was doing great things."

"Then why didn't you stay with him? With us? You could have stopped this."

He hung his head, the shadows creeping across his eyes. "I tried to see our parents, and everything went wrong. They hated what I'd done with my past. Maybe they were embarrassed. Said they never wanted to see me again and shut me out of their lives. I was a mess. I thought they could forgive me, but it'd never happen. I went back to drinkin' that night. That was the last time I had a drink, but it was the worst time to do it."

"That's when Dave found you," Anna said. She remembered all too well the story Dave had told her.

John looked up at her. Tears sparkled in his eyes. "It was my fault what happened to Thomas. If I hadn't said anything that night, Dave would never have gone after him."

It was true, she thought. John had tipped Dave off about her father's work. If that one night had never happened, he would still be alive, and they would still be a family.

He turned to face the painting. "I wish I could take it all back. I wish I had never come back to see him." He wiped the tears from his eyes, and he laughed a bit. "It was just like him, though, to get this thing painted. He always was the one wanting attention, sitting there in his fancy suit and that . . . weird thing in his hand."

Weird thing? Her eyes moved to her father's open hand, a thing she had seen hundreds of times, but never before like this. She stood from the chair, taking the lantern in her hand, and walked around the desk. The painting loomed closer as she examined his hand under the light.

Within the space of his outstretched fingers was a faint sphere of blue light. The sphere fit within the palm of his hand and held a series of small decorations. She moved closer to the painting, and her eyes widened at what she saw.

"I can't believe it," she muttered to herself as she withdrew the journal from her apron. She had seen those marks just the other night. The light fell on the yellowed page where she had left off and found the identical marks as the object in the hand of the painting.

Every one of them was an astrological symbol, the same marks she had scrawled into the journal from that morning in the tower in Rhode Island. And they were in the same order as she had written them, the same order that they had illuminated during sunrise.

"What is it?" John asked and peered over her shoulder to the book.

"The painting. It's not just some portrait. It's a marker. A clue."

"You see that?" she said and pointed up at the painting. John followed her gaze and furrows formed in his forehead. "Look at the way he's holding his hand. It's not natural. It's almost like he's pointing at something."

With the lantern held up, she stepped up to the painting and then traced her gaze along an invisible tangent. She stepped along the fireplace, her boots tapping on the hardwood floor with each step. The bookshelves had remained undisturbed as had the tea table along the wall. Was this where he pointed? She approached the shelves, the spines of all the books now in clearer view.

Another step forward and a floorboard creaked and shifted under her foot.

She held her breath and gazed down at the board. Its edges had worn differently than its neighbors. She rolled the ball of her foot over it, and it creaked again.

Would her father really have kept such a secret hidden in their house?

She dropped to her knees and set the lantern down. Uncle John moved to her side and knelt down beside her.

"What's going on?" he said.

"The floorboard. I think there's something underneath it."

Her fingers worked at the edges, but couldn't find a place to lift.

"Wait a second. I've got it," he said and withdrew a knife from his belt. He wedged the tip at the edge of the board and pried it up until it popped free.

Blood raced into her head until it made her dizzy. She gripped the board and slid it away, revealing a definite space under the floor. The lantern light made the shadows dance in the cavity, and she gazed at it until she had her breathing under better control. It wouldn't do her any good to hyperventilate with excitement now.

She bit her lip and reached into the dark space. Please don't let there be spiders. She closed her eyes as her fingers searched into the cavity. Her arm craned down to the elbow until the tips of her fingers found a solid object wrapped in some sort of cloth, carefully concealed within the hollow under the floor.

Anna pulled it out into the light and set it on the floor. Wrapped in burlap, it fit in the palm of her hand but still carried a distinct heft to it. Her gaze flashed up to John, and now his eyes had grown wide. With shaking fingers, she opened the burlap, and the lantern light shone on the brightest brass she had ever seen. Symbols etched in dark oil decorated the dials.

An astrolabe.

An astrolabe with the same astronomical symbols she had found at the Newport tower.

It wasn't hidden away in some dusty old museum. It was right here.

"Oh my gosh," she said.

"What is it?"

"I'll show you. Find that map."

He scrambled out of the room and downstairs as she set to work dialing in the astrological symbols into the astrolabe. She wrote down the corresponding numbers that the device interpreted for her. John returned and spread the map across on the floor. He watched quietly as she dialed the tool and wrote down what she saw.

"This device is a navigation tool. But this particular astrolabe is also a decoder. It was designed that way as a tool to guide someone to the treasure."

She moved to the map and plotted out the coordinates. Using the spine of the book she traced straight lines down the map. Then she sat back on her heels and looked down to the intersection of lines.

John cocked his head to the side and looked at the map.

"That's where the coordinates lead," she said and pointed at the intersection of the lines.

He scanned the lines. "That's Oak Island. In Nova Scotia. It's probably a day's sail from here."

"I thought we were going home," William's voice spoke out from the door.

Anna's heart almost pounded out of her chest. She had been so involved in the map that she had forgotten how loud they had become. He padded over to her and knelt down between her and John.

"I don't want to go anywhere else, especially not Oak Island," he said and rubbed at his eyes.

"Don't worry. We're all going home tomorrow."

"What is that thing?" another voice came from the doorway to see Jackson standing there, his hands in his pockets. The whole house had now stirred because of her discovery. "That's the thing Dave wants, isn't it?"

She nodded. "But he doesn't know it's here. And it's going to stay that way."

A crease formed between his eyebrows. "We need to get out of here."

"Before sunrise," John said and shot a glance to him as well. Anna wrapped the astrolabe back in the burlap when he leaned closer to her. "When we get home, I think it might be a good idea to destroy all of these things."

# CHAPTER 31

**B**efore daylight peeked through the windows, Anna was up. Sleep didn't touch her well last night, not with nightmares of Dave hiding in the shadows and a bullet whistling past her ear. John was up and packing their few things. With Jackson's help, they had the horses brushed and saddled. Then, they all worked at closing up the house again, hoping to leave it the way they had found it.

Anna sealed up the board in the study floor and covered the desk with the linen "shroud" sheet. This could possibly be the last time she would ever see this room again, and she watched the portrait for a few minutes. He would never talk to her. He would never move. But he had passed on the last secret he had in this room. She tore her eyes away from the painting and closed up the room with a heavy click of the door latch.

She moved down the stairs to find Jackson covering the rest of the furniture with the discarded sheets. Uncle John passed a pack of dried fruit and jerky to William.

"Get these on the saddles," he told him. William nodded and gathered the packs. He hurried out the back porch to the carriage house where the horses had spent the night.

She descended to the last step when John turned toward her and tossed the water bladders into her arms.

"Fill those," he said and worked on the final leather pack of their belongings.

She carried them into the kitchen and placed them under the pump. She cranked the handle, and a rush of water poured into the sink. It ran a ruddy brown at first and then cleared. The pump hadn't run in a while, so it wasn't much of a surprise that it argued with her for a moment. She filled the bladders and then tied them with burlap string.

John hefted his pack onto the cutting block in the center of the kitchen. Anna added the water bladders when Jackson entered the room, his pack slung over his shoulder.

He scanned the room while John pulled his coat on and situated the hat on his head.

"Where's William?" Jackson asked

Anna peered around Uncle John to the porch door. He should have been done with the saddle packs by now. Typical. Just when they needed his help to carry the rest of his stuff, he decided to go out and play.

"I'll go get him," she said with an exasperated sigh.

She grabbed her coat as she walked out the back door and trudged across the stone way to the carriage house.

"William," she called out to him as she opened the side door of the carriage house. "Get back into the house. We don't have time for this."

She stepped inside, and the smell of sweet hay lilted through the open doorway. The horses shifted in their stalls as she approached. Her eyes adjusted to the dark of the house enough for her to see into the stalls.

"William?"

The horses watched her as she gazed between them. He hadn't even bothered to tie the packs to the saddles yet. She clenched her teeth, her mind swirling with all the angry words she would point at him when she found him. Not in the stalls. Not in the main room. Maybe the tack room. She stepped to the end of the house and pulled open the door to the tack room, but it stood dark and otherwise empty.

Her jaw loosened and a quiver of nerves jangled in her stomach. It wasn't like William to keep up a game of hide and seek like this. One of the horses snorted with a loud huff, and she jumped. *Cursed creature. Why did it have to do that now?*

She marched back to the end of the house and yanked open the side access door. The click of metal on metal made her halt, and her spine went stiff. The silver barrel of a pistol pointed at her head, and one of Dave's men stood just on the other side of the doorway.

"Well, well. Dave said you'd be here," the man spoke, his dirty yellow teeth evident even in the poor light. He held his gun steady and aimed it right at her. "He done broke into this place once, told me right where it was."

Another click of a pistol hammer echoed in the space, but it didn't come from the man's gun. He froze, and his eyes grew wide. The gun twitched in his hand as he shifted his gaze to the left. John moved around from behind him, his pistol pointed at the man's head

"Hold up there, John," the man said. "I'm not here to hurt no one. I'm just deliverin' a message." He held his hands up, the gun dangling from his index finger.

"You better start talkin' then," John said and aimed the gun between the man's eyes as he eyed him with a piercing glare.

The man smiled. "Dave says if I don't come back alive, then he's gonna kill the boy."

The gun in John's hand remained as steady as ever.

"And he says to meet him at Oak Island tomorrow at dusk," the man continued.

"How does he know about that?" Anna said and stepped closer to John.

"Little boys talk a lot when they scared," he said and winked at her.

He glanced back to John. "So I suggest y'all get ready for a sea voyage. We'll be seeing ya' tomorrow."

With that, the man lowered his weapon and backed out of the carriage house, each step careful. There was nothing that Uncle John could do. Dave had found them. They thought they were being so clever, coming home like they did. But Dave had always known where they lived. The house had been broken into a month or so before they had moved. The police had never found the suspects, and that's when Mother had decided it was time to move on.

Dave was the suspect all along. He had come here, probably looking for the journal and the map when father hadn't given them to him.

And now he had William.

The man slipped out the door as desperate rage rose in her chest. He was just getting away, and Uncle John allowed it to happen. She rushed out the door after him, but her vision blurred with tears.

"Where's my brother?" she shouted in between choked sobs.

But John caught her, his thick arms wrapped around her, and despite her pounding at him with her angry fists, he held her back as the man stepped away with a smile. Soon, he was gone, and she was left to cry at the door of the carriage house.

When she stopped fighting him, John released her. She stumbled to the wall and slumped down to the ground, crying. He placed a hand on her shoulder, but she batted him away.

They were supposed to be going home. That was how it was going to be, but things had changed, and now she was drawn into this horrible treasure hunt once more. She had to face Dave again, too. What she wanted more than anything right now was to just go home, eat some of Maria's wonderful tortillas and sleep in her own bed with her mother caressing her hair and singing her to sleep. But they were so far from any of that now. She would do anything to get her brother back, and Dave knew it. There was no other alternative. They would be off to Oak Island by morning. And what they would find there could be the greatest mystery of all.

With the back of her hands, she wiped away her tears, cleared her throat and stood. She took in a deep breath.

"Looks like we need to find ourselves a ship to take us to Oak Island," she said to John and marched past him into the house.


The early morning air over the water carried cold mist that crawled through every layer of clothing Anna had put on. She sat on the bench along the bow of the little steamboat, gazing out over the dark waters as they left Boston harbor on the way to Nova Scotia.

Jackson settled down next to her and hugged his coat around his chest. The cold spray off the ocean must have chilled him as well.

"Are you okay?" he asked.

"Not really. I wish everyone would stop asking me that."

He looked out toward the coming dawn that left glowing orange sparkles on the ocean ahead of them. "It's because we all care."

"I've kept him safe this whole time," she said and rubbed at her sore eyes again. "And he leaves my sight for a few minutes. That's all it took."

"It wasn't your fault."

"Oh really? None of this would have happened if I hadn't walked into that silver mine."

"If you hadn't done that, I wouldn't be here. I would never have run into you two, and I would still be stuck in Kansas City."

She looked at him as he watched the horizon. "I wish it didn't take such a drastic measure for that to happen."

"But it did, and here we are, and we'll find him."

"I hope you're right."

"I'm never wrong." He glanced at her with a wink. "Now, when we get to Oak Island, what's next on the map?"

She withdrew the journal from her apron and opened it into the growing morning light. The spine felt more tattered than it had since she had first discovered it. She flipped beyond the pages of her scrawled astrological symbols. This was awfully close the end, and it was a brief notation. She flipped past it, and the remainder of the pages were blank. This was the last of her father's entries, the final notation regarding the treasure.

"The last one?" Jackson said, his eyebrows raised. "Better be a good one."

She read the entry aloud to him. "A remarkable lock, and only I know the whereabouts of the key. I have only come as far as this door, but I dare not tread further, for beyond this gate lies the spoils of a hundred wars waged upon holy ground. Here lies the relics removed from ancient lands, or perhaps here lies damnation."

"That's it?" he asked.

She nodded. "Nothing else."

"That doesn't tell us very much."

"It says he found the treasure's location."

He tilted his head. "But he never actually saw it."

True. What if they actually found the location and it was empty? With Dave standing there, guns in hand and William in his grasp. That would be the end.

"I can't worry about that right now. We just need to get William and get out of there."

She glanced down the length of the boat to where Uncle John sat near the keel, arms folded across his chest and his hat over his eyes. At least he was with them this time. He was her only chess piece left in this game, and she needed him now more than ever.

The journey on the water was long. She had seen the sun arc from one side of the ocean to the other. The further they traveled, skimming the surface of the water, the air chilled with each spray that rose over the edge of the stern. But not all of the cold came from the water. Anna shivered with a hollow breeze that came from inside of her, and it whispered of dark places and terrifying things ahead of them.

"Land, ho!" the captain shouted from his station on the bridge. In the fading evening light, she looked across the horizon and saw the outline of a slip of land in the distance. It stood like a shadow in the water, with a hill of trees rising above the rocky sea shore.

That had to be Oak Island.

Uncle John and Jackson stepped to the stern as well and gazed out over the water.

The engines slowed, drawing the loud pumping sound with them. The captain stepped from his station and dropped an anchor off the side of the boat.

"No docks here," he called out to them and nodded to Uncle John. "Need to take the dinghy to shore. You able to row?"

"I can manage," he said.

John and the captain pitched the dinghy overboard, and they climbed into it, but every board creaked and moaned as it sloughed white paint chips from its sea-weathered sides. John rowed the boat toward the shoreline. A thick of oak trees stretched from the inner shore and up the hills, disappearing over the top of the largest hill on the edge of the island.

A group of dark figures stood along the shore. Six of them, as best as Anna could see in the fading light.

It had to be Dave and his men.

Her fingers clutched the side of the boat until her knuckles had gone white.

"When we get over there, let me do the talking. Stay calm, and we'll get William out of this," John said as he pulled the oars through the water.

The boat neared the shore, and a couple of the men trudged through the water to aid the small craft into the bay. One of those six figures standing along the sand was William, his small form next to Dave, who kept a hand on his shoulder. He looked okay save for a small bruise above his left eye.

A small twinge of satisfaction settled over Anna, though. In the fading light, she saw the swelling purple bruise on Dave's nose that extended under both of his eyes, thanks to her sturdy boot heel.

"Welcome to Oak Island, boys and girls," Dave called out to them.

John jumped from the edge of the boat to the water that lapped around his knees. He pulled the craft further to the shore with the aid of Dave's men. The keel scraped along the rocks and sand and wouldn't pull in any further. Anna and Jackson stepped from the boat onto the wet rocks, her dress skimming the edge of the water as she jumped from rock to rock until she touched down on the sand.

Once she stopped beside John, she noticed a pistol in each man's hand.

Dave stepped away from William and into the circle of men. "Now, John, would you kindly give up your weapons while we conduct a bit of business?"

One of Dave's men walked up to John and pulled his gun from the holster at his hip. Then a knife from inside his coat. And another snub-nosed pistol from a pocket deep inside John's duster. And another knife. No wonder John always wore that coat. Lots of places to stash any kind of weapon he might need.

"Well, now that we have finished that, y'all might be interested to see what we found while waiting here for you." Dave turned and started into the thick of oak trees that led up the hill.

Before William moved with him, Anna caught his eye.

*Are you all right?* she mouthed. He nodded and then spun around to start up the hill as well. That had to be good enough for now.

Jackson stayed right at her side with John ahead of them as they moved up the hill. In the dark, she stumbled a few times but kept the pace with the rest of the men until they came to the peak and a clearing that opened up at the top.

In the center of the clearing, a great tree loomed with a single jutting branch. An old, frayed roped dangled from the branch, swaying ever so slightly in the faint breeze that drifted over the hill.

Was that a hangman's noose? Is that why he had brought them all this way, for a hanging?

As they neared the tree, the fluttering in her stomach intensified, sending zips of adrenaline in her veins. The rope wasn't a noose at all. It dangled over a pit, at least five-feet across, and it cut deep into the earth. Someone had taken the trouble to dig this hole below the tree, and the rope looked like a pulley system. Probably to move stuff in and out of the pit. That hole was deeper than it looked. The fading twilight cast only a view of the first few feet of it.

"I am a betting man," Dave said and gazed down into the hole. "I would bet that this is our next stop." He crouched down, picked up a pebble and tossed it into the pit. It fell and fell into the abyss until a distant thud finally echoed back to them. "You see that there hole? I believe there's something down there for us."

Unfortunately, he was probably right.

He looked up at Anna. "And you're gonna go get it for me."

# CHAPTER 32

Anna stepped to the edge of the abyss. "I'm not going down there."

He withdrew one of his pistols and pointed it at her. "Oh, yes you are. Look at it this way. You go down there. Scout it out, get what I need, then you and your family go free. Even Uncle Johnny, here. If you don't do it, I shoot all y'all right now and go down there and get it anyway."

He waved his pistol at each of them.

"I'll go," John said and stepped closer to the hole.

"You most certainly will not," Dave said and pointed the pistol at John's chest. "My deal was with the lady."

Her head spun with thought of the inky blackness down in the hole. The distant echo of the pebble Dave had thrown in there still bounced around in her thoughts. But it was either this, or they all die.

The air above the hole shifted around her boots like tendrils wrapping around her legs. The chills moved into her spine as she gazed into the abyss. "You promise to let my family go if I do this?"

"I'll keep my word."

Blood drained from her face. "Okay."

She could only stand there, helpless, as the men situated the rope and pulley toward her. There was a loop at the end of the rope that dangled above the hole. She pulled her long hair back and tied it in bun. It just wouldn't do for it to get tangled up in the rope.

Jackson and John stepped up to her. She pulled off her coat and handed it to her uncle.

"Just hold on tight," he said. One of Dave's men passed a lit lantern to her. John moved the rope toward her, and she fit her boot into the loop. "Holler if anything is too dangerous down there."

"And then what?" she said and met his gaze, her head cocked to the side. This wasn't a time to be soft. "You think they'll just pull me back up?"

"See you soon," Jackson said. His jaw had clenched tight, and he stepped back from the edge of the hole.

"Enough," Dave called out. "Time to get going." He signaled to his men, and John stepped back. She held the lantern in one hand and wrapped her elbow around the slack rope. The handle of the lantern slipped around in her damp palm.

The four other men with Dave hoisted on the line, and the rope went tight, showering her with a sprinkle of dust. It pulled against her boot, and the ground vanished below her feet. The rope swung her over the pit. She held her breath and closed her eyes. *Don't let go. Don't look down.* Vibrations zinged down the rope where she pressed her body against it with each heave of the rope from the pulley.

Her breath escaped in little gasps through her lips. *Get it together.* All of this would fall apart if she passed out now. She opened her eyes, and in that moment, she saw William, standing beside Dave. The knit of creases between his wide eyes scared her.

The rope jerked again and lowered her into the pit, one heave at a time. Foot by foot. Cold heavy air surrounded her as it oozed from the earthen walls. The lantern light surrounded her space in the hole. *Don't look down*, she reminded herself. Not that she would see anything anyways. That pebble travelled a long way down before it struck bottom. Blood pounded in her brain and ears with such force it made her head hurt.

The sound of her breathing echoed against the walls. The pit surrounded her now. She wrapped her arms around the rope even tighter and closed her eyes as the walls of the hole threatened to creep in on her. Vibrations shook down the length of the cord, rubbing and burning against her arm.

She glanced back up. The faces of those that gazed down at her grew smaller with each foot she descended and the lantern light no longer illuminated them. Just silhouettes in the dark.

The smell of cold, damp earth rose up, and it reminded her of a grave. The rope descended in brief spasms of movement, further and further into the deep. She closed her eyes again and hugged the rope despite the vibrations.

The rope jerked, and something struck her foot. The rope went slack, and she stumbled backward on solid ground. Her eyes flew open as she grasped for the rope. No more shaking at the bottom of a rope and dangling like bait in the darkness. Her trembling knees held her upright, but her fingers and knuckles hurt from holding onto the cord so tight.

She was alive. She made it to the bottom of the endless abyss.

The glass in the lantern rattled as she held it with her trembling hands. The light fell on the earthen walls of her tomb. She turned while she steadied herself with the rope.

And then she found it. The thing they had sent her down to discover.

A stone slab, the height and width of a great door, faced the south side of the hole. A collection of pegs and protrusions decorated the otherwise smooth surface. She touched the stone, as cold as everything else down here. One shove to it did nothing. It stood firm and unmoving. No door handle. No way to open it. Her fingers moved over the pegs.

This had to be where her father once stood. She removed the journal from her pocket and opened it once again to his final entry.

*A remarkable lock, and only I know the whereabouts of the key.*

A key. What key? And how would it even open the door?

She stepped back. Her father once said that in order to solve a puzzle, one must take it in its entirety. She had done this with the Kensington stone at the Ohmans farm, and that had worked out well for her. Pegs. Protrusions. Grooves. In patterns, maybe? Symbols? No.

In groupings. The marks were grouped together in bundles. Three pegs here. Two grooves there. All scattered over the center face of the slab. She stepped back further until she pressed her back against the opposite wall.

What groupings would make sense? Think of the whole picture.

A grouping of pegs stood out to her, to the right of center. Could it be that simple?

*Only I know the whereabouts of the key.*

Was it possible that she had the key the entire time?

She pulled the pendant from under her bodice, the iron warm in her hand from her own body heat. Lantern light danced over its polished curves. She pulled the string from around her neck and turned the pendant over in her hand. Deep into the backside of it were a series of four notches: just large enough for four stone pegs.

It couldn't be.

Her father had given her the key for safekeeping.

With shaking hands, she approached the slab and eyed the four pegs that had caught her attention. She released a steady and slow breath. The pendant shimmered in the light as she placed it over the pegs and pressed it into place. The stone fit into the grooves, and it slid in with a sharp click.

And then nothing happened.

She pressed on the iron surface of the pendant, but it didn't budge. Her brow furrowed as she turned her head and examined it from all sides.

She searched the whole slab again. Perhaps she missed something. But there couldn't be anything else. The pendant fit too perfectly. That had to be the key.

Anna stepped back.

A remarkable lock . . .

That it was, so how did it open?

The pendant was definitely the key. She stepped up to the slab and ran her fingers over the iron and pressed it toward the stone. Solid, just like the last time she had tried it. Maybe it wasn't fitting right. Her fingers slid around the side of the pendant, but it didn't move. *Great.* It was stuck now. She wedged it to the right to try and get her fingers underneath. A sharp pop resonated through the stone, and she jumped back, her heart pounding against her ribs.

Wait a minute. This was a key. And keys turn. That's how they work.

A wide grin spread across her lips. Her father used to say something only associated with the pendant.

I'll always be two steps to your right.

Right; clockwise.

She placed her fingers over the pendant and forced it in a clockwise direction, just as she had tried to do when she attempted to pry it free. The pendant and pegs underneath it spun with ease. Click. Click. Two steps, two clicks.

Immediately after the second click, the slab shuddered, and the ground vibrated. Cogs and wheels or whatever inner workings that moved behind the stone clicked and echoed around her.

This kind of shaking could bring down the whole pit. She stumbled backward and fell against the far wall. With a deep grating sound, the slab shifted and sunk back into the wall of the hole. It slid into the shadows and then disappeared to the right. And then everything fell quiet and still.

She didn't dare move in case the shuddering started again, or the slab could slam shut and trap her on the other side. The lantern light only glowed a few feet into the tunnel beyond where the slab once stood. A breath of damp, stale air exhaled from the dark tunnel and across her face.

This was all too familiar. Just her and a lantern exploring a dark cavern, just like the silver mine. And that hadn't turned out so well.

She stood and walked toward the opening. The lantern glowed further into the tunnel, revealing a smooth stone walk down a corridor that plunged deep into the earth.

Her father had never been this far. He had only ever stood at the door with the key in hand. And he had never been in this tunnel because the man at the top of the hole had killed him. That man waited for her right now.

"I found a door," she shouted up to them.

It only took a few minutes for the rope on which she had descended to disappear on up to the top of the hole. One by one, Dave sent everyone down. All except two men he left at the top. Need to have someone up there to drag up all the loot he planned on obtaining. Even with Dave down here, it was nice to no longer be alone at the bottom of the pit.

"You okay?" John said when he stepped off the rope.

She nodded, but his eyes wandered to the tunnel entrance. He and Dave held up their own lanterns and gazed into the corridor just as she had.

Jackson stepped from the rope, his eyes wide again. But he didn't care about the tunnel. He stepped toward her and threw his arms around her.

"How did you do that by yourself?" he said. His strong frame trembled against her. "That was the scariest thing I've ever done."

She pulled back from him. "Well, the night's not over." She ticked her head toward the tunnel entrance.

He stood with the others as they gaped into the tunnel. William then stepped from the rope and approached her. She crouched down, her hands on his shoulders.

"You sure you're okay?" she whispered to him.

"Yeah."

"You need to be brave for this next part. It might get a little dark, but just hold my hand."

"Okay." He grasped her hand. He had never felt smaller to her than he did right now.

Dave straightened and examined the crew. Everyone was accounted for. "Okay, let's go."

He motioned Anna to the front of the line. The nervous flutters started in her chest again. She raised the lantern high and stepped into the tunnel ahead of them with William at her side. Her hand moved along the smooth walls, and the ground sloped downward. They descended with careful steps, John, her brother and Jackson right behind her. Dave moved in line behind them.

Someone had carved out this tunnel hundreds of years ago. And nobody had walked this path since that time. The Knights Templar were the last people to tread within this corridor, and now she walked in their footsteps. Her father hadn't even been able to do that.

An archway and central keystone supported the ceiling about every ten feet, carved with such craftsmanship. Of course, it was perfect. The men who had constructed this were skilled masons. She half-expected to see drawings on the walls, but she reminded herself this wasn't an Egyptian tomb. It was something greater.

The corridor sloped again, and the echoing sounds of their footsteps changed. The humidity in the air thickened. The circle of lantern light dropped away with each step, and the end of the corridor opened into a grand chamber. Her mouth gaped open as she gazed upward. The lantern light barely touched the high walls, all smoothed stone cut away by the makers of the tunnel. The room opened wide across a vast expanse of rock.

Anna stepped across the room. The voices of everyone behind them echoed in gasps throughout the space. She moved to the center to find the smooth floor give way to a deep canal. It had been cut through and divided the length of the chamber, starting midway up the left wall, and coursed through the room to the lower aspect of the right wall. Stone steps descended on one side of the channel and then up the other side. Anna followed her light along the stairs and across the canal where it landed on the opening to another corridor.

"So, is this the treasure room?" Dave asked.

"No," she said and pointed toward the other corridor.

Jackson stepped beside her as Dave moved around her and hurried down the steps. "What is this room?"

She scanned the channel again, stretched from one wall to the next. "I'm not sure."

The others had continued on, climbing the steps on the other side of the channel, but she and Jackson just gazed over the room.

"Look," he nudged her with his elbow. He pointed to the west wall. Her eyes caught the image carved in the stone just above a stone protrusion.

Four wavy lines.

"The water trap," they both whispered together.

"This is it," she said and held the lantern over the canal.

"Come on," William said from across the canal. He frowned at them and waved them forward.

With her blood pumping even faster, she hurried into the canal, each step echoing against the stone. At the deepest, the canal rose at least three body lengths high and cut until the stone was smooth as glass. They ascended to the other side and caught up with the group in the second corridor.

The tunnel moved straight into the earth, not sloped like the first tunnel. Footsteps and voices ahead of her changed, echoing louder than ever before. Whatever was ahead of them had to be big. The tunnel opened into another chamber and to broad stone steps that descended onto a platform.

Aged bundles of dry wood were set in great spires at the edges of the platform, overlooking the grand room where Anna's lantern light wouldn't reach. Nobody spoke, not even Dave. They stood around the platform, gazing into the dark recesses of the room. Her fingers buzzed as she stepped toward one of the wood bundles.

"What is that?" Dave asked and moved with her. She was sure he didn't want to miss a thing.

She was just going to show him. The dry wood still smelled like cedar, after all these years down in the cavern. She removed the flint strike from the bottom of her lantern and stepped up to the bundle. If this worked, it could be brilliant. She set the lantern on the ground and struck the flint against the bundle. After a few strikes, the spark caught on the wood. It popped and blazed quickly. The fire grew and accelerated to the top of the spire in an impressive flame that towered over the platform.

# CHAPTER 33

All eyes turned toward the room in hushed silence. The massive torch illuminated the deep cavern but still didn't reach the furthest recesses. The fire glistened off a room filled with gold, statues, shimmering jewels and millions of other trinkets stacked from floor to wall. An occasional path wound between piles of gold and stretched back even further than the torchlight could reach. Carved slabs decorated with hieroglyphs that Anna recognized from Egyptian, Sumerian and Etruscan texts were stacked to the ceiling at one end of the room. On the other, large wooden chests, hundreds of them, were organized and undoubtedly filled with more gold.

In all her reading about the Knights Templar, the most intriguing story to her was the possibility that they had even collected the Holy Grail. What if it was in here, somewhere among those chests or piles of jewels and coins?

Or even the Ark written about in the book of *Exodus*. Rumor was that the Templars had possession of that as well. And this was the sort of place to keep something like that hidden.

Which meant that this could be a holy place. A place so sacred that no man should be walking here.

And her father had suspected it. He even wrote it in his journal: *This could be their damnation should they tread any further.*

"Whoo-hoo!" Dave shouted and bounded down the steps from the platform and into the room. His two men followed him, leaving the rest of them on the platform.

John stepped beside her. "You did it. I can't believe you found this."

"I didn't," she said. "It was father. This was his life's work."

Dave and his men ran about the room, filling their pockets with as many coins and trinkets as they could carry. Her stomach churned as she watched them. Their obnoxious voices carried throughout the room and likely into the corridors.

Dave's greed tainted this place like sin. This was not what this room was meant for. Deep within the recesses of this place hid holy relics collected from far-away lands. These things were not only of wealth and status, but they also held cultural and religious significance. They were never meant to be profaned by the likes of Dave and his men.

"This isn't meant for him," she said. "It's not meant for any of us." No. It belonged to the hundred, the thousand unseen souls that watched from the shadows. This treasure was a collection of ages of history and culture, taken from people that had died to keep these things safe. If their ghosts were here, protecting this place, they wouldn't want to see it tainted.

"There's nothing we can do," John said.

"It's not right," she said.

Dave turned toward them, gold coins dripping from his fingers. "Miss Anna, John, you fulfilled your end of the deal. You and your family can get going."

William grasped her hand and tugged on her to pull her back into the corridor. She glanced up to Uncle John, but his face had gone pale, and he hung his head.

"Come on, Anna. He said we can go," William said.

"What is it?" she whispered to Uncle John, despite William tugging on her arm. "Something bad, right?"

"He never intended to just let us go," Jackson said from her other side.

John looked up at him. "You're too smart for your own good, kid."

"What do you mean?" She shot glances at both of them.

"Those two men at the top of the hole will kill us as soon as we get up there. There was no leaving this place once we got here." John said, his voice lowering.

Her stomach dropped like she had fallen from a great height. She hadn't seen it, but Jackson and Uncle John did. Dave wanted all of this for himself. He had never planned to let them go. After all, they could come back and get some of the treasure for themselves. Or tell others about it. He probably didn't plan on sharing it with his own men, leaving himself as the only one to walk out of this pit alive.

Tears flooded her eyes. Mother would never know what happened to her entire family. No way out. No way home.

A lump formed in her throat and an idea flashed through her brain. But there was a way out. Just one.

She wiped away her tears and blinked her vision clear. Anna turned away from them and marched back down the corridor that lead from the treasure room. Her light opened into the canal room.

The others followed her, leaving Dave and his men to bask in the gold.

"Do you want to let me in on what you're thinking?" John said, quickening his pace to keep up with her.

She raised her light and gazed at the four wavy lines carved into the wall.

"Oh, hell," Jackson muttered.

"Oh, hell what?" John said and stood before her.

"I might have a plan." Her eyes widened as she looked between the three of them. "The original architects built a fail-safe. There was no way they could get back up and out of the hole once they went in. There had to be a back door. I also found a passage in father's journal about a trap that they built to keep everything in here safe from intruders. And that's it." She ticked her head toward the carving and the stone latch on the wall.

John followed her eyes to the symbol. "It's a water trap. And this channel, I think it's the flush. If we trigger it, we'll only have a few minutes. But I think it could work."

Uncle John ran his fingers across the stubble on his chin. "Oh, hell is right."

"I don't see any other way," she said.

"And this channel, where does it go?" he asked.

She shrugged. "I don't know. Probably out to the ocean."

He dropped down on one knee and pulled them all around him. "Do you believe that it will work? In your soul, do you believe it?"

In that dim light, Uncle John's eyes were her father's eyes. His voice, too.

"I believe it."

He nodded and looked down, silent and pondering.

John glanced up at Jackson. "What do you think?"

"I would trust her. She hasn't been wrong so far." He smiled at her, something wan and pale and scared. "I would follow her anywhere."

Her heart pounded in her ears.

"And you, William boy?" John turned to her brother.

"I know it'll work." He must have had no idea what she was talking about because he didn't look scared enough.

"Okay," John said and rose to his feet. "Then it's the only way out. We'll follow your lead on this one."

Everybody put all their faith in her, and her knees trembled. They had no alternative, but she hoped more than ever that she wasn't wrong about it this time.

With the lantern raised, she stepped to the symbol and the stone latch. The group stayed close beside her.

"What do we do now?" John said.

"I think we just pull the latch down and it triggers the trap."

"And then what?"

Her fingers went cold. "And then there's no turning back."

This was going to end right now. One way or another.

Anna stepped toward the latch, but John held out his arm to stop her. "I'll do it."

He rubbed his hands together like he warmed them against a fire. Anything to delay the inevitable. He grasped the toggle and pulled it down. At first, it didn't slip, but he leaned his body weight into it. The latch moved with the grating sound of rock against rock. Just like with the stone slab, the whirring of a mechanism behind the stone sounded, and each of them stepped away from the latch.

The ground quaked, and the walls rumbled. A rolling stone rose from the wall to the left, where the channel crept upward. The stones shifted, and a gaping hole opened up above the canal. A roar like a freight train chugged from the dark gap in the stone. At first, all Anna saw was a trickling stream of water pour into the canal, but the roar rose to a deafening sound, and a crashing wave of ocean water rushed and careened into the channel from the opening. Stones on the opposite wall shifted, creating a passage for the water to course somewhere deep into the hillside. The water trap was an enormous flush from left to right.

"That's it," she shouted to John above the roar of crashing water. "The channel should open up outside, probably at the beach. We should be able to get out that way."

But it would only be open for a short time. In the end, the flush portal would close and flood everything, keeping this entire structure safe from intruders. Forever.

The color drained from his face as he watched the water move with tremendous force into the canal carved into the earth, disappearing into heaven-knows-what.

The roar of the water-chute pounded through the cavern, and the stones rumbled, dust raining down into the room. William wrapped his trembling arms around her waist.

From the other side of the canal, Dave and his men emerged from the treasure room at the tremendous sound of roaring water, their pockets stuffed full of gold. He shouted at them above the sound of the water.

"What did you do?" He reached for the gun in his holster.

The corridor behind them rumbled as more inner-workings of the trap sprung to life. A large limestone slab rolled from the walls, just like the slab in the first tunnel. Dave turned on his heel and ran to the door. His fingers grasped at the edge and pulled, but the stone dragged him with it. He got his hands out of the way just as it slammed shut, protecting the treasure room from what would come next. Like a child having a tantrum, he screamed at his men to try and open door.

"We've gotta go now," Anna said to John and tugged on his sleeve.

He turned and glanced at Jackson. His voice rose over the rushing water. "We need to go in pairs of two. I need you to hold on to William. Don't let go of him."

Jackson's jaw had gone slack, but he nodded.

"Anna," John said and turned to her. "You will hold on to me."

William let go of Anna and stepped by Jackson's side. Uncle John crouched down to face William. His small chest rose with quick and nervous breaths. "We have one shot at this. It's gonna be a wild ride, but you will take a real big breath and jump into that water. It's gonna take you someplace safe."

William's eyes grew wide, and he looked up with doubt to Anna. "It will be okay," she said. "We have to do this if we want to go home." She glanced up at Jackson. "Don't let go of him."

"I won't. I promise. We'll make it to the other side. I swear it. We'll make it, and then we'll go to New Mexico."

She pulled him into an embrace, and his arm wrapped around her back. "Double swear it."

"I double swear it."

"Okay," John said and faced them.

Anna let go of Jackson.

"Go now! We'll be right behind you," John said and nodded to the canal. He walked them to the edge, the roar of the fast-moving water deafening.

She blinked fast, but the tears welled in her eyes. They had to do this themselves. She couldn't go with them. William glanced back to her, his face strained and afraid. Anna nodded to him.

He nodded with his hand clutched tight to Jackson. For only a few seconds, they stood at the canal's edge. Jackson's chest rose and sank in quick bursts of air. He strengthened his grip on William's hand. William drew his other hand to his nose and pinched it closed. Jackson looked down at him as he took in a big gulp of air.

They leaped into the water, and Anna's heart almost stopped. As soon as their bodies had plunged into the chute, they were lost in the dark tunnel that opened into rock.

She gasped as they disappeared. What if she was wrong?

John turned back to her and held out his hand. Her legs felt like stone and didn't want to move, but she forced them forward. She grasped his extended hand. Ringing started in her ears.

"Now, hold on," he shouted over the water. "Don't let go. No matter what."

A grinding growl sounded over the roar of the water. Anna glanced down the chute to see a slab of stone settling down over the exit tunnel. The flush was closing, ready to flood the entire room.

"We need to go now," he shouted again. "I'll see you on the other side."

She couldn't speak. She only nodded and clasped her cold hand around his even tighter.

"Ready?" he asked.

She took in a deep breath and nodded again.

John moved, and she jumped with him, even when her mind screamed in terror at her.

Their feet hit the channel, and the water grabbed them in an icy cold rush. Roaring water filled her ears, and she fought against the urge to scream. Her fingers wrapped tighter around John's hand. Together, they plunged into darkness. It was so black, like oil, and the water tumbled them over and over again. The force of the water churned them to the left of the channel in a powerful punch. John collided into the wall. The one thing she dreaded the most in these last few seconds happened. His hand slipped out of hers. She clambered to find him again, but his hand was gone. The air bubbled out of her lungs as she cried out for him.

No. He was gone. There was no more air. This is how she would die, in a dark and dismal place as cold and lonely as Purgatory.

Then the world went black.

# CHAPTER 34

So cold. And dark.

Everything hurt, and her lungs burned. Anna coughed until her throat ached, but it wasn't enough. She needed to cough more, to get the water out.

Something warm touched her face, and she opened her eyes. It was all still so dark, but an angelic face looked down on her.

No. Not an angel. It was even better.

"Anna," William's voice called out to her. "I thought you were dead."

Her throat spasmed again, and another cough erupted from deep in her lungs. She turned to her side and coughed until it didn't hurt anymore. Sweet oxygen filled her lungs and cleared the pounding in her head.

"I got you," Jackson's voice came from her side, and his hand rested on her back.

She pushed herself upright enough to see their faces. Water dripped from their hair and soaked through their clothes. Jackson had a new scratch on his cheek.

What had happened? The last moments she remembered were only a blur of light and sound. So much water; the sound was too loud. They had to get away. This was their last chance. She held onto Uncle John's hand and then . . .

She bolted upright and staggered to her feet. Jackson rushed to her side as she teetered on the uneven ground. "Where's Uncle John?" She wiped away the water that dripped down her face and gazed around in the dark. The moonless night left a blanket of shadows over everything.

"I don't know. We were lucky to find you," Jackson said.

"No," she said and pushed away from him. She stumbled toward a tree, her body still starved for oxygen. "That's not good enough."

She ran along the shoreline, tripping along the rocks and sand. Water sloshed and gurgled along the beach where the rush of the canal had disturbed the ground.

"John!" she shouted into the night. She lurched forward and fell into the sand, her lungs wracking with another cough.

"Anna, stop," Jackson ran after her and knelt in the sand beside her.

Her eyes blurred, and it wasn't the water dripping from her hair. "I tried to hold on."

"I know you did."

"I let go of him."

"It wasn't your fault," he said and placed his hand on her back again.

"Yes, it was. He told me to hold on, and I didn't," she cried and pushed herself to her feet. She staggered toward the marsh and collapsed at the grassy bank. The water was so dark and surrounded by trees. The open channel had disturbed the mud and left the water a murky mess. The cooling night turned the ocean spray into a mist that settled over everything like a ghostly veil. Even in the daylight, John could have sunk to the bottom, and they would never find him in these conditions.

She sat on the bank in a heap of tears and wet clothes. The mist collecting from the crashing surf sprayed over her wet head and chilled her, curling its death-cold grip into her bones. Jackson settled beside her on the grass and placed his arm over her shoulder, pulling her into his side.

John was gone, and it was her fault. It had been her idea to escape through the channel, and he had believed in her. Maybe if she could have held on just a little tighter, then she would never have lost him.

Her memory went to the picture of her father in the study. She at least had that one thing to remember her father's face. But she had nothing of Uncle John, only her guilt that she had hated him at one time. Now, she would give anything to have him back, to ride with him to New Mexico and to see her mother. She wanted to hold his hand and tell him that she was sorry that she had doubted him.

"What is that?" William said from behind her.

She looked at him and then followed his pointing finger across the marsh. A shadow moved in the mist like a spirit of Avalon. Anna held her breath and stood on shaking knees.

In the dark of night, the figure staggered along the bank of the marsh, his left arm cradled against his ribs. This play of shadows teetered toward them, sloshing through the reeds and mud.

Anna gathered her damp skirt and ran toward him. The closer she got, the better she could see his face, dripping with pond water and streaked in mud. As she approached him, John's knees staggered, and he collapsed just as Anna caught him in an embrace. William ran close behind her and flung himself at his uncle as well. John winced as they collected him and he panted for breath.

"I thought I lost you," Anna cried.

He turned to her and pulled her wet hair from her face. "I'm not going anywhere."

John hugged them with his good arm and then glanced up at Jackson as he walked up to them.

"You did good, kid," John said with a smile. He turned to Anna and William and lifted up their heads to examine them. "Everybody okay?"

"All good," Anna said and wiped a tear from her cheek. "What about you?" She glanced down at his arm.

"Oh, this," he said. "It'll heal. Just needs a little love, that's all. And a warm fire."

Anna and Jackson helped him to his feet, and they moved together away from the marsh. He headed toward the shoreline where their dinghy waited, but Anna pulled back.

"There's one thing I need to do before we go," she said and gazed back up the hill.

Jackson followed her gaze. "I'm coming with you."

They left John and William at the boat and climbed up the hill together. Just as she had suspected, Dave's men had disappeared. It probably happened with the water channel opened. They had left everything behind, including John's guns and her coat.

They stepped up to the edge of the pit, but so much had changed since she last stood here. Water had filled the entire hole to within a few feet of the rim, leaving only a black and endless abyss of water that plunged into the center of the world. Good. Nobody would be able to search into the bottom of this water trap, and with the rope pulley overhead, it just looked like any old well.

She reached into her apron and found a coin from the collection at the silver mine.

One last wish before they departed.

She flicked the coin into the water, and it sank into the black abyss.

Now they could go home.

# CHAPTER 35

**W**arm spring air drifted through the open window, billowing the lace curtains and drifting across the writing desk. The sounds of the collected crowd down in the garden carried up into Anna's room. It wouldn't be long before Maria summoned her. There was quite an event about to happen, and it would be improper if Anna wasn't there and ready when it started.

She peered through her window and down to the crowd in the garden. Everyone dressed in their finest. And there he was.

Jackson looked up at her as though he felt her gaze on him. He smiled one of those half grins. The dimple in his chin formed when he did that. His hair was combed and his suit clean, the very one that he had purchased at the tailor with his own money earned by working on the farm for Uncle John.

He ticked his head and waved his hand for her to come down. Just one more minute. She pulled away from the window and sat at the writing desk. She picked up the fountain pen and opened up the crisp pages of her new and empty journal.

She had to finish this one last thing while it was still on her mind.

*April 7, 1893*

*This is the beginning of the journal of Anna Holloway. Like my father before me, I intend on recording my life's work. I would certainly like to provide you with the details of my adventures to this date, but I must take this secret to my* grave, for the things which I have seen many months ago are sacred and wholly unbelievable. My father, Thomas Holloway, understood this as well.

I begin this day in writing regarding my adventures because today I embark on a new chapter in my life. Today, my mother will remarry, and her husband is none other than my Uncle John Holloway. I have now become quite fond of him, and I confess to you, dear Journal, that I see much of my father in him.

This day I honor my father as well by beginning this journal just as he had. As I complete my schooling, I intend on applying to the university in Boston where I wish to study linguistics of the ancient people of Europe, as did my father before me.

I must also tell you of my new friend, Mr. Jackson T. Belford. He has followed me across this vast country, during the hardest of times, and appears determined to follow me forever. I cannot say that I mind, however. I suspect that we may have many more adventures together, as he has secretly asked for my hand in marriage on my seventeenth birthday and has devoted himself to coming with me to Boston. However, I have insisted that he ask Uncle John for my hand, as it is only proper. This is something that my father would have wanted.

Many secrets have I seen, but there are many more which I shall discover.

Anna Holloway

"Anna, dear," Maria's voice called to her from the hallway. "You must hurry. The ceremony is about to begin."

The orange tabby meowed from where he lay on her bed, which was a much better place to sleep than his usual place in the barn loft. His tired eyes glanced at her as though he did not have enough time to deal with Anna's problems today.

She rose from her journal, closed its pages, stroked the cat's head, and then looked at herself in the mirror. Her long dark locks were curled and pinned about the crown of her head with silver clips. The white dress still remained smooth and flawless, the lace perky at the cuffs of her sleeves. Then she joined Maria and stepped down to the wedding at the back garden of the ranch house where she greeted Jackson with a wink and a smile before she stepped next to William, who stood beside the minister.

The breeze shifted against her hair, and she turned toward it. At that moment, Uncle John smiled at her. He stood across the aisle, on the other side of the minister. She smiled back at him, and, together, they waited at the end of the aisle for the bride to appear.

Fresh spring air drifted over the new crop of corn that peeked their smooth green strands above the tilled soil, and a new season opened its eyes.

## THE END

While this is a fictional tale, there are some aspects that are based on historical fact.

• The Kensington Rune Stone is an actual artifact, unearthed in Kensington, Minnesota, just as it was described in this story by Mr. Olof Ohman. After its discovery, Mr. Ohman was endlessly ridiculed as many thought he was the author of a hoax. However, after much scientific study of the stone, it is thought by many to be an authentic medieval marker placed in the ground in Minnesota by ancient people who had trekked across the American continent. It did indeed bear the marking of an X with a notched arm, which was often used in Templar writings and codes.

• The Newport Tower in Rhode Island is also an actual medieval structure that was built upon this continent much earlier than the day Christopher Columbus set foot upon this land. It is believed by researchers to be a guide marker to several other important archeological sites across the country, including the Kensington stone. The quartz as described in this story is fictional, however.

• Although it seems fantastical, the Oak Island pit is also a true archeological discovery. Often termed "The Oak Island Money Pit," it was discovered by two young men in 1795 as a depression in the dirt and overhanging it was a rope dangling from a nearby tree. They started the initial and unofficial excavation of the pit. Since that time, it has been excavated deeply into the earth by several different investigational groups. The mystery that continues to plague researchers, however, is that the structure was man-made and consists of layer upon layer of carefully laid platforms of thatched wood, stone, and other vegetation that has never been native to Oak Island. About 90 feet into the dig, a stone was found with an inscription that was once interpreted to state "forty feet below, two million pounds lie buried." At one point during excavation, the drill struck "something" which subsequently flooded the entire pit, and to this date, despite exhaustive efforts to drain the pit, nobody has ever been able to stop the flooding. One theory suggests that this may have been a booby-trap set to hide something deeper within the hole and that those who would know that the trap was there would be able to avoid the flooding.

According to Mark Finnan's book *Oak Island Secrets*, it is suggested that the pit and its unusual structuring appears to be related to some Masonic rituals and that it could be the doorway to a secret treasure vault. In many historical accounts, the Masons are a direct relation to the Knights Templar.

Despite endless man hours and funding, the Oak Island Pit still holds a mystery within its watery depths.

For further information regarding the Kensington Stone, the Newport Tower as well as their possible Templar connections, please read *The Hooked X* by Scott F. Wolter.

• Anna and the boys meet a stranger at the World's Fair in Chicago. Mr. Henry Holmes (also known as H. H. Holmes, or Herman Mudgett) was a real person, and likely one of the first documented serial killers in the United States. He built a hotel just blocks from the World's Fair and lured unsuspecting tourists to it, where he subsequently murdered them and disposed of their bodies within the building. He was later captured, tried, and convicted of murder, shortly after this story has him meeting with the kids in Chicago. For more information, read *Devil in the White City* by Erik Larson.

# ABOUT THE AUTHOR

When she isn't delivering babies, Carrie Merrill is a prolific writer who has put pen to paper since the age of 8, when she wrote her first story about a dragon that lived in a cave across the river from her house in Idaho. A day has not gone by since that time when she didn't have a story floating around in her head. Her Angel Blade Series includes *Angel Blade*, *Daemon* and *Archangel* and has received great praise. She is currently a full-time OB/GYN in Wyoming with her six rescue cats when she isn't writing about the things that lurk in the dark.

## The Angel Blade Series

**Book 1:** *Angel Blade* is a new adult paranormal novel that involves a strong female protagonist in a supernatural setting, dealing with issues such as loss of home and family, the burden of being female in a male-dominated realm, and romantic entanglements that can jeopardize her future. Nikka is dying of cancer until a stranger provides her with a cure, but it comes at a steep cost: she must become a Seraph, an angelic being with the power to exorcise and destroy demons. With Gideon, the stranger who introduced her to this life, she learns of the battle between Heaven and Hell and about the part she must play to fight the demon horde and destroy Abaddon, the Prince of Demons.

Then she meets Jason, a man with a troubled past who also brings the promise of a normal life, and his offer may be too good to let go.

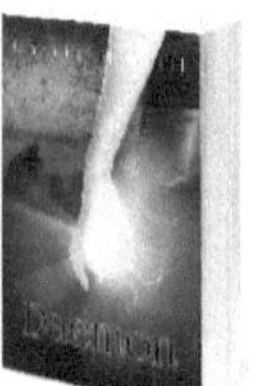

**Book 2:** *Daemon* In this sequel to *Angel Blade*, Abaddon has fallen, and Nikka, the seraph, and Jason go into hiding as the rest of the world makes sense of the chaos that had occurred in the battle. But as Nikka struggles to face the impact of the events that took Gideon from her, she receives a disturbing vision about the end of the world.

Now, with Jason at her side, she must find another ally foretold in her vision and fight to stop the demon horde from bringing about the final Apocalypse.

**Book 3:** *Archangel* Demon hordes now rule a post-apocalyptic world. As the new seraph, Jason is bound to Gideon, even though Jason blames him for Nikka's disappearance and the loss of her unborn child. Someday, he will kill Gideon or die trying. Until then, he must wait and learn all he can about being a seraph.

When he sees a vision of Nikka, alive and well, Jason is determined to find her despite the demons hunting them. And with the help of a woman they meet along the way, they may be able to answer the question of Nikka's vanishing.